JUDGE

Michele Lee

Cover Photo: Golden Czermak FuriousFotog
Cover Model: Andrew Flanagan
Cover Design: Brittany St Thomas
Interior Formatting: Silla Webb |
Masque of the Red Pen

To K.L. Savage for bringing these besties turned writing duo together with your Ruthless Underworld.

To Queen Erica, you are the best wingman a fictional character ever had!

Also, for Libby. You know why. #JudgeisLibbys

Carolyn Rumsey. Words cannot express how saddened we are to hear of your passing. You became one of our biggest supporters, and we will forever hold your words of encouragement in our hearts. You were taken way too soon. Rest in paradise, Care.

PROLOGUE

*** Present ***

When I was younger, I never understood the dynamic of a happy family, I am sure I had one until the age of three, but I have no memory of that. I only have the small smattering of pictures that I was handed throughout the years from the social workers as they shuttled me from house to house.

Nothing like the eyes I see looking back at me in the mirror these days, broken and jaded from the shit I took in the foster system. I see a small kid with deep chocolate eyes that looks so vibrant and happy in those pictures, with a matching sparkle of mischief like the older man right alongside me. Then there was the woman whose deep muddy brown hair sparkled almost black in some of the pictures, who I assumed was with her husband. He looked upon her with adoring eyes, and the warmest, most beautiful smile graced her lips when she looked at the trouble-making toddler with matching hair.

That's all I took away from them, the sparkle in his eyes, her hair, nothing more. No memories, no quirks or traits. Even if I actually did have them, who was around to share them with me anyways? I was alone, a victim of circumstance and the system.

When Theo and I got busted, at twelve years old, for driving our abusive Foster Fuckers' car right into the middle school's gymnasium, that's what the judge called me, a victim of circumstance. In that hearing, Theo and I talked about the Foster Fucker and what he did to us; what he tried to do to one of the foster girls was with us. After what he tried to do, Theo and her swapped rooms, so she was now in the room between ours. The moment we heard any noise, *all of a sudden* one of us needed to piss or get a drink, never really allowing him the chance to go into her room again.

We were labeled problem children after that. We were doing what was needed to keep her safe; the system had us deemed unwelcoming, uncontrollable, and hard to work with. Because of that, no family wanted us, so we were put in group homes, and those were even worse than the private homes.

We were given garbage bags to carry our things in. We were a paycheck, a job to do; we were not treated like children. The harsh reality was that we didn't matter. Not to any of them.

That was the truth to our stories; we were all children who lost everything.

We were nothing more, yet somehow, everything less. When it came to anything hard labor that had to be done around the home, we were used because we were free while getting paid to make us do all the heavy lifting. I ain't talking standard household chores or simple tasks like doing the dishes. In one of the group homes we were at, the people who ran it just sat and took over the TV, and we older kids were left to do all the cooking, cleaning, and taking care of the younger kids.

It got to the point where I dreaded going to school. If there was an emergency baby in the house, I knew that minimal care would be done for that child until we got home. I also hated that the little kids there would have to walk home from the bus stop by themselves. A couple of blocks could mean the difference between life and death in a shadier part of town.

I may have been raised in the system for what almost equates to my whole life but, I knew when shit didn't fly. The way Theo and I grew up, I knew it wasn't normal. Even for the foster system, I knew we were dealt the shit end of the stick. However, I wasn't going to allow that to bend me into some piece of shit human being because they raised us. No. We were going to be better and do better. That was a promise we made to each other that no matter where we went, Theo and I always held onto it.

We held onto it as tight as we held onto ourselves, our sanity, and each other throughout the years.

High school was rough. Because we stuck so close together, everyone thought that we were gay. Which is fine, it didn't faze us, but unfortunately, others had an issue. Those issues caused fights and made high school hell sometimes. But high school is supposed to be hell, right?

It didn't matter, though, because we made it. Now, I look back at the shit Theo, and I went through, and I am fucking proud.

Our operation is one of a kind. I mean, who else has a fully functional cattle ranch, mechanics shop, bar, illegal gun and drug operation, MC, and children's group home all under one umbrella? It is a unique way of life, and with the crew I have, my loving wife, who really is the brains of this whole operation, by my side, I know deep down that is why we are successful.

Wanting to help kids stay away from the hardships and often torturous times we went through, we make sure to keep the kids free from the unsavory side of what we do. We give them skills and confidence to be who they need to be in life and give them the shot Theo, the guys, and I never really had.

We give them a cheering section at every school play, sporting event, and graduation. Those kids that are too old in the system are our bread and butter here. We take the *undesirable* children from the foster care system and give them all the kinds of love they need to become the best human beings they can be.

Theo and I started the MC to help kids in the area that were being abused in any aspect and give them the backing to go after their abuser. Then we dish out our own brand of justice once a child has their closure. Making sure to give *just enough* time that the law doesn't catch on and the abuser has that false hope that they are okay. Spoiler alert, they aren't. Our body count is high when you tally just the pedos we have rid this world of. I know I should feel bad, but I just can't. The thought of someone touching my kids, biological or not, sends me into a dark, twisted tailspin. The only way out is the bloodbath of the sinner.

Those thoughts have found me here looking at my computer, trying to balance the income and feed expenses for the cattle. We just sold fifty head at the last cattle auction, and the checks just came in. Now I need to allocate that to the rest of the two hundred and twenty-five head of Highlanders out on the thousand plus acres we have. But my head isn't in the present right now; it's in the past.

I need help. I need my numbers bunny to hop on in here and help me out. Maybe hop on me first. The thought of my wife bouncing on top of me has a groan slipping from my lips, but the thought doesn't stick around. I hear a commotion outside the office door, and I take that extra distraction to not only pull myself out of the delicious gutter I was in but to get away from the numbers that are driving me crazy and to see if I can be of any service.

In the kitchen, I find the love of my life directing our latest group of kids on making lunch for the MC boys, our Cowboys, and the young boys learning a few hands-on skills.

Manda came to us four months ago and has turned sixteen in her time here. We celebrated it like any kid, with a party, cake, presents, balloons and a bonfire. She even got to invite friends over, and we moved her bunkmate out of their room so she could have a sleepover and everything a sixteen-year-old could want.

You only get one sweet-sixteen, and we wanted her to feel like we cared about it because we truly did. She was a good kid before, but since her birthday, she has been even better. She is currently helping our newest little friend, Karma, make sandwiches.

Karma is six and only here temporarily as an emergency case. Her mom passed away from a drug overdose a few weeks back, and her dad isn't in the picture. The good news? They found her dad's parents, who are more than happy to take her and experience being first-time grandparents. They need to get a few more things squared away, and we are more than happy to help her in the meantime.

Speaking of my numbers bunny, I see Elvira helping Kathy-Rae and Caleb with the soup and setting the table out in the sunroom for everyone close by. I watch her hips sway as she moves back and forth between the kitchen and setting the table. Her short, fire engine red hair halos around her head. This is her tight ship to run; she was built to be a mom, a business owner, but most of all, she was built for me.

"PawPaw?" I hear a little voice, down by my knees.

"Now, who said that?" I look around, pretending not to feel the tiny fingers pulling at my jeans. That little grip pulls harder, and I finally look down at the intruder who has stolen everyone's hearts. "Oh, Miss Marley! There you are!"

I scoop up her giggling body and toss her in the air a few times. This tiny four-year-old started as an emergency placement at four months old and has been in and out of our care since. With her mother's revolving door of the prisons and halfway houses, we never know when we're getting and/or losing Marley, but we will never say no. Bonus, she is also the best chicken wrangler we have ever had.

"Can you help me ring the lunch bell?" She asks when I settle her on my hip.

"But of course!" I boom, and we make our way to the front of the house to call in the troops for some grub.

Marley rings the bell as best she can then I take my turn and call them in. Watching my MC, Cowboys, and kids coming to the house brings me back to when I found out about this place. When I discovered that my luck had really changed, and it only took thirty-five years for that to happen.

ONE

JUDGE

-15 Years Ago-

"What do you mean you can't give me the loan?" I am trying to keep my calm sitting here with the bank's mortgage officer, but the situation is proving harder and harder to remain that way.

"There are notes on your account that you are to contact a law firm in Colorado. A Spek, Duiker and Michaud firm. They're located in Wyman, Colorado, about two and a half hours away from Denver." She continues to type away on the computer, trying to find more information about the hold on my account, which I am still baffled was placed legally.

I worked hard from eighteen till thirty-five, saving, putting as much as I could away every check, living on next to nothing for months at a time. Taking the bus from eighteen till twenty-five until I bought myself a bike, using the skills I learned from the garage to fix it up and get it operational. I still drive it to this day ten years later.

Not much use for anything else in California, and it is better on gas than a big car or truck. Plus, the freedom I feel while riding is indescribable. Growing up the way I did, any amount of freedom, of ownership, was cherished. Yet, even thinking of the way my bike made me feel normal, I could not calm my raging mind.

Here I was trying to make my dream come true and buy a hobby farm. I had more than enough for a down payment in my account, I wasn't sure what was going on, but I was determined to find out.

Believe it or not, I had never been on the wrong side of the law as an adult. I had no parking tickets, speeding tickets, even all those nights at the bar pulling Theo off some guy who pissed him off; I was never charged with anything. This situation was doing my head in with worry.

"I have the contact information here, but that is all. It seems that the courts put a hold on your savings last week; they have been trying to reach out to you for a few years. It looks like there is one other note stating, 'due to no response from multiple attempts, we will be holding your accounts' then it provides their contact information."

"Is this even legal? I have never gotten a letter, nor a phone call. Hell, I would think that this is something that they would have someone serve me. You can't do this!"

"I am sorry, I truly am, but we're not the ones doing this. There isn't much I can do about this. Again, I am so sorry, Mr. Kelley." She really did look like she felt for me, which is not a reaction I got much with my long hair, tattoos, and the bike that I rode everywhere.

I knew that I couldn't take my frustration out on her. It wasn't fair. She was just the messenger, after all.

"It's all right. Thank you for the information." I take the post-it note from her with the contact number. The only thing that I could do was call them and figure out why they did this to me. Did fraud happen? Do they think I killed someone? Every reason I could think of for this happening wasn't a good one.

Why the fuck would a judge sign off on placing a hold on my money? I may be a guy with nothing but friends. I may be a former foster kid who aged out of the system, but I was a good, hardworking man. I paid my taxes, volunteered with other foster kids to help them take the advantages they were given and not dwell on the disadvantages.

"Take the free secondary schooling the state is giving and be better than what they expect from you." That's what I instilled in those kids day in and day out. I wanted them to be better than I was. I wanted them to do better. They had the opportunity. They just had to take it.

The whole ride home, I was playing my life repeatedly in my head, trying to pinpoint anything I did that would cause my assets to be frozen. Still, nothing but the worst came to mind.

Not your assets, just your savings account. I told myself, but that did little to ease the knot in my belly, the stress in my head. I walked in the door to Theo drinking a beer on the couch. He was talking to me, but I didn't hear him. I only saw his lips moving. I continued on my path to the kitchen to make the call. I don't remember dialing the phone number, and I barely know what is going on when the receptionist answers the phone.

"Spek, Duiker, and Michaud, how may I direct your call?" The soft voice said on the other end of the line; I couldn't say anything. Was she the one that held my life in her hands?

"Hello?' She asked a bit louder. I cleared my throat and finally found words.

"Hi. Uhm, I am not sure who I need to speak to," I said, trying to find my balls again to get this settled.

"Okay, what is the nature of your issue? And I can try and get you to the right person." She was sweet. I needed that right about now.

"I was trying to get a mortgage, and they said my account was on hold and I needed to contact someone at this law firm. I am just outside San Bernardino, California. So, I must say, having to call someone in Colorado was a bit unexpected." *There you go; your head is officially out of your ass.*

"Okay, so you will want one of the partners. What is your name?" I can hear her typing away, probably an email, to whomever I needed to talk to.

"Kenneth Kelley," I said simply, there was a pause in the typing, and I could hear a mild gasp in her breath.

"Okay, just one moment, Mr. Kelley, I will get you to who you need to talk to."

The line clicked, and there was trashy hold music playing. I took a deep breath, closed my eyes, and when I opened them, Theo's ugly ass face was right there, causing me to jump back. I cursed under my breath, but before I could say anything to him, the line clicked back to a male voice.

"Mr. Kelley?"

"Yes, I'm here, hi!" I rushed out the words, getting an odd look from my friend and roommate. I wasn't keeping the control that I normally had.

"Mr. Kelley, my name is Pontaleon Michaud, and I am sorry that this is what it came to, but we have been trying to reach you for many years, sir. There is someone who is looking for you, and you also have an inheritance waiting for you here in Colorado." He says, sounding like he is really excited and on the edge of his seat.

"I'm sorry, you're telling me that you guys froze my accounts because you have money for me?" This is the stupidest thing I have ever heard in my life, but I was floored. Theo's eyes went huge as he sat across from me on the kitchen counter. "This sounds like a badly plotted movie on Hallmark or horror movie." I release a humorless laugh. "Do I have to stay forty-eight hours in a haunted house to get said money?" I didn't want to believe it. This also sounded like one of those emails that trap older people into thinking a prince will love them and give them all their money.

"No, sir, but you will need to come here for all the details. I promise it will be worth all the trouble. Now that you have contacted us, we can release the money once you give us your travel plans to come here."

"Forgive me but, how the fuck do I know that you aren't full of shit? That this isn't some ploy to rob me of everything I have. Even though, in some way, you already have. You want me to get to you yet; you froze my money."

"Only your savings accounts. I know that you have checking accounts. We froze the larger account so you would take notice. I really do apologize, but we needed to contact you. All previous attempts have gone unanswered. I promise I want nothing to do with the funds that are rightfully yours. I know that I am asking a lot, but I am asking you to trust me."

"Right, trust a lawyer."

He chuckled, and I could tell that that was either something he heard a lot and didn't phase him, or my snide comment didn't bother him because he was telling the truth.

"Yeah, I can see how my title makes me seem shady as hell. Please. I have the documents ready to go. You just need to come here. In the worst case, after you hear what I have to say, all you have wasted is a drive. But I promise you, the reward is worth it." He says.

I now hear doors opening and closing, computers typing, taking notes, or getting the paperwork ready; I wasn't sure. But he was right. I really had nothing to lose, and if I trusted him, everything to gain. I take my mouth away from the phone, looking Theo dead in the eye.

"Wanna move to Colorado?"

It took a few days, but Theo and I loaded up his truck with my bike and anything we thought we would need, which honestly was not much. Being foster kids most of our lives, we were used to traveling light because nowhere would keep us long. Unfortunately, it is a tough habit to break.

I stood outside the law office, wondering again if this was a trick. Was this something they said to bring me here to arrest me for something I didn't do? I know I was letting my imagination run away with me, but this was just insane. How could a kid with nothing and no family end up with an inheritance? I know not one of those foster families left me anything. It was just too good to be true.

"Are you going to stand here or go in?" A brash female voice said from beside me.

I look and see my hand is on the handle, and I have just been standing here. I mumble an apology, not looking at the woman while I open the door for her. I guess there is no time like the present to get this done. I walk in, and it feels like all eyes are on me; I am used to that. I don't look like I should be in here. I feel as out of place as I look, but I keep my head high as I make my way to the reception.

"Welcome to Spek, Duiker and Michaud. How can I help you today?" The same soft voice from over the phone asks me. Her voice matches her eyes. A soft blue, hidden behind dark-framed glasses. She is older than me, hinted at by her head full of grey hair. She calms me, if only for a moment.

"I am here to meet with Mr. Pant- Mr.Ponte-." I am struggling with pronouncing his name as he flew through it on the phone and in the follow-up email, fuck if I could pronounce it.

"Mr. Michaud?" She asked with a small smile, making me feel at ease and not judging me for not remembering his name. I nodded yes, returning the smile. "Who may I tell him is here?"

"Kenneth Kelley," I say simply.

Her eyes shot to me again, and she was gone from her chair to the offices in the back. I stood there for a whole three seconds before she returned, leading me down a long hallway, and again, it seemed all eyes were on me. I was not sure what that meant. Was this a trap, was everyone in on a secret that I wasn't?

"Mr. Kelley?" I heard the lawyer's voice.

"Ken." I corrected, reaching for his hand to return the proffered handshake. "Fancy place you got here," I say, looking around the office. He closed the door and followed me to the desk. "I am not sure what is going on, but it seems the whole office knows about me."

I am trying to break the tension that is building. I am sure it is one-sided; I mean, this guy has stated there is an inheritance.

Once it is all said and done, he will be getting a cut, so he is more excited about that than my being here.

While he pulled files from his desk, I studied the man, he was in his mid to late fifties, slightly greying around the temples, and honestly, you can tell he spent most of his life sitting in an office and very little time in the courtrooms these days.

"Mr. Kelley, Ken. I am an estate attorney, and I have been with the firm representing this estate for more than thirty years. Not only that, our firm as a whole has been working with the Faulkner Family Ranch for over eighty years."

My eyes go wide.

"I'm sorry, did you say, Faulkner Family *Ranch*?" My heart was going a million miles a minute. The reason I was at the bank is now right here in front of my face.

"Yes, sir. It seems your mother left the ranch and never looked back. Your grandparents didn't know of your existence until sometime after she had passed, and by then, you were in the system. Sadly, they could not find you because you had – have - your father's last name. When they did find you, you were eighteen and already aged out of the system. Sadly, they couldn't reach you then. Every attempt made ended in disconnected phones, or you had already moved on. It took a long time and another death in your family for the courts to allow us to freeze one of your accounts, just to get your attention." He flipped open the folder and started pulling out sheets.

"I have grandparents?" I said softly. I am struggling to breathe at this point. I had a family that actually wanted me. Yet, they couldn't get in contact with me because of how I was raised. Once I turned eighteen, I tried to keep a phone, I tried to have ways for others to communicate with me, but other means of survival were more important.

"I am sorry to say that your grandfather passed last year at the age of eighty-six. His health had been failing for many years, but he wanted to find you." He slid a paper to me, and the name jumped out at me.

"Kenneth Levoy Faulkner is the third generation to own and run the family's Cattle Ranch. He was hoping to pass it along to his daughter, but then after her unfortunate death, they would have to sell the ranch. However, after some digging, they discovered she had a son. You were about ten when the search started."

My mind was racing; I started to hyperventilate, jumping from the chair and starting to pace.

"I was put in the system at three. THREE!" I was freaking out, running my hands through my shoulder-length hair. "I was in a system where I was abused, beaten, starved, and I had a family that wanted me? The whole fucking time, I could have had a better life. I could have been loved!"

The look on this man's face tells me he was unaware of everything that I went through. As I pace, I replay my childhood and wonder if it would have been so different. Would I be as hard-working and strong-willed as I am now? Would I have been a different person and knew more about my parents than the few pictures I had left? SO many questions, so many thoughts. I should have told Theo to come with me; he would slap me and get me focused again.

"Mr. Kelley, Ken, please sit. I have much more to tell you about your family, what is going on with the Ranch, and the money in the Faulkner name." He stood but spoke softly, trying to get me to refocus. It worked. Something in his tone, I shook it off and took a seat.

"Now, I know this is a shock, but there is more news, good news. While your grandfather has passed, your grandmother is still very much alive and living at the ranch house."

I wanted to cry. Over thirty years of thinking I have no real family, I found out that I not only have a blood family, but they wanted me and were actively looking for me. So much emotion was screaming to be released, but I needed to listen and hear more about what was coming to me before I rushed out the door into my grandmother's arms.

"Ken, due to your grandmother's advanced age, she wants you to take over the Ranch. She wants you to learn about how it works, and when you have learned as much as you can, she wants you to become the rightful owner of the place. That includes all titles of land and buildings. As well as access to any and all accounts." He concludes by handing over the papers in the folder; it is the latest appraisal of the land and all bank statements in the Ranch's name.

The numbers were staggering. She wanted me to have it. I wasn't worthy of it. She doesn't know me.

"She doesn't even know me," I whisper, speaking aloud what I had just thought. Looking at the numbers and the will with my late grandfather's name on it.

"But we have done a background check, and she sees how long you were in the system, and because the judge allowed us to look into and share your bank information with the parties involved, she knows you are good with your money and hardworking. She also knows you are family, and family is everything, blood or not. She wants you and your travel companion to accompany me to the ranch."

"Right now?" I asked, still in shock.

"Yes, I booked the rest of today to help you get everything you needed in order with her." He had this smile that proved that he knew how hard they were looking for me for her and how much she wanted this.

While everything as a whole was a huge invasion of my personal life, I was already starting to feel grateful for the intrusion.

I made a phone call to Theo, and he swung by to get me in the truck. We followed the small car that the lawyer drove the whole way there. We watched the older man go into the house from the truck, waiting to see what would happen when he told her that they had found me and that I wanted to learn. I couldn't believe that my lifelong dream to own and operate a Cattle Ranch was on its way to becoming a reality.

"I think that outbuilding there would be good for me to set up a mechanics shop," Theo said, trying to get me out of my own head.

"I think that is a bunkhouse, dude," I replied, looking at him. "After all these years, we have a family, man," I say, looking at him, getting the thoughts out.

"You have a family; I am just along for the ride." He said, with nothing but love in the tone, his hand on my shoulder. But how wrong he was. He was just as much a part of this newfound family. After all, he's been the only family I have ever had constantly. I wasn't getting rid of him now.

"Nah, man, you were my only family for so many years. This is your family too! This is our dream, and we will make it work." I reach across the seat and pull him into a hug.

When we pull back, we see an older woman on the wraparound porch beside the lawyer. She looked pretty spry for a woman in her eighties, but that just meant that I had time to learn and get to know her.

We vacated the truck and made our way over to them. The woman hobbles down the steps quickly until she is right in front of me. She is tiny; she cannot be more than five feet tall. Only coming up to mid-chest on Theo and me. She looks me up and down, then tears form in her eyes.

Every cell in my body screams to scoop this woman up close and hold her as my life depended on it. So, I did. She cried on my chest as I held her. Letting my own tears fall freely, I didn't care anymore. I was home. She felt at home. After a moment, we pulled away. She brought her life-worn hands up to my face, inspected my eyes, my hair, and all of my facial features. Her eyes then flicked to Theo, my best friend, brother in life, then back to me.

"Your husband is a real looker." That was all she said with a wink and walked back up the steps, leaving us shocked and too stunned to correct her.

TWO

JUDGE

- Past -

After we had followed my grandmother into the house, she guided us into the large kitchen. She shooed us to take a seat as she got baked treats set up on plates, along with tea and coffee, for all of us to take. Theo was eyeing the cookies good and hard while watching this woman glide about the kitchen like that is where she was the most comfortable. If a woman could be graceful opening and closing cabinets, my grandmother was the epitome of grace.

As she made her way to the table to take her seat. I had to guess that she saw Theo take a cookie out of the corner of her eye and bite into it. I don't know how she did it or how fast it happened, but she produced a wooden spoon from her apron pocket and knocked Theo square in the back of the head. This caused him to spit the cookie he was chewing across the table, between the lawyer and me, and hit the wall beside my head.

"It's not polite to start eating until the host or hostess is seated and ready for the visit. Aren't all you homosexuals about manners and proper etiquette?" She asked, taking the leftover cookie from his hand and popping it in her mouth as she took her seat beside him.

"We aren't gay, ma'am." He mumbles, rubbing the point of contact on the back of his head.

"Really? You were all loving up on each other in the truck, I just assumed. You make a mighty fine couple; I wouldn't put it past ya." She shrugged and started doctoring up her tea the way she liked it. I should jump in and correct her, but watching Theo try to navigate this is just too funny to stop.

"Well, you know what they say when you assume…." Theo said, reaching for another cookie.

The older woman, quick as ever, whipped the wooden spoon out yet again—this time smacking the back of his hand, causing him to lose another cookie to her. I am in tears laughing at this point. I'm not sure if it's because my best friend is getting served by an old lady or simply because she assumed we were gay, just because he hugged me. Nonetheless, I enjoyed the free show, judging by the snorts coming from the lawyer; he was also.

"In this house, there will be no sass, backtalk, smart mouthing, and sure as hell no swearing. My name is Matilda Marie May Faulkner, born Morrisson, but you can call me Yaya. A god-fearing man raised me, and he didn't take no shit from no one. Taught me how to do the same. This Ranch is your home for as long as you want it, but in this house, there are rules, and I expect you to abide by them no matter how old you are. Understood?" She looked from me to Theo, my eyes wide while I slowly nodded my reply.

"You said there was no swearing. But you swore. Twice!" Theo pointed out, earning him yet another smack and a lost cookie from my grand- from Yaya.

"I also said no back talk! Is he always this thick?" She asks me, and I'm done by this point. This woman has brought so much joy and life into my world, and I've only known about her for forty-five minutes.

"I think with a few more rounds with the wooden spoon, he will start to see things your way." I chuckle while taking a big gulp of hot coffee. Theo goes to flip me off out of reflex, and that earns him one more good smack with the wooden spoon. I wouldn't be surprised if, right about now, he is second-guessing coming with me.

"Now, go clean that cookie off my wall and floor. We live on a ranch; that's a surefire way to get vermin in the house!"

She barks at him; he listens and makes sure to keep his grumbling to a minimum.

Judging by the self-satisfied smirk on her face, as she takes her first sip of tea, Yaya hears him but is cutting him a slight break at this point. Which, in turn, makes me laugh even harder. Her eyes are now drawn to me, which I notice because I am still aware of every little move she makes.

"You look like your grandfather when he was young. But a bit more tired around the eyes. Tell me about your life, was it hard? Were you loved?" She folded her hands in front of her, almost in prayer, hoping I would tell her I was loved. I wasn't sure if I should spare her and lie, but at the same time, something told me that she would know that I was, and I would be on the receiving end of that damn spoon.

"I… I had a hard life from the age three and up." I cleared my throat, not realizing the emotions that were just below the surface. "When my parents were killed in the accident, I was put into a special home to help me with the few broken bones I sustained.

They didn't do everything needed, and I still have some issues with my right knee when the weather shifts.

Then I was moved to an all-boys group home for a few years, then to a private home. A few months after that, Theo came into the home. I was about eight or nine, and he wasn't that much younger. He instantly became the little brother that I had never had yet always wanted. We fought to stay together, so the only time we were separated was when I aged out of the system and had to wait for Theo to do the same.

We continued that back-and-forth path until I left the system. I started working hard learning how cars and engines worked, honed my skills, and got myself a place to live. When Theo aged out two years later, he joined me, and we have been working and living together ever since." I shoot my best friend a smile and look back at Yaya.

She looks heartbroken, tears gathering in her eyes, her small hand reaches for Theo's. But, given their most recent interactions, he flinches and pulls himself away from her. We all chuckle as she takes his hand in hers and kisses the back of it. She places her free hand on his cheek and pulls him close so she can look him in the eyes.

"Thank you for being there for him when we couldn't." She pats his cheek, takes a deep breath, looking between us again. "Are you sure you are not homosexuals? As I said, you do make a handsome couple."

"Oh, I am sure Mrs. Faulkner," Theo started. "We are just best friends. But to clarify, if we were, he would totally be the wife." This got him another smack upside the head, only it was from me and my big mit this time.

"That is Yaya to you, boy!" She sassed him. It made me believe, because she ignored the wife comment, that even if we were a couple, she truly wouldn't care.

"Well, I hate to put a damper on this, but we have some legal documents and paperwork to go through together here." Mr. Michaud said before Theo could point out she had broken her own rule again.

I had forgotten that he was even here by this point. He allowed us to have a moment before everything got heavy because this type of paperwork was emotionally draining. He allowed part of the emotional heaviness to get out of the way, which I appreciated more than he could ever know.

"Now, here in your grandfather's last will, he leaves the ranch house and personal vehicles to your grandmother as well as a sizable bank account to spend the rest of her days comfortably. Anything left within the account after she passes will go to you, Ken. As well as the house and vehicles. To you, his only other living blood relative, he leaves you the Ranch, all one thousand two hundred and thirty-two acres, and buildings residing on this land, less the ranch house. Again, that is to be yours once your grandmother passes. As well as full control and access of all business accounts in the farm's name. You are to train and learn how the Ranch operates from the lead Cowboy and Head Ranch hand, Robert Davidson, as well as taking courses in animal husbandry at the learning annex in town."

He cleared his throat, looking up at me, half expecting an objection to this clause, before continuing.

"Once you have control, you are to run the ranch as you see fit. Upgrade with the times and change the livestock as you deem necessary. This Ranch may be your heritage, but it is also yours to someday pass on to your children. You are not allowed to sell it. Should you face dire life circumstances, you are to offer it to Robert first. Should he choose not to accept it, you may then sell it. Dire circumstances include a child being sick and needing medical attention that you cannot pay for otherwise, every single animal dying, etc. This ranch shall remain in this family at all costs. Make it something you would be proud to pass on."

I look at Yaya, and she is dabbing the corner of her eye with her apron. Theo has his arm around her, pulling her close, giving her some comfort. He has never had someone that he could smother in this kind of comfort before, besides me. I took the words the lawyer read to heart; they were a direct quote from my grandfather to me on his deathbed, and I wanted to make him proud. Which I could tell he was all too happy to give. This was my dream before I even knew about this part of my life. This ranch would have an even longer legacy than either of us had ever dreamed of if it was the last thing I did.

"The Ranch carries over 350 head of Highland cattle, 25 Scots Grey chickens, 3 Scots Grey roosters, 15 Scottish Blackface Sheep, 2 Clydesdale horses, 6 quarter horses, 2 Bearded Collies and 2 Border Collies. All records of breeding are on the computer in the cattle office, as well as a list of all breeders that have been used in the past." He continues to list the vehicles, tractors, and trailers that are also the property of the Faulkner Ranch. He even goes over the last vet visits and results. Even though that is something that I knew Robert would be going over.

"We have cattle pastures, sheep pastures, land that we grow crops for our own consumption as well as for sale." Yaya states.

My head starts to spin. This is all mine, but with Yaya owning the house, does that mean I will have to live in town and commute? Will I have to live in the barn? When can I set up the one outbuilding for Theo to open his mechanics shop? I am sure he would be super useful in fixing any and all mechanical objects on the land. How many cowboys do we have? There is so much, I feel myself start to get overwhelmed again, but this time, I can't handle it.

My world fades to black before I can even ask for help.

I came around sometime later. I can hear Yaya and Theo talking with the lawyer. As he is still here, I must not have been out as long as I had thought. I can't believe that I passed out. What did that say about me? How can Yaya trust me to handle all of this if hearing about it all makes me pass out?

"He will be fine, Yaya."

"Has this ever happened before?"

"Honestly, no. But, he also hasn't been told that he has a long-lost family, met that family, and then told he is not only gaining a ranch that he has wanted his whole life but also inheriting millions of dollars. On top of that, he is now responsible for so many lives. It's been him and I against the world for a long time. He was trying to get a loan less than a week ago to start his own little ranch. He has just been given a fully functioning one. It's a lot to take on. He will be okay, though. He needs to process it."

"Maybe we should hold off on giving him so much. Is that something we can do, Mr. Michaud?"

"Yes, but...."

His voice fades as the one in my head grows louder. I can't allow that to happen. I can't let Yaya down. What Theo said is right. This was a lot of information handed to me, and my world did a complete one-eighty. It was only a few short days ago when I thought that the worst had happened, only to find out that the one thing I wanted in life was my new normal.

I needed them to know that I was okay. That I would be able to do this without any issue. I was strong-willed, hardheaded, and I could make this work. Nothing was going to stop me.

"No. Do not change the plan. I am fine, honestly."

"Ken! Oh my goodness, boy. You nearly put me in an early grave. Something I will not tolerate before you give me great grandbabies to love on."

"Whoa there, Yaya, hold it down for just a moment. I'm not there just yet. I wanna do right by you first and get this ranch going the way it should. Great grandbabies aren't coming anytime soon."

As soon as the last word left my lips, I felt the smack of the wooden spoon.

"Ah! What the hell was that for?"

Immediately, I felt two more smacks.

"What the hell did I say about back talking and swearin' boy? When I tell you to give me grandbabies, you best reckon that I expect them from you. I will not leave this earth without getting the chance to spoil babies."

"Okay, and what were the other two smacks for?"

"For almost making me see Jesus today. Watching you hit the floor was too much for my heart. Never again, child. Never. Do. That. Again." I knew she was serious as I am pretty sure the Devil just came out in her tone just now.

I could see the fear in Yaya's eyes. She had just got me, and I went and did a fucking dumbass thing like pass out. I couldn't tolerate knowing that I made this woman so upset. That I scared her so badly. I pulled her into my embrace and let her know that I wasn't going anywhere, and reluctantly, I told her I'd work on the great-grandbabies thing even though that was the farthest thing from my mind.

After all, I just got here. Who the hell was I going to find that would let me knock them up that quickly?

THREE

ELVIRA

-Past -

"Guys, let's get a move on!" I usually like to do my shopping once a week, but with two growing boys and a daughter who has decided to be pickier than my budget can afford, I seem to be going daily. "I swear to the good Lord below that if I am stuck bringing home the bruised vegetables, you ain't eating nothing but oatmeal and bologna for a week!"

"MOM! You can't threaten us like that." J.J. whines at me

"Oh, am I mistaken? Can you please show me where you became the one in charge, the one making money, the one cleaning your clothes, keeping a roof over your head, and making sure you live a good life? No. Shut the hell up and get in the car." He huffs, tossing my bags for the product into the back of the SUV.

I swear these kids do nothing but test me daily. I can't tolerate them from 8 am to 6 pm, but I love them more than life itself. They remind me that getting away from their daddy was worth all the pain I was going through. The trouble would be worth it in the end. I just had to get to the end.

However, I wish the boys could be more like their little sister. She doesn't complain nearly as much. She is a saint in comparison. I was blessed with her. I think the man above saw what he'd given me with Jonathan and Robert and felt terrible. Elenor was golden.

"Mom, why do R.J. and I need to go with you? Ellie loves this shit. Why can't you just take her and leave us home?"

One, two, three, four, five. Breathe in. Breathe out.

"Boy, what have I told you about that language? I don't give a rat's ass if you *think* you are grown. You are barely fifteen years old. I will paddle that ass of yours if you continue to backtalk; you aren't grown enough for me not to take you over my knee. And as for why you are coming, I need no other reason than 'I told you so.' Now, get in the damn car."

Sometimes, I felt that Jonathan and Robert took the worst parts of their father and became almost replicas. It was bad enough that they looked like him. Although while I would never admit it to my piece of shit soon-to-be-ex, I would never regret my time with him because although they drive me crazy, these kids are the very best parts of him and me as well.

Sure, the boys took some of the worst parts from their father, like his short fuse mixed with a hot temper, but they also took what was once great. Before the shit hit the fan, their father was sweet, caring, and he loved me hard, almost too hard; that should have been a red flag. It wasn't until years after we had gotten married that the devil came out. The devil tried to blacken my soul and crush my desire to live. He failed, though. He underestimated just how powerful my will to live was. How powerful it still is.

"Mommy, why don't we just go? We can have a girls' day?" Ellie piped up from the front seat.

She took only the best from the two of us. She was my little mini-me in every way except she got her father's muddy brown hair over my deep auburn curls. She is also the reason why I was strong enough to walk away from that monster that blessed me with these three. We are a rag-tag group of mismatched people, but we fit, and we love each other.

"As much as I love the thought of that baby girl, this is the only day that I get all three of you together. So come on, let's go." I pointed, again, to the car and watched as the sullen teenage boys crawled in the back seat.

With the kids finally in the car, I was about to lock up the house so we could head out to the farmers market when the phone rang. The only one that should be calling me was my lawyer. Thankfully, the windows in the car were manual, and it wasn't hot enough out yet for them to be down. The kids could wait for a moment while I see what my lawyer needs.

"Hello?" I couldn't hide the slight quiver in my voice as I answered.

"Mrs. May, do you have a moment?" A meek man spoke on the phone.

"Sure, Mr. Spek, what can I help you with?" I cleared my throat and tried to shake the ominous feeling off.

"I need you to come to my office as soon as you possibly can." There was a mild sense of urgency in his tone that wasn't there when I answered; the last time I heard that tone, I was hospitalized

"I can't right now. I have my kids with me." My mind was racing. What in the world was going on?

"This involves them too; your ex violated his parole, again. The Judge signed off on your request to expedite your divorce, grant you sole physical and legal custody of the kids, and only supervised visitation once a month with your ex. I need you to come to sign the updated paperwork, and then you are finally free of him." This was all I wanted, but there was still an edge to what he was saying.

I couldn't breathe. I didn't think that this day would come. Travis was lower than low yet somehow kept convincing the Judge that he deserved to be in the kid's life. That he wasn't a threat to them. Why would he be? He didn't beat them, only me. The fight against him was starting to take its toll on me not only mentally but physically as well. So getting this call, a weight had been lifted. There was still so much at stake, though. Supervised visitation meant he still had access to the kids in some capacity, and then there was the fact he violated the terms of his parole *again*. What was it this time, guns, drugs, or did he cross the county border without telling his PO about it and got busted.... Oh, I can't even think about how close he might have gotten to us.

"I'll be there in 20 minutes."

We said our goodbyes, and I rushed out to the car. I didn't have to hide this news from the kids. They all testified against their father, but his disgusting lawyer twisted it, stating that I had possibly made them say the things they did. All because some desperate women do that in the heat of a custody battle. They still have to see him, but there will be an impartial third party watching and monitoring how he is with the kids.

"Kids, change of plans. We're going to my lawyer's office first." I try to hide the shaking in my hands as I buckle up.

"What? Why?" J.J. is at full attention. He was the one who was privy to most of the violence between his father and me.

"What happened?" R.J. was just as on edge and practically climbed in the front seat with me.

"Your father violated parole, again. The judge had no choice but to grant the speedy divorce and grant me full custody of you three. You all still have visitation with him once a month, but it's at the visitation centers, and there are people always watching and listening. I know it's not 100% what we wanted, but it's still so close to it that we cannot be that upset about it. I need to sign some papers, and it's official."

The shouts of joy told me that I was doing the right thing by them. They understood the position that I was in and knew this was one of the best outcomes after so many shitty ones. With a smile on my face and three additional smiles in the car with me, I headed to my lawyers' office to start the rest of our lives.

I get the kids situated in the car, promising that I won't be long, and rush down the sidewalk to the office. There I am, stopped by this man who is just standing at the door. Frozen in place, I couldn't get around him because he had his big meaty hand on the handle. I gently clear my throat in hopes he would snap out of whatever he needs to deal with. He didn't move; he didn't flinch, almost like he didn't hear me, so I tried again. And still nothing. I was antsy to get the paperwork signed and filed with the Judge. I was bouncing on my toes and trying to think of ways to get his attention; I cleared my throat for the third time, only louder, and still, he did not move. Finally, I had enough, I was so close to freedom from my ex I could taste it, and now all that stood in my way was this guy!

"Are you going to stand there or go in?" It came out harsher than I wanted, but nothing else was working.

He snapped out of it, kind of mumbled something, and opened the door for me. I rushed past him, waved at Anita at the front desk, and hurried my way down to Mr. Spek's office. I practically slid to a stop in front of his office and knocked before entering his open door.

"Mrs. May, you made it in record time." He seems a little shocked at how fast I was.

"We were already out the door on the way to the farmers market." I take the seat offered at the front of his desk. "I am really excited about this ruling. Does this mean my Order Of Protection was extended as well?" I ask, hoping that he just forgot to mention that in the phone call.

The look on his face made my heart sink. He not only has access to the kids now, but he also has access to me. He can come to our new home and talk to me; he can reach me and hurt me even more than he ever has. He will because he has had time to fester and stew on the fact I dared to leave him, I dared to better myself, and in his eyes, I turned the kids against him.

"I am sorry, Elvira, but because he stuck to the agreed-upon email-only communication, took the anger management course, and has shown change to his PO and the Judge, they don't feel he is a threat to you, or the children, anymore. The original end date stays; it was just the extension that was denied." You could hear the disdain in his voice for that ruling as well.

"But, that's only six more weeks! You also said he broke parole! What the hell did he do then to break parole?" I was trying not to shout; I went to run my fingers through my hair but stopped myself and started pulling at my cuticles instead.

"He was caught gambling at the track and drinking. Conditions of his parole were no drugs, alcohol, gambling, and no firearms. He broke the basic conditions and had nothing to do with you and has abided by the conditions of his release when it came to you and the kids. Given your history with him and the testimony from the kids, they have agreed to supervised visitation, and then they are going to revisit it in six months." He explained, showing me the outline on the paperwork with the Judge's signature.

I can feel the nerves and the stress get to me more and more; my hands shake. He can get to me, to the kids; I have no more lines of defense after these next six weeks are up. What is to stop him from following us home after visitation? There is nothing left that the police and the courts can do for me until I am bruised, broken, and dead in a ditch and my kids are left alone. I need to take matters into my own hands now. I need to bring myself up and defend my kids and myself since there is nothing the law can do for me now.

"Okay, so when is the first visitation?" I ask. The thickness in my throat causes me to almost choke on the words.

"He will email you when he has made the appointment at the visitation center. The visitation is one weekend a month, and he is in charge of making the appointment at the center and communicating that to you." Mr. Spek pointed that out in the paperwork as well.

I signed it all.

He told me my copies would be in the mail as soon as Travis signed his copy. I shook his hand and left. Feeling more deflated than happy that I was leaving divorced but not fully protected. I don't know how the boys are going to react to that at all. I kind of do, but I will try to be upbeat about it and bring the positivity they need and deal with the rest.

I know many look down at being open about a divorce and custody issues with your kids, but it's their life too. J.J. is almost fifteen, R.J. is thirteen, and Ellie is ten; they are well aware of everything that is going on. Ellie saw the last big altercation between their father and me, which was why we packed up and left him. My kids gave me the strength to find myself again and make a better life for us here.

I don't even remember the walk back to the car. I was in a fog. The kids were sitting on the hood of the car talking to each other when I walked up. I didn't have time to school my features before they saw me. J.J. hopped off the car and wrapped me up, he may only be fourteen, but he is already taller than me. I hold him close and feel R.J. and Ellie join our group hug. At that moment, I knew I would do anything and everything I needed to keep them happy and safe, even if that means sacrificing myself in the process.

The weekend went by without a hitch. We never did make it to the farmers market, but the kids humored me and helped me stress clean the whole house. J.J. and R.J. even tried to cook for us, and as much as I appreciated that effort, I almost killed them for messing up my clean and organized kitchen.

Monday came; I got the kids up, breakfast cooked, and lunch made. The boys were back to normal, grumbling that they were the only kids who brought their lunches to school while all their friends bought theirs. I make another sandwich, a piece of fruit, and a baggie of veggies and slide them in J.J.'s backpack. He watches me and knows why I am doing it and why we don't talk about it. He confided in me about a friend, and we are doing what little we can to make his life easier.

I get the kids on the bus, and off to work I go. I hate my job. Well, I love working with numbers and balancing budgets but doing it here with all these fucking men who think that they can just spend what they want and I am going to pull more money out of my ass is ridiculous.

We are a small town feed store, a lot of farmers grow their own for large cattle, so I don't know why we keep all that feed in our sheds. Maybe it's just for the mice? We are forced to throw out so much and just take the loss on it. It's a waste of money, but I don't know what I am talking about because I am just a woman. I walk into the back office and see more receipts and invoices just tossed all over the place, no rhyme or reason.

"Hey, Karl?" I called out on the floor, on my way to find him.

"What?" He called back from the front of the store.

"Karl, what's all over the desk? I balanced our inventory and receipts on Friday before I left for the day. I know we were not due any other shipments, seeding is done for the season, and no one has that many chickens around here."

"I was looking for something and couldn't figure out your filing system, so I pulled it all out. It's not like you have a lot to do today. You can work them all back into the cabinet." He shrugged like it wasn't that big of a deal.

"Karl!" I exclaim, trying to keep some semblance of calm. "It's payroll, and bills are due to our distributors this week. Mondays are the worst! Why didn't you just call me and I would have helped you. Now I have two weeks of filing and sorting to do on top of payroll!" I can't even keep my cool anymore.

All the stress from Friday afternoon, this, and just life in general, has come to a boiling point. I was done with all of this, and I was going to explode in the middle of the shop in front of God and all the customers in here. I started to breathe deeply and walked back to the office. I started sorting through it all, trying to find the bottom of the pile. I am not an emotional person, but I cry when I hit a certain level of anger. I reached that level, and as I am trying to sort myself out as well as the papers, Karl comes huffing back to me.

“Are you on your period or something?” He shouts.

“Excuse me?”

“You heard me! That can be the only reason why you have the balls to come after me in my shop, in front of my employees and customers, like that. Questioning me like you know more than me, and I have been at this a lot longer than you have been alive, honey.” He starts menacingly approaching me; I can feel my heart pounding in my chest. Everything about him right now is exactly how Travis was. His demeanor, his tone, the balled fists. I don’t know if I will be able to hold myself up. I want to curl into a ball and protect myself from the fists that I am sure will be swinging at me at any time. Why is Travis doing this? No. Not Travis. This is Karl. I’m at work. He won’t hit me. I pull myself together as best as I know and decided that I will not back down from this man. I will do what I should have done sooner with my ex.

“You also had your wife manage the books, and since she left your misogynistic ass, you practically begged me and my accounting degree to work for you! So, when I asked, it wasn’t against you!” I yell back, tears blurring my vision and dripping down on the paper on the desk.

“Listen here bitch! I don’t need you or your fucking attitude!” He spat at me, his neck turning purple. “You can just pack up your shit and take your hormonal ass out the door. I don’t care what happens to you and your fucking crotch goblins! Get the fuck out of here! I will make sure you never work in this town again!”

He turns to leave, and we see a crowd has gathered to watch the festivities unfold. For a small town, the feed shop was filled up with people. Perfect, just what I fucking needed, more humiliation on top of everything else that is going on in my life. My personal and professional life is falling apart.

"Sir, I think you need to apologize to the lady." I heard a voice out of view say, a gravelly voice that made my whole body tingle.

"Who the fuck are you to tell me what to do?" Karl demanded. I busied myself cleaning up my personal things but keeping my ear open for this conversation.

"If you have truly fired her, I'm her new boss and a gentleman. My outlook is that you treat people the way you want to be treated. If I were you, I would apologize to the lady." He started again. I could hear whispers out the door.

Wait, I thought. *"New Boss?"*

FOUR

JUDGE

-Past -

I tried to keep my composure as I tried to get this gorilla of a man to apologize to the fiery woman hidden away in the back room, which I assume is her office. No woman should be spoken to like that. I am sure Yaya would have words for this Karl fellow if she were here and not at her quilting club meeting at the community center.

"You just got the ranch, and you are hiring some random person?" Theo said, only loud enough for me to hear. He was right in questioning me, though. What kind of business person states that they are going to hire someone out of the blue? How can I be successful in this if I act impulsively?

However, I also knew that this woman didn't deserve to be spoken to in that manner. From what I could hear of their fight, this putz of a man begged her to work here. She claims to have an accounting degree. Shit. What the hell did I just offer?

"I am not saying shit to her. No one, including you and especially her, can come into my business and yell at me as she did. I am her boss, not the other way around."

"From what I could hear, you fucked up her filing. She keeps this in order, not you. So going in there and doing whatever it is that you did, is unacceptable. Firing her because she stated that you could have just called her is horseshit."

I was fuming at this point, and I didn't understand why. I have never met this woman. Why was I coming to her defense so quickly? Almost irrationally so. But I started this fight, and I was determined to finish it. Even if I now realized how dumb it is.

"Look, I don't care if this is your business and you're her boss. She doesn't deserve to be spoken to like that. No one does. Be a gentleman and apologize to the lady." He huffed a deep breath and exhaled loudly.

"Fine. Elvira, get out here."

"This isn't so hard now, is it?" Theo mumbled behind me.

I smirked at him, and he grumbled something under his breath. This was going to remain a challenge, and I was aware of this fact instantly. This man is horrible. My guess is Elvira isn't the only woman he treats this way. I am also almost positive that he is only in business since he is the only feed store in the immediate vicinity.

I hear shuffling, and I look up just as Elvira is closing the door to the office. Her back is facing towards us, and I take a moment to appreciate her stunning red hair; it's the most beautiful color of auburn I have ever seen. It almost doesn't look real. But the way the light hits it through the skylights, I can tell that it is.

She is still standing at the door, locking it, maybe? I am not sure, but I do the least gentlemanly thing, and I look down. Her waist comes in, and her hips are far out in comparison to her ass. Mmnnnhh. Her ass is plump. Her jeans hug it tight, and it's big. It isn't overly large, but it is juicy, and I want to take a bite out of it immediately. If I had to, I'd say it's like a Honeycrisp Apple. Large, firm yet juicy, delicious. My cock stirs slightly. I have always been an ass man, and hers, wow.

I clear my throat and mentally berate myself for even looking. This is not the time to check this woman out. Just then, Theo hits my arm, and I look over at him. He knows *exactly* what I'm seeing and what I'm thinking. He gives me a smug look, and I tell him to fuck off with my eyes.

"Any goddamn time today, Elvira."

Her back straightens, and she turns. Holy. Fucking. Fuck. Me.

Gone. I'm a damn goner. She is, without a doubt, the most beautiful woman I have ever fucking laid my eyes on. She has an oval-shaped face and the most creamy complexion I have ever seen. A slightly squared chin and the most stunning blue eyes. Those eyes are rimmed in red. She'd been crying. She wasn't anymore, though. Now, those eyes held fire.

She made her way over to the man, and my eyes made their way down her body. I couldn't help myself. I tried. I fucking tried, but I had failed. Her chest was covered thoroughly, but it was evident that it was substantial. I immediately visioned my dick sliding between them; then, I pictured myself suffocating between them and dying the most glorious death. I wanted her - bad.

A low growl had Theo hitting me again and bringing me out of the trance that Elvira had put me in.

"Yes, Karl?"

"You're fired."

"I quit."

"You can't quit; I just fired you."

"Well, too fucking bad, Karl, because I quit."

"Excuse me? You can't fucking speak to me like that. I am your boss."

"Last I fucking checked, you attempted to fire me, and I quit. Have fun doing payroll this week and making sure everyone gets their money. You fucked yourself by not calling me. I hope you continue to fuck yourself and this store tanks. You're a fucking dick, and I honestly understand why your wife left you."

"Yuh bitch!"

That brought me out of the trance she yet again put me in because she stood up for herself. I stepped in between them and put my arm out, hitting him against his shoulder.

"I told you to apologize, and you called her a bitch, again. As of ten minutes ago, you fired her; she quit, it doesn't fucking matter. What matters is, she is no longer in your employ. She is now a consumer. She is a human being that deserves to be treated with respect. I will not tell you again; apologize to the woman."

"Fuck you, cunt."

That was it. I allowed my temper to get the best of me, and I punched Karl across the face. The gasp I heard from behind me is what worried me. I didn't want her to think that I was some bad man. I was anything but. Did I just ruin my chances with her? *What chances are you talking about? She doesn't know you.* True. But I wanted her to.

From the corner of my eye, I see Theo taking her out of the store. I look up, and the patrons that were in the store are smiling. Some even clapped. My guess, Karl treats everyone like shit, and this was a long time coming.

"You son of a bitch, you broke my damn nose!"

"You'll fucking live. Word of advice, stop being a fucking dick. You may be the only store in town, but you will close if you continue to act like this. You're a piece of shit. Judging by people's reactions, you deserve this. Now that I have called you out, don't be surprised if others finally let you know how they feel."

With that, I walked away. I needed to find Elvira. Hopefully, Theo had my back and kept her around. I wasn't sure I should stick to my plan of hiring her before, but now I need to. It would be the easiest way to get to know her, to have her around. I wanted her. The feelings that she evoked within me were almost unbearable. She was everything I have ever desired and everything I knew I needed. The craving I felt wouldn't go away. It wouldn't dwindle. I was going to make her mine: one way or another.

Once I am outside, I look both directions and find Theo and Elvira over to the store's left. I can see that they are talking but that it is awkward as hell. Striding up to them, I clear my throat.

"Are you okay?"

"Yeah, I'm fine. Thank you for trying to get him to apologize. He's always been a dick, but it got worse when his wife left. I just..."

She blew out a breath and started to reach for her hair. She stopped and just let her hands fall to her lap. "Just, thanks."

"You're welcome. I'm Ken, by the way."

"Elvira. But I am sure you knew that already."

I chuckle, "I did."

"Did you also mean that you're my boss now?"

"Yes." I wanted to be her everything. Her boss, her lover, her man, her life. I wasn't going to let her know that just yet, though.

"Why would I come work for you? I don't know you. I don't know what you do. Hell, you don't even know what I do or what my qualifications are and, you just witnessed me telling my now ex-boss to go fuck himself. Pretty sure that isn't professional or what someone would want in an employee."

"All valid points. I don't care about you telling him to fuck off. He deserved it. As for your qualifications, I heard you yelling. I get the gist. You know numbers. I need a numbers person. I just inherited my family's ranch and…."

"Faulkner Ranch?"

"Uh, yeah. You know it?"

"Everyone around here does. It was a big deal when Kenny died. We all tried to do what we could for Yaya, but that woman is stubborn as a mule. She… Wait. Your name is Ken, and you inherited the ranch? Who are you?"

"I'm their grandson."

"Holy fuck. I thought. Wow. That's incredible. I'm…um, I am sorry for your loss. Please excuse me but, where the hell have you been?"

She was brash and straightforward. I was attracted to it completely. I also understood the question. Yet, at the same time, I knew that questions like that took balls. Or, in her case, giant fucking tits.

"I, unfortunately, didn't grow up knowing I was related to them and only recently found out. That's a long-ass story for another time, though. Would you like to come work at the ranch? I don't know the numbers fully yet. I can't offer you what you're worth until everything is straightened out and I see the Profit and Loss statements. In the meantime, I can give you the minimum wage. If you can get me up to speed, say by the end of next week, I'll pay you what you should be making, and I'll give you a $2000 bonus for doing this for me."

I knew Theo thought I was crazy, but I really did need the help. If I wanted this Ranch to survive, I needed someone to give me the numbers breakdown, and a small bonus was a good enough incentive to work for a week and a bit.

"I don't know. Again, I don't know you."

"You're right, you don't know me, but you do know Yaya. I'm just asking for just a little under two weeks of your time. I'll pay you a minimum for hours worked, and then I will still give you the $2000 bonus at the end. Please."

She sat and thought about it. I could see the apprehension on her face. I knew I wasn't offering a lot, but I was only asking for one day shy of two weeks' worth of work. Outloud. Internally, I wanted so much longer. Elvira was the one woman that I would never get out of my head. No matter what. She can say no and walk away, and I will always be left thinking about her.

"Okay. I'll do it, but I have my own condition."

"What is it?" I wasn't sure if her making conditions was something she should be doing right now, but I was interested in what she had to say.

"I have three kids. I need to be home by 5:30 PM at the absolute latest. Preferably by five. I can start working at 7:30 in the morning, but I need to be home to make them dinner and help with schoolwork."

"Done."

"Done? Just like that?"

"Yep. Your kids matter more than the work. I will never keep you from being with your children. That's a promise."

The look of relief that passed through her features told me that this was a problem before. I know what it's like to grow up without the love of your parents. Without them being there. I will never be the reason that her kids don't have their mother around.

"Okay then. Where do I meet you tomorrow?"

"Come out to the ranch. I'll be in the main house. Am I safe to assume you know where it is?"

"Yes," she chuckled, "I know where it is. I'll see you at 7:30 AM."

With that, she got up and walked away. I followed her with my eyes until I couldn't see her anymore. Theo started laughing next to me.

"What the hell is your problem?" I grumble at him, trying to think of ways to get chicken feed now.

"Dude, you are so fucking fucked. That woman walked away with your balls in her purse."

"Man, fuck you." I shoved him, almost pushing him off the narrow walkway.

"No thanks. I'm sure you'll be getting it from her in no time anyways. If you have your way."

I wanted to get my way so badly. I wanted to know everything about her. I wanted her story. I wanted her smiles, her laughs, her kisses. She captivated me. I would never admit it out loud, but Theo is right. She grabbed me by the balls, and I didn't give a shit if I never got them back.

I. Am. Fucked.

FIVE

ELVIRA

-Past -

Making dinner that night was nice; there was no rush, but there was so much going on in my head that I needed all that extra time to compartmentalize. First, there was the fact that I was no longer employed. I also have nothing permanent lined up. Second, I only had just under two weeks to look through and decipher a *one hundred* plus year old family ranch's financial records. Finally, what the hell was going on with my body?

I had just a small interaction with him in front of Karl, and at that moment, there were sensations all over my body, mainly in a part of me I thought was long dead and buried. I thought it was just because he was new around town and fresh meat is hard to come by in such a small community. But his friend escorted me outside when the fight started. I use the term "fight" *very* loosely as Karl really stood no chance in hell against the long-haired cowboy.

His friend did nothing for me. The same tingle wasn't there. The want to be closer and closer, the tingle and need, was only for my hero in a backward ball cap.

Thinking back to the moments before I was rushed away, there was something about him that pulled me in. It wasn't just the fact that I have never seen a man look at me like he did before, or even a man that looked like him in general. Well, okay, online, on tv, in movies, but never in real life. He was just pure perfection in real life, and I haven't even seen all of him. His long hair, thick, somewhat curls at the ends, was at his shoulders. Chocolate in color that is just starting to grey around the temples. His beard cut close to his face yet still thick. Deep expressive blue eyes pierced directly into my soul.

What the hell was happening to me?

"Are you okay?" His friend asked as we sat outside.

"Hmmm?" I was still wrapped up in the fact a man was fighting *for* me, not fighting *with* me.

"I said, are you okay? That wasn't something that I reckon you go through normally. That man was a complete asshole to you and in front of everyone. *Is* that normal?" He looks back at the feed shop, almost wishing he was the one fighting.

"Oh. Karl. Unfortunately, yeah. He has always been a dick. I have, well, had to put up with it because I needed my job. There aren't many opportunities here in town for accounting that are not at a bank. I put up with it."

"That's bullshit." He snorted.

Who the hell was he to tell me what I already fucking knew? I knew that I shouldn't have put up with all the shit I did from Karl. I *really* knew that it was a bullshit reason to stay but, I also knew that I had three kids to feed. There is only so much a single mother can do in the middle of nowhere, Colorado, to make sure you are home for those kids at the drop of a hat. Sure, I could spend hours in traffic to get to Boulder or even move to Denver, but my time was limited with my kids until last week. My suffering was worth all the time I had with them. So, to hell with this guy.

"Thanks, but I don't need you telling me that my reasons for working here are bullshit. I don't fucking know you." I huff, seriously contemplating just leaving and forgetting all about the new Rancher in Town.

He threw his hands up and took a step back, "whoa, whoa, whoa. I wasn't saying you and your reasons are bullshit. I was saying him being a dick is complete and total bullshit. That's no way to treat an employee, customer, or just a person in general. I know I don't know you, but I also know it's a damn good thing you got out of there. That fucker is toxic."

"Yeah, he really is. I'm sorry for snapping." I felt my face heat with embarrassment. I really am a fiery redhead.

"Hey, it's not a big deal, really. I'm Theo Loveitt." He holds out his hand, and I tentatively place mine in his knowing full well there wasn't going to be the spark I so desperately wanted to be there—something to tell me that my body is just reacting to the new faces.

Theo isn't an unattractive man. He is wearing a tight t-shirt, and from what I can see of his exposed skin, he has many tattoos. It makes me wonder if the long-haired man inside is also covered. That man has my complete attention.

Theo and I just stand there for a moment before it starts to get awkward. I want to say something, maybe even ask for the other man's name, when I hear a throat clear behind me.

"Mom? Mom. MOM!" A distant voice called and, as it got louder, snapped me from my memory of earlier that day.

"What, what?" I was startled out of my thoughts, which was probably a good thing because I could finally smell the burnt chicken. Pulling open the oven, I grab the chicken out and inspect it. Thankfully, dinner wasn't completely ruined.

"Mom, are you okay?" My oldest eyes me suspiciously.

"Yeah, J.J, why do you ask?"

"You were just standing there. I don't even think you saw me come into the kitchen. Then dinner almost burned. Are you sure you're fine?"

The concern that my son showed towards me was heartwarming. He was at the age that everything was a fight; I didn't know shit and was also the biggest embarrassment in his life. Yet, there were times when he clearly shows he loves me and cares about what I am going through.

"Yes, baby, I am fine. I just have a lot on my mind, and I am just trying to get it all sorted in my head, is all. I'm good, though, I promise. Go get your brother and sister and set the table."

"Alright, momma." He says, giving me a small peck on the cheek before leaving the room.

That boy may be a hard ass on the outside ninety-five percent of the time lately, but he loves something fierce. I hope he never loses that part of him. That whoever snags his heart cherishes it forever. But then again, isn't that every mother's wish for her children?

The rest of last night and our normal morning rush flew by, and I was now standing on the dirt driveway at the ranch.

I was nervous as hell.

Reason number one - how bad were these books going to be? I had such a short time to accomplish it all. Sure, I would get paid for all the hours worked plus that $2000 bonus but, this ranch is old. If the books weren't kept properly, I don't know if I will get it all done. However, my only saving grace is that the ranch has been successful for as long as it's been open. Someone had to be doing the bookkeeping. Right?

Hell, I hope so.

Reason number two - Ken. That man was the subject of my dreams all night, as well as the name I whispered out in the shower after touching myself to thoughts of him. How the hell am I going to be able to work if he is around? I can only hope that I will have an office when I am here and that he won't be in it. I'll just have to tell him to email me, send his correspondence through Theo, or maybe use a damn chicken. What the hell am I going to do?

I have been asking myself that question since I agreed to this job. Once again asking myself and not having an answer. I continue to fight with my Shoulder Angel and my Shoulder Devil on what the best course was. That asshole devil was currently winning with *"just fuck him."*

I felt the heat of my blush creep up my neck when the front door to the house opened. My breath released, and I smiled. Thank you! I needed this little break.

"Well, Miss Elvira. I haven't seen you in Lord knows how long it feels like. Get on up here and gimme some lovin' before my spoon meets ya." I couldn't help but laugh and pick up my pace.

"Yes, Yaya." I am up the steps and bringing the little old woman into my embrace. "I have missed you, Yaya. I'm sorry it's been a minute since I've been out. So much has been happening."

"You're lucky I love you, and I understand. You get that divorce yet?"

"Yes, thank the Lord."

"Good. I never did like that Travis fellow." It was obvious too. Yaya demands that everyone, and I mean everyone, calls her Yaya. Once you come into her life, you're hers to keep and love except for Travis. It was always Mrs. Faulkner. He thought it was because he didn't grow up here. I knew better. It was another red flag. It should have stopped me from everything but, I can't regret it all.

"I know, Yaya. But I wouldn't change it. He gave me my babies."

"I guess that's true." She winks and starts to lead me into the house. "Now, wanna tell me why I am getting to look at your beautiful face so early in the morning?"

"She's here for me."

That voice stopped me dead in my tracks. I looked up and saw Ken coming down the stairs, and the curiosity I had about tattoos was answered. He was shirtless, chiseled, his chest covered in ink, which connected to his left arm and went all the way down to his wrist.

Holy hell, this man is delicious.

"Young man, you march yourself back up those stairs and get decent. What in the world are you thinking coming down here like that?" He smirked and winked at me, I turned to go, and he put his shirt on over his head.

"I'm decent, Yaya. It won't happen again."

"You see that it doesn't. You may be grown, but you're livin' in my house, and I won't have you walking around, looking like a hussy. 'Specially not in front of the ladies," she winked at me before continuing, "ya rude ass."

Both Ken and I start laughing, and I see the smile on Yaya's face. That woman is the sunshine that everyone should be so lucky to bask in. My joy is cut short when I no longer know how to breathe. Ken is standing in front of me, bringing his thumb up under my chin, lifting my eyes to his.

"Why don't we head to the office in the barn, and you can take a look at the books."

"What in the world? Kenneth, why does she need to look at the books? I...."

"I offered her a job helping me to figure out the books," He faces her. However, I am still in a trance because he is still touching me ever so slightly, "we need help managing them and getting them updated."

"Oh. Alright then."

He turned back to me and flashed that million-dollar smirk. If his smirk was so expensive, I don't think I would be able to handle the price tag of a full-blown smile.

He leads the way to the barn, and once inside, there is an office over to the right. Before I even have a chance to sit down, Theo comes running in.

"You tell her?"

"We just got here man, calm down."

"Tell me what?"

"I want to add a shop on the south end of the land far enough away from the animals and easier access for people. I want to build a mechanics shop; there isn't one in town. It would make a lot of money people currently have to go to Boulder or Denver to get serviced; it would make a *KILLING*." Did he even breathe saying all of that to me? He looked like a puppy, bouncing on the balls of his feet.

"Okay, first of all, breathe. Second, why are you telling me?"

"I need to know if we can afford it. What will our P&L look like if we make this venture? It takes a lot to start up, but I know that Super Theo's Auto Repair will be a hit."

"I'm sorry, what?" Really? What kind of five-year-old name was that?

"Super Theo's. Or I have Sexy Theo, or reverse it, Theo's Sexy Auto Repair. Or Sittin Theo's Lap Auto repair. Hehe, get it? Stallion Theo? Studmuffin Theo. Endless possibilities."

I couldn't even get a word in before he continued. I could only hope it wasn't with more ridiculous names.

"But for real. The shop would make money instantly. We can service cars, trucks, motorcycles. Especially motorcycles. I can build a bike from the ground up, completely custom, with my eyes closed. It would be full service, including body repair and paint. It wouldn't be cheap to start it, but I know it would make a profit. I just need to know what the damage will be to start. I need this to be feasible."

"Okay there, Shit Disturber," I said to Theo once he finished his long-winded, whatever the hell that was. His nonstop rambling gave me a moment to think of names. I think I came up with a great one. Definitely better than the bullshit he was spewing.

"Shit Disturber? Jesus, I haven't been called that in years." He says with a chuckle in his voice, tossing a quick look to Ken.

"Well, I have only been around you collectively for twenty-five minutes, and I already know I am gonna have my hands full with the shit you are sending my way." I cross my arms under my breasts and hear a sharp breath intake from Ken.

"Well, can you think of something else to call me then? Because that one holds memories I don't want around you." He half explains while subconsciously rubbing the outside of his left thigh.

"Hmm, I think I can come up with a few." I think about it for a moment and start tossing them out there. "Shit head?" No. "Shit Stick?" No. "Gob Shit?"

"No-ah! Why do they all have shit in them?" He asks, kind of whining about it now.

"Because I can tell you are going to be full of the stuff, so it's not hard to think of names that reflect that! OH! What about Shi-." He cuts me off.

"Why not just use the first and last letter… There are a lot of words and names that start with S and T." He pleaded with me, trying to put those ice-blue eyes to use.

"Okay, what about Storm?" I ask, acting like I am conceding to his plan.

"Yes! I like that. I can go by that for a while. Storm!" He turns on his heels and walks away before I can change my mind.

"Your next suggestion was Shit Storm, wasn't it?" I felt the warm breath from Ken down my cheek, along my neck, and cooling as it reached the front neckline of my shirt.

"He doesn't need to know that I still win." I turn my head to meet his eye, our noses slightly graze one another, and the shock from our earlier touch has nothing on what this accidentally intimate moment just did to me.

"What would you say is my nickname from you?" There was a soft rumble from his chest when he finished asking. His neck showed him swallowing hard, his cheeks slightly tinge pink as he tried to keep eye contact.

I pull back from our closeness and give him a quick once over with just my eyes. They linger on his dark muddy shoulder-length hair and candy red lips that look like they are begging for my lips. I meet his eye again and see a small glimmer of vulnerability in what I am about to say to him. I take his one hand in mine, not breaking eye contact once.

"You are Judge. You have the ability to judge a person's worth accordingly. You know in that snap but accurate judgment who is worth your time, energy, and generosity and who is not worth more than the wrath of your fists or the taste of your dirt as you walk away. It's that judgment in that chance encounter that you gave me a job sight unseen on my qualifications. It's also that judgment, a legend among the Faulkner men in our county and the next two over, that tells me you will make this ranch bigger and better than it has ever been. So, Judge, what do you think of that one?" I finish, trying to pull my hand back from his.

But he won't let go; in normal circumstances, I would pull away harder or scream, but this didn't bother me. His eyes were searching mine hard like he was worried I was lying. Before I could say any more, he pulls me forward and crashes his lips to mine.

This shouldn't be happening. I shouldn't be enjoying the lips of this man that I barely know, but I couldn't help it. He tastes like coffee and sin. All the good things that I have always been told are bad.

His hand grips the back of my head, slightly pulling my hair. I moan into his mouth, and he deepens the kiss. He pushes me back into the wall, and I feel the hardness of the wall behind me, which is nothing compared to the hard body pinning me to it.

He pushed himself closer to me, and I felt his leg push between mine. My arms, finally able to move from the shock of it all, go to grip his waist and bring him even closer to me. I hear a deep growl permeate from his chest as I make a move.

I want to feel more of what I believe is not just his thigh rubbing against me. I make my move when he bites down on my bottom lip, and there is a slight taste of copper. He pulls back, anger and shock written across his face.

"What the fu...."

"Finish that sentence, boy. I dare you."

Ken, I can tell, is trying to hold his tongue while Yaya is fuming. I can barely see the wooden spoon hanging from her right hand. She goes to smack him again, but he ducks out of the way.

"Yaya, stop. What are you doing?"

"I should be asking *you* that! What are you doing to that girl? She is supposed to be your employee, helping out on this ranch, and you have her pinned up against the wall like she's a little harlot. I should beat the stupid outta you for not knowing any better."

I can't help but smile. Here I am, doing everything that I normally would never do, with a man I barely know, and she is trying to protect my virtue. This is the Yaya that I know and love. The one that I got to grow up around. Always making sure that I was taken care of and treated fairly. I wouldn't be surprised if she truly feels like Ken is taking advantage of me. What she doesn't need to know is that I want him to in every way possible.

"How could you act like this?" She asks, seeming truly baffled at what she came upon.

"She wanted it as well, Yaya." He shot back, obviously without thinking, again.

Yaya's face turns almost purple. I can see the devil in that woman's eyes. I smirk and walk away. This is something that Ken got himself into, and he can attempt to get himself out. I am almost to the door before I hear him shouting and begging for her to stop.

SIX

ELVIRA

-Present -

The house is quiet. The calm that I don't always get has embraced me in a warm hug, and I don't want to let it go. Most days, there are loud noises, screaming, laughing, crashing, glass breaking, anything that would give most people a headache. I love those days. I also love when everything calms, and it's just me, even if it's for a moment.

In times like this, I would generally love to sit down and just read. My reading count for the year isn't as high as I'd like it to be, but I can't bring myself to do that tonight. Tonight, I am happy standing at the sink and washing dishes, looking out the big picture window above my sink.

It's dark outside, but the sky is clear, and the moon is full. Living on the ranch, when the moon is full, it lights up the pastures. I can see the cows that are still out. It's relaxing. I can also see the red lights that are placed outside of the barn, indicating that Church is in session and they are not to be disturbed.

I am fine with that. I'll leave them alone. We had what we refer to as "Staff Meeting" earlier. Those I attend. I handle the money; there is no getting out of it. Church though, I have no part in that.

I have no issue with what they discuss and what they do. I know that my husband and those men are not always within the law. However, not knowing the details gives me plausible deniability. Something that I need if anything were to go wrong and Ken was taken from me. If any of those men were taken from me. I love this MC more than anything but these kids of mine; I love them more.

If I had to pick between the MC and the kids, I'd pick the kids. Every. Single. Time.

Lost in the motions of washing dishes and the quiet I don't typically have, I nearly jump out of my skin when my phone rings. I dry my hands while glancing at the clock. It's nine o'clock at night. When I know all my kids are home, it can only mean one thing - I'm about to gain at least one more mouth to feed, one more heart to love.

Checking the ID, I see that it's Sheriff Anderson.

"Sheriff. Whatdya got for me?"

"Elvira, I'm sorry to call you this late, but it's an emergency. Hey! Make sure that those two are wrapped up, and you have documented each photo. Get the gun in an evidence bag. Come on, you guys. I'm sorry, one moment."

I hear shuffling, and I can tell the Sheriff is frustrated. He is a nice man, and he knows what goes on behind the walls of the MC. Small town living brings a sense of family with the most unlikely people. Pasts and stories that aren't mine to tell brought the Sheriff to our side.

"Keep it clean and clear of you having had anything to do with this. Anything that points to you will go back to you. You make it so it doesn't, and it never will."

I remember hearing him tell Ken and Theo that, handing over the okay to do what needed to be done. That night, a child molester that kept escaping jail time for molesting ten little boys went missing and was never found.

"Elviria, did you hear me?"

"I am so sorry, Sheriff, the phone cut out. Can you please repeat that?"

"I have two little ones that I need you to come get from the station. One is about one, the other 4. Dad murdered mom, and dad was suicide by us. I shouldn't even tell you this information, El, and you know that, but these kids are in bad shape. I am honestly disgusted by the state of the room I found them in, and I am not talking about the one where the mother's head was blown to bits.

These babies were living in filth. Shit and piss everywhere. They were naked. The bigger one held onto the younger one for dear life when we came in—bruises all over their little bodies. I can see the ribs on both of them.

Medical checked them out. They are too small, dirty, and were starving but otherwise okay, given the shit circumstance. I don't know how they are okay and how they don't need to be in the hospital, but they are. Surprisingly, they aren't dehydrated. It's, it's fucking bad, El. Could you take them? I need you to take them. Please tell me you can."

"Without question, Sheriff."

"Thank fuck. Look, I know I don't need to tell you but, you don't know shit about what happened to these kids, just that they need the placement. I....something inside me snapped. Seeing these babies, thinking of my own. Just...." He lets out a loud exhale before continuing. "When can you get to the station?"

Judge and I were known for being the Emergency Placement for foster care. We built our home with more than enough room to accommodate more children than we would ever have at any given point.

"Ken and I can be there in thirty minutes."

I hang up and rush out of the house to head towards the barn. Ken and I, when it comes to picking up the kids, always go together. I wasn't about to change that fact just because they were in Church. This man had been by my side for fifteen years. If he doesn't realize that I will interrupt due to the kids, he never will.

I bang open the doors, and all of the men stand. Some even have their guns drawn. We're going to talk about *that* later.

"El, what the fuck?"

"Shut up, Theo. Judge, we gotta go." Even in these situations, I try to show him the respect he deserves as President when he is in front of his club. The man worked hard to make this club what it is. The least I could do is give him this. Theo, on the other hand, that Shit Storm can fuck himself.

"What's wrong? What happened to the kids? Are the kids okay?"

"Our kids are fine. We have two emergency placements we have to go get. One is one, and one is four. Murder/Suicide. I don't have time to fucking waste," I turn to the other men, "I need you all to put a stop to this. Go to the main house, get a bucket from the one year & four-five year shelves. Take both of them to the baby room. Make sure there are two beds with clean sheets and ready to go. I'll take care of the rest when we get back. Let's go, Ken."

Well, the keyword when it came to calling him Judge was *try*.

His face hardens. My husband shows his emotions when it comes to things like this. Well, at least I see them. Most see a hardass that doesn't take shit from anyone and will kill you should you cross him. Me? I see the man that loves his family more than himself. That will give others whatever they need without question. The man brought together a group of men with the same goal.

One of the many reasons why I love him as much as I do is because of how much he loves. I wouldn't be anywhere near where I am today without him.

We make it to the station, and as we're walking up, an officer is coming towards us. I've seen him before. Not in a "this is a small town." seen you before. This is in the "my kids were arrested, I gotta go." seen you before.

The cop that arrested my kids is walking toward us, and I instantly fall into the memory of that day.

"Ms. May, this is Officer Baiseur from the police station. I have Jonathon James and Robert Jackson May here. They were caught shoplifting, and the store owner is pressing charges. Please come into the station immediately."

The voicemail was short and to the point. I had missed the call and was freaking out listening to it. I had only missed it by five minutes. Who knows what the hell could have happened in such a short amount of time.

I am on my way to pick up my children for being arrested*, and I am breaking almost every law to get to them. Fucking Ironic. The worst part in all of this, though? Why? Why would they be stealin' when I know they have money? What the hell is going on?*

I get to the station, park, and start to head inside. I stop dead in my tracks because coming up the walkway is Travis. My ex. He sees me and gets a smug as fuck expression on his face.

"Well, well, well. It looks like our children have become delinquents under your care." He tsks a few times while shaking his head. I am trying to control my rage and not do something stupid, like murder him in front of the police station.

"How bad this will look for you, Elvira. You can't even handle our children. Shameful."

"Don't start with me, Travis. What the fuck are you doing here?"

"Seems the police caught your delinquent sons and couldn't get a hold of you. Apple doesn't fall far, does it? What exactly were you doing that was so important you couldn't answer the cops when they rang? Obviously not taking care of these kids you so desperately had to have."

Do not murder him, do not murder him, do not fucking murder him.

"Not that it is any of your damn concern, but, given the time of day, you should be able to figure it out. I was working, Travis. You know, that thing normal people do. From the hours of nine to five for most. Now, leave before I have you arrested."

"They called me. What exactly do you think you can do?"

"In case you have forgotten, I was granted a temporary restraining order against you, and it is still valid. They may have called you, but I will have you in there and in cuffs within the next two minutes if you don't. Fucking. Leave."

His face morphs into a sinister snarl. I don't even know what the circumstances are. I knew bringing up the fact that he legally can't be here would piss him off but, trying to pin this issue as something that is my fault because I was working crossed the line. I refuse to believe my children are now delinquents because of a mistake. On the other hand, he would make sure they only believed that about themselves and nothing else.

"Mark my words, Elvira. I will get those kids, and I will end you."

"Is that a threat, Travis?"

"It's a fucking promise."

Before I can respond, he turns and walks away. I get inside and immediately ask the front desk who the fuck called my ex.

"It says here that Officer Baiseur called him when he couldn't reach you."

"Interesting. I want him and your Captain out here now."

"I am sorry, but the Captain...."

"Will get his ass out here before I come back with a lawyer. Both of them. Now."

I wasn't normally this way. My heart was pounding, and I needed to get out of here. I needed to call my lawyer. My ex was threatening me, and I needed to make a note of it but, I needed to yell at the fucker that caused this problem in the first place.

"Ma'am? I'm Captain Anderson. This is Officer Baiseur. What can we help you with?"

"Two things. One. I want my kids. I don't care what they did. I want them now. Two, you," I point to Baiseur, "Needs to learn how to fucking read files."

"Excuse me?" The officer in question asked.

"Had you read *the file that is attached to each kid and me, you would have seen that their father has a restraining order against him. He is not allowed within 500 feet of his kids or me. YOU almost let him be. YOU almost let my kids leave with that man. Had they left, it would have been because of YOU that I would never have seen them again. Give. Me. My. Kids."*

"Ma'am, I. I'm sorry, I didn't know."

"No, you didn't, because you can't fucking read. What did they even do?"

"The shop owner says that they took candy bars."

"Are you fucking kidding me?!" I scream.

I lost it. There was no being calm. My world is upside down because Travis was outside and threatened my life. My kids were arrested because of some bullshit. I am about to go momma bear and threaten this asshole's life. However, the Captain steps in.

"We were actually about to release them. There is no video, and the kids don't have anything on them. Officer Baiseur, go get them."

"El? Baby, are you okay?"

I shake my head and clear my thoughts. I didn't realize that I would be able to get so sucked into a memory just from seeing Officer Baiseur.

"Baby, why are you shaking?"

Thinking about Travis does this to me. It puts me in a state that I hate to be in. It's one that I can't afford to be in right now. Not when these babies need me.

"Just the whole situation. Let's go get these babies and bring them home."

"After you, my love."

SEVEN

ELVIRA

-Past-

The past two weeks flew by. I quickly got into a routine after the first day. That day Yaya made me work in the kitchen and tried to show me what she knew about the books; it really wasn't much. She told me that Robert would be the best source of information; as Kenny's' eyesight and memories had continued to deteriorate near the end, he passed as much information along to him as he could. Robert started taking over the paperwork at the end of it all. He was more than happy to spend time with me if it meant all that work was coming off his to-do pile.

He was not a numbers man in any way, shape, or form; he knew where the money came in and when it came out and made a note of both. I loved looking through all the years of paper ledgers, and it felt like I was touching history. All of the ranches' hard years were noted in these books. You could see the handwriting of all the Faulkner men throughout the years. You could truly feel their frustration in every loss and the absolute elation when they had more gains than losses.

I wasn't ready for this to end. I liked this job. I had secretly hoped that Ken would ask me to stay. The whole operation here fascinated me. However, that would take seeing him for him to ask me to stay. Ever since that first day, that amazing, panty-melting kiss, I haven't seen him once.

I wouldn't be surprised if Yaya had something to do with it. She beat the hell out of him with that spoon. Afterward, she came and found me and kept me busy the rest of the day. I didn't even get to say goodbye. I wasn't sure where I stood with this farm or with Ken.

I was sitting in the office, dwelling on the fact that it was my last day here. I truly did not want to leave, and I loved the numbers and the independent atmosphere. I wanted to keep this job, but most of all, I wanted to keep Ken.

"Do you have a minute?" His voice seems to pop out of my thoughts and end up right behind me.

"Uh, sure? What's up, boss?" Really... What's up, boss? I mentally facepalmed myself. He chuckled at me shaking his head; I guess my face is more readable than I would like it to be.

"I wanted to talk to you about all the hard work you have been doing here. I have been working with Robert, and he says you have a great head for the numbers most of us don't." He slowly starts to prowl towards me; it's almost like we have danced this dance before. "I do not have a head for numbers, nor do most of the people here. I have talked to Yaya and-."

He was cut off by another swift smack to the backside, causing him to just forward a bit, while the tiny, anything but the frail woman appeared from behind him.

"Child, I told you not to go on without me. I may be old and small, but I will still take you over my knee as needed!" She chastised him before looking at me. "El, dear, we have talked about it and would like you to come on full time. We can pay you what you are worth, and when the harvest and auctions are good, you will see a bonus with the rest of the men. You can keep the same hours, so those children of yours aren't running wild like we know they want to."

I felt like a weight had been lifted. While I loved it here, the time and energy here plus at home had left me with no time to look for a long-term solution for gainful employment past the two-week mark. This was a gift that I really needed, but before I could say anything about it, my phone started blaring from my purse.

"Please hold," I said to Yaya and Ken while rooting through my bag, ready to silence it before noting it was Ellie's school calling. I gave Yaya an apologetic expression before answering it.

"Hello?"

"Mrs. May, I'm sorry to bother you, but Ellie May has been in here in the nurse's office for the past hour. She first came saying that her stomach hurt and wanted to lay down. She didn't have a fever, so I had her rest on one of the cots. About thirty minutes into her rest, she started saying her head was hurting. Unfortunately, about five minutes ago, she started crying and screaming from the pain she is in. Please come to get her. I know I shouldn't give my opinion on this matter, but I really feel like something is wrong."

I was about to respond when I heard Ellie screaming in the background. "I am on my way." I hang up before the nurse can say anything. I shoot up from my seat, causing Ken to have a panicked look on his face.

"What's going on?"

"I…I'm sorry, but I have to go. Something is wrong with Ellie. I..she started screaming. I have to, I'm sorry. I need to leave." I could feel my eyes welling with tears. I wasn't sure how I was going to be able to even see. My baby was in pain, and I wasn't with her.

"El, wait. El! Let me take you. You're panicking, and it's not safe for you to drive. Please."

I didn't fight him and handed him my keys. I knew he was right, and I needed to get to Ellie. I couldn't get to her if I were dead in a ditch somewhere because I couldn't focus on my driving. We rush out and get into my car. Thankfully, I don't have to tell him where to go. The school is the only one here for her grade. It doesn't take any time before we are parked, and I am rushing out the door and into the school.

I push through the front doors and head to the desk. "The nurse's office, where is it."

"Can I get your name, please?"

I slam my fist on the top of the desk, pissed off and desperate to get to my child.

"No! Tell me where it is. My kid is there."

"I'm sorry, ma'am, but I need to know your name."

I couldn't believe this. I was about to open my mouth again when I heard Ellie scream.

"Ellie!"

I ran towards her screams. I could feel her pain radiating throughout my own body. She was still screaming, and hard sobs were now mixed in. I was able to find her in no time.

"Ellie! Ellie, mama's here, baby. I'm here."

I kneel beside her and start rubbing her head. Just as the nurse said, she doesn't have a fever, but something is very wrong. My baby is in so much pain was killing me. I couldn't do anything about it.

"Mommy, mommy, it hurts so bad. My head is pounding, and my stomach, I need to…."

She turns her head and vomits all over the floor. It misses me by a hair.

"Let's go."

I turn in time to see Ken walking in. He comes right up to me, slightly pushing me out of the way, and scoops Ellie up into his arms. She doesn't hesitate, and her arms go around his neck, and her head curls into his chest, her body still wracked with sobs. He nods towards the door and walks out with her. I look at the nurse, "thank you for taking care of her. I am really sorry about your floor." She smiles sympathetically, and I leave to find Ken and Ellie.

"Ma'am, I am sorry, but I need you to sign her out. Please."

I take a deep breath and nod. I know that Ellie is safe with Ken. I can give the five seconds it takes to sign her out. "I'm sorry about earlier. Have a good day."

I walk out, and Ellie is still clinging to Ken. He looks at me like he doesn't know what to do.

"She won't let me put her down."

"That's okay. If you can get in with her, please do so. It's only a quick drive to our house. I have a sneaky suspicion that this is a migraine. I have never seen it this bad before, but I have the medication she needs at home. I would like to get it into her system first before taking her to the hospital. It's fast reacting. If she isn't better within half an hour, we can go to the hospital."

"You've got it, babe."

He gets situated in the back seat with her, looking very uncomfortable. I'm sure the angle he has to sit at to keep her upright isn't easy. I am heading towards home when I take a pause. Did he call me babe? I want it to mean something more than I think it does, but I also can't dwell on that right now. I needed to get my baby girl home and let her rest before things went from bad to worse.

We made it home in record time, and I made a point to take as many shortcuts to avoid high trafficked areas and the chances of being pulled over. Ken wiggled his way out of the back with a slightly calmer Ellie still in his grasp, being held like I wish he would hold me. *Focus woman!* I shake the thought from my head and hurry to unlock the door and guide him to her bedroom while I retrieve the pills and some water from the kitchen.

I walk back into her room, and I just smile, followed by a slight chuckle. Ken has one hand supporting Ellie's head, the other trying to reach behind his neck to pry her little hands. I can tell she has a death grip on his neck, and he isn't going to be able to get out of this on his own. I place the meds and water on her nightstand and reach for her hands.

"Here, let me help you."

"Thank you. I wouldn't think that a girl this little would be so strong." He looks up at me, "she must get it from her momma."

I blush and glance down. I don't think he understands what he does to me, and now is definitely *not* the time to let those feelings take over.

I can get Ellie's hands pried of him, and she lays down. I sit down next to her, trying to ease her head back up.

"Sweetie, I need you to take this. You'll feel better soon."

She nods and thankfully takes her pill. She lays back down, and I lean forward to kiss her forehead. "I'll be just outside your door in the living room, baby. I love you."

"I love you too, momma."

With that, Ken and I leave her room. I close her door slightly, leaving it ajar. Letting out a sigh of relief as I sit down on the couch. Ken excuses himself to call Theo in the kitchen; I have left with my thoughts again, which is currently scary. I take the time to look around, realizing I let the man from all my dirty fantasies in my house, and it looks like a frat house. The boys had their friends over last night, and there are pizza boxes, soda cans, and random articles of clothing all over the living room. I am mortified when I remember that there are about two days worth of dishes in the kitchen sink. Good lord, what is he going to think of me? I feel the couch beside me sag as his large frame sits rather close to me. My eyes meet his as he leans over and places his elbows on his knees.

"So…" He is cut off by three sharp knocks on the front door." Stay, I'll get it for you."

"Thank you." I was exhausted at this point and grateful that I didn't have to get up and take the five steps to the door.

Ken spoke softly with the person at the door but then led two sharply dressed men into my messy, teenage lived-in, looking house. Ken stood behind the couch while the two men stood side by side in front of me. I had never seen them before in my life.

"El, these men here say they are friends of your husband." Ken starts.

"Ex-husband." 'Really, what is wrong with my brain today?' I quickly corrected, needing him to know that I was a single pringle when we shared any moments.

"Yes, Mrs. May, we are acquaintances with Mr. May, and he seems to owe my father and boss a lot of money." The taller of the two starts. "He gave us your address and said that you were holding the money for him." My body went rigid at his claim.

"I don't have anything of his. He has been out of my house for more than two years and permanently out of my life for the last six months. I know nothing about him owing anyone anything."

"That's not what he said."

"I don't care what he said. Listen to what I am telling you, and I don't know what you are talking about!"

"Mrs. May, I am a reasonable man, but I will not take your attitude lightly."

"Then you can fucking deal with mine. She said she doesn't know anything. She fucking doesn't know anything. You can do yourself a favor and get the fuck outta my house."

"Funny, Mr. May said it was his house."

"Mr. May is full of shit. You want whatever amount…."

"$20,000."

"WHAT?! I…How the fuck does he owe that much? You know what? No. I don't fucking care. He is not my problem. Your problem is with him. Like my man said, get the fuck out of our house!"

I can't believe the lies that I told this man, but it feels so right calling Ken mine. And, he started it all, claiming that this was his house. That should tell me something, right? That he wants to be with me as much as I want to be with him. I wanted nothing more than to focus on him now, but the asswipe in the suit was still standing in my living room.

"Who the fuck are you?" Ken demands, coming out from behind the couch. Anger radiating off him. It was so incredibly sexy. *Not the fucking time, Elvira.*

The man in the suit, who was glaring at me, turns his black orbs towards Ken. He has a sneer on his face, but he answers Ken.

"Artem Sidorov," He speaks, venom lacing each syllable of his name.

"That supposed to mean something to me?"

"My last name is a name you should know. If not, learn it, remember it, fear it." He looks at me and very calmly states, "we'll be in touch."

"Mother fucker, if you come near here again."

The man standing next to Artem pulls a gun and points it at Ken's head. I freeze. My body seizes, and I can no longer feel my limbs, but I shake myself out of it. I need to get to Ellie. There is a man in my house, pointing a gun, and I am nowhere near my child. Oh shit. Please, PLEASE, do not let my boys come home.

"I am not one to be messed with, Kenneth Kelly. Do. Not. Threaten. Me."

"How...how do you know my name?"

"Rumors of your homecoming have spread, even to the biggest of cities. I have ways of knowing. Always. Again, we will be in touch. Rafe, not now. Pozvol'te nam uyti."

Rafe lowers his weapon, and they are out the door, Ken rushing to lock it. He turns back to face me, and I take off towards Ellie's room. I open the door, and I sigh with relief, seeing she is still passed out in her bed, completely unharmed. Closing the door all the way this time, I head back out to the living room.

"Are you okay?"

"That piece of shit told them I have his money! Am I okay? How the hell can I be okay? No, I am not okay."

Ken walks over to me, and we both sit on the couch. He lets out a loud, deep breath and grabs my hands. Looking me dead in the eye, "it's time you tell me about this piece of shit you married."

EIGHT

JUDGE

-Past-

She looked nervous, keeping her eyes everywhere but on me, and I loved when her eyes were on me. But this time, they needed to tell me she wasn't lying. They needed to tell me how much trouble this man has caused her now and in the past. She was tough as nails, holding her own at those men in her house while they pointed a gun at my head. It wasn't the first time I had looked down the barrel of a .45, and I am almost positive it won't be the last either.

"El, babe, you have to talk to me. I need to know, or I can't help you." I plead with her, trying to get her to look at me again. When I said babe, her eyes flew to me. There was a fire in them.

"You need to stop with that Babe shit. What the hell was that 'your house' bullshit too?" She shot up like a rocket from the couch and started pacing.

"You sit here, laying all this claim on me. Why? I am nothing to you! I am just your employee. You can't come in here and start saying what's mine is yours, that *I'm* yours. That isn't how this works!"

She is frantically picking up everything around her home. Slamming drawers, throwing clothes into baskets, I've never seen anyone clean this fast.

"Babe."

"Stop it! I am not your babe. I am not yours. I am not anyone's!"

I walk over to her, knock whatever was in her hands to the ground, grab her by the sides of her face and pull her to me. My lips crash into hers, and I soak in the feeling. Pushing my tongue out to meet hers, she opens willingly and moans at the connection. This pushes me further. I start walking back towards the couch, turning and pushing her down onto it, with me falling on top of her.

Her legs open freely, and I place myself within them. Grinding into her, making not only her moan but myself as well. Her hands are in my hair, pulling tightly at the strands. Right on the spot that is still tender from my beatdown, giving me PTSD that a wooden spoon is about to hit me upside the head.

I shake the thoughts away and pull back slightly. "I claimed you because I needed to. Because I want you so fucking much." I push my cock into her and grind up. Her moan captures me completely. I want to fuck her. "I have wanted you since the moment I saw you. Fuck El, let me claim you. Please."

I wasn't above begging. This woman was everything I have ever wanted in my life. Her curves, her beauty, her heart. She was perfect. My left hand is still holding me up on the couch while my right grips her tit. It's soft, full, and so damn perfect.

"Baby, please say something."

"Yes. Please. Claim me, Ken. I want you in me. So fucking much."

Her moan is deep and feral. I drag my hand lower, starting to undo her pants. The loud banging on the door has me stopping.

"Hey, guys! It's me. Open up!"

"Fucking Theo," El says as she tries to even out her breathing and covers her face. I completely forgot that he was on his way to come and get me. Of all the times to not have my bike with me. Fuck! Cock-blocked by my best fucking friend.

"Stay here, baby. I'll get rid of him."

I stand up, and she follows me by sitting. She grabs my hand to stop me from going any further. "Maybe you should just go."

"What? Why?" I thought that we were enjoying ourselves. That she wanted this as much as I did. Did I completely misinterpret her reactions? Shit. I crossed a line. I am about to say how sorry I am when she cuts me off.

"Ellie is home. The boys should be home soon. The last thing I want is for any of them to see me with your dick buried to the hilt within me." Her choice of words has my cock aching and pushing against my zipper.

"I want you, Ken. So much. But I also don't want to rush. So, thank you for today. For everything. You don't know how much I needed it. How much I needed you." She stands up and gives me a slight kiss on the cheek. As she pulls back, I grab the back of her head and turn her to face me, sealing my lips to hers once more.

The kiss is powerful, deep, and all-consuming. That's when it really solidified it. She's it for me.

I pull back and rub my thumbs along her jaw. "Go out with me tomorrow. Dinner?"

She takes longer than I would like to respond. Theo is once again banging against the door. My patience with him is gone. I turn towards the door.

"Chill the fuck out, dude. Ill be out in a minute!" I turned back to El, "please, baby?"

"Okay. I'll go out with you tomorrow."

I kiss her again and tell her I'll be here to pick her up at 6. I walk out the door and see my best friend just sitting on the steps, with a smug as hell look on his face.

"Kept me waiting long enough. Why the hell did you call me if you were going to be getting your dick wet?"

I punched him in the arm and kept walking towards his truck. "Fuck you, ya dick. That didn't happen. It was a crazy fucking day. We dealt with her daughter, and these Russian pricks showed up demanding money. She went off on a rant about me claiming her. And,"

"Hold the fuck on. People came over demanding money?"

"Yes. Her piece of shit ex said that she had what he owes."

"Mother fucker."

We both get in the truck, and once the doors are shut, Theo turns and looks me dead in the eye. "What are we going to do about it?"

This is why he is my best friend, no real questions asked, just ready to jump in and defend my girl's honor. But, I wasn't sure just yet what we were going to do. I just knew her exes' days were numbered.

I was sitting in the car, trying to figure out how I could get El out of this horrible situation that her ex put her in. However, I wasn't sure how that would be possible because she didn't tell me anything. The second I was hopefully going to get information out of her was the second that Artem guy left after claiming she had the $20,000 that her ex owed. I scoffed. I was fuming. I couldn't believe that he would do this to her. To their kids.

"What's wrong, man? Tell me what happened."

"This man Artem shows up. Claiming that her ex owes 20,000 dollars to his boss, who also happens to be his father, and then practically threatens her that he will be back. He isn't going to stop until he has the money owed."

"Okay, so we get the ex."

"That's the damn problem, man. I don't know who the ex is. The guy showed up, made claims, and left, I then told her she needed to tell me, but then things took a turn. She started screaming at me. I didn't know what else to do so I kissed her. One thing led to another. I was about to have," I paused. I didn't need to say it. He knew. "And then your ass showed up and killed the mood."

"Man, I am really sorry." He shrugged, not really sorry.

"No. She pointed out that Ellie was home, and her sons could come home at any time. It wasn't the time. But now. Now I am fucking pissed. I know that this threat from this Artem guy is real, and I can't do shit because I know jack shit about who her ex is."

"We'll figure it out, man."

I just nodded. There wasn't any more that I could say. Would we figure it out? It wasn't like I had all the resources in the world. I sat and thought about who I could ask to find out any information regarding this piece of shit.

"Fuck." Theo exclaimed, causing me to jump.

"What, man?"

"I know who to ask to find out more information." He side-eyes me with a kind of devious smirk; I wasn't sure I liked that look on him.

"Who?" I was skeptical he could come up with a logical answer as he had been in town the same length as me.

"Yaya."

Theo must see the fear in my face because he busts out laughing. He has been beaten with that damn wooden spoon as much as I have, if not more, yet he finds immense joy out of my suffering. He gets hit because he's Theo. He's a dumbass. I get hit because I am falling for a woman, and Yaya doesn't like it, doesn't think I'm worthy of her, or both. Because let's face it. I'm not worthy of Elvira.

Walking up the steps to the farmhouse, I could feel the weight of it all on my shoulders, mainly because I knew I would have to explain myself as to why I needed the information, and I was sure that it was going to end with me getting pelted with that damn spoon again. I made it to the kitchen, and there she was cooking dinner for the crew and us out in the fields.

"Yaya?" I called her, and she stopped abruptly, turning to me. Wooden spoon in hand, causing me to flinch at its sight, I knew it was going to meet my head soon. I wasn't sure why she was determined to keep me from Elvira, but I had to take the chance with her and figure out what was going on.

"Whaddya need, Ken?"

"I need to know everything about Elvira's ex."

Yaya's eyes held a storm deep within their depths. I loved this woman, but her anger towards my desire for Elvira needed to calm. I would never do anything to harm her. If she only knew my full want for her, maybe she would calm that spoon-twitching hand.

"What on earth do you need to know about that miscreant?" I did not miss the venom in her tone.

"Some men came by Elvira's house today, looking for him."

"You were at her house? Boy, what in the world are you doing at her house?"

"Yaya," I let out a breath, "You know why I was there, and even if you didn't, that's beside the point. Her ex. I need to know about him."

She narrowed her eyes at me and let out a small hmmm.

"Travis is no good. I never liked that no-good snake in the grass. He treated Elvira horribly. He was constantly bringing her down. Degrading her in front of anyone that would watch."

"Did no one do anything?"

"People that tried to meddle, for a while, she denied it all. Even if people saw it, she said they misunderstood or it was an inside joke. She hid a lot from everyone. It was hard for her, though. She loved him with everything that she had. She gave him everything. When she had the kids, she did what she could to keep their family together. It started to take a toll on her, though.

We started seeing her less and less. When we did, she always had caked-on make-up or long sleeve shirts. It was obvious to us all, but you can only tell someone so much what to do. It becomes their choice on if they are going to listen or not."

"What about the kids? Did he ever hurt the kids?" I held my breath. I was already mad enough at what Yaya was telling me about what El went through. If he hurt the kids, I'd find him, and I would kill him. It was hard enough not to do so now.

"Thankfully, no. Jonathan witnessed most of it at the end. He took out all his anger, hell, even his happiness, on Elvira. Ellie was who helped her find the strength she needed to put an end to it all finally.

Travis made court hell for Elvira, but she didn't stop fighting. Now, tell me, why is it that you need to know about him?" She had turned back to what she was mixing before.

"I told you, some men came…."

"Yes, some men came, but why? What did he do?"

There was no point in trying to hide what really happened at El's house. She would find out one way or another.

"They came in saying that he owed them $20,000 and that he told them she had it."

The spoon of death clatters to the counter. Yaya turns around and walks over to me. Tiny hands grip my shirt as she pulls me down to look into her eyes. Eyes laced with fear.

"She doesn't have it. If Travis has money owed to someone, he doesn't have it either, Ken. He deals with bad men. Evil men. He is a rotten apple, straight to the fucking core. She is now on their radar, whoever they are. Her kids will be next. Ken, just pay it."

"What?"

"I said to pay it. Take the money out of my funds. It's not like I need every penny that was left to me. If we don't pay it, anything can happen to her and the kids. If something did, knowing that I had the means to stop it, I wouldn't be able to live with myself."

I wrap my arms around Yaya and hold her tight to my chest. Her love for the people she cares about shows no bounds. To willingly hand over that kind of money to keep El and her kids safe, I couldn't help but smile. This woman was the definition of a Goddess. I wasn't sure how anyone could live up to her.

"Yaya, I, thank you." The words came out, choked with emotion. "You have no idea what this means to me."

"Yeah, speaking of that. Why are you acting like you're in love with her?"

I opened my mouth, but I stopped myself. I was about to say, 'because I am.' I knew it was crazy, though. It was too soon, but she was perfect. She was perfect for me. The second that I noticed her, I knew she was it for me. But telling Yaya that I loved her before I told El, was that wrong? Could I do that?

"Oh my lord, you do. You love her."

"Yaya," I let out a sigh and looked at the ground, "she's it for me. The first time I saw her, my world stopped. The second I heard her voice, all others became muted. That first touch, though light, knocked me down like a bolt of lightning. The first time I felt her lips, it was more than just a kiss. It was my future. She's just… mine."

"Be still my heart." I looked up at her now, and tears were streaming down her face. She wiped them away and smiled at me. "Ken, you sound just like your grandfather."

I smiled. Even though I didn't know him, every time she told me I did something as he had, or I looked just like him, I felt close to him. It was my way of getting to know him.

"I was so worried about you trying to swoon her because of everything that she has been through. I should have had more faith in you, though. I should have known you would treat her like nothing less than a Queen."

Yaya went back to her mixing bowl, and I sat for just a moment, realizing that this was her way of giving me her blessing to be with El.

"Thank you, Yaya. As much as I love talking about El, I need to get back to why I am here. Travis, do you know where he lives?"

"If I tell you, you're just going to go over there and do something that you definitely shouldn't. I can't have you getting in trouble or making the situation worse. Believe me, if I could get away with killing that man, I would. So, I'm not telling you. Do what you need to do to pay what he owes and move on. You're no good to Elvira if you're in jail. Lord knows I won't bail your ass out if you get caught."

"No swearing, Yaya." I couldn't help it. I needed to make her smile after spilling some hard truths about Travis. It was the wrong move, though. That old, frail-looking woman proved me wrong yet again with her speed and strength. That spoon clocked me right upside the head.

"I also said no back-talk!" She winked at me and turned back to her mixing bowl. I couldn't help but smile as I turned and walked out of the kitchen. I needed to find Theo, and we needed to do some work regarding how to find Artem. I was going to end this for El.

NINE

JUDGE

-Past-

Theo and I had a long talk about what we would do and how to get this handled. It was clear that Artem had men backing him.

Theo and I were just that, Theo and I.

I didn't have a group of men behind me when I felt that I needed them.

"We need a club. Let's start a club," Theo said.

"Yeah, let's do that. I gotta get the treehouse built first. The rope ladder is proving tricky, though." I shook my head. Leave it to Theo to make some dumbass comment like starting a club.

"You damn dickhead. An MC. We should start a motorcycle club. Then we would have the backing we need in moments like this. The brotherhood that would help us stand strong when dealing with people like Artem. People that we know have no issue killing others and will always show a united and strong front. If we had a backing like that, moments like this wouldn't seem so daunting."

It wasn't a bad idea. But El didn't have the time to wait for us to create this club. She needed help now, and I was going to give it to her.

"It's not a bad idea, man, but right now, we can't focus on that. We need to deal with Artem and the money that Travis owes."

"Yet how do we do that when we know fuck all about him? It's not like he gave you a card with his phone number or a 1-800-contact-the-mob line."

"We can get it figured out. There has to be a way to find him. If he is in the mob and is here in a small town, people must know about him."

"What if we have El ask Travis?"

"No."

"He may be the only way to get ahold of him, though."

"I said no, Theo! We're not having El reach out to him. If we need his help, I'll get the information. She isn't going anywhere near him."

Theo mumbles something under his breath and holds his hands up in defeat. "Okay, man, no need to jump down my throat."

"Fuck, man. I'm sorry. But I wouldn't say I like the idea of her having any more to do with him than needed. If I can keep her out of this, I'm going to."

"Are you going to tell her that you paid the money that fucker owes? She doesn't come off as the type of woman to accept that type of help."

"What the fuck does that mean?"

"Hey! No need to get angry. It means that she is strong as fuck. She comes off as the type of woman who stands on her own two feet and doesn't beg or ask for things when she knows full damn well that she is a bad bitch that can handle it on her own."

He was right. El was strong as fuck and wouldn't let me help her. Sure, we almost had sex on her couch, but we weren't together. We weren't married. I had zero reasons to help her like this. I, along with Yaya, wanted to help. There was only one way to do this. I had to keep her out of it.

"I'm not going to tell her. I'll work it out with Artem and keep her out of it. I want to keep that man far away from her and those kids. The last thing I want is him retaliating against her or her kids. It would kill me. I can stop the what-ifs and make sure she is safe."

Theo nods in agreement and headed out the door. I needed to do the same. It had been a few days since the incident at El's house. I hadn't seen her, and I needed to. She called the day after to say that she wouldn't be coming in. That Ellie was feeling better but wasn't one hundred percent yet.

We missed our date. She felt bad, but I told her repeatedly that I understood. I would never hold a grudge towards her because she chose her kids over me.

Grabbing my keys, I headed out to my bike. Getting to El was all that was on my mind now. It didn't take long for me to get to her house. I knew she heard me pull up. That was evident when she opened the door while I was getting ready to turn off my engine. She's so damn beautiful. Wearing a white t-shirt and jeans, her hair pulled up in a tight bun on her head. Such a simple, classic look. I'd never seen anything better.

I walk up to her and envelop her within my arms, bringing my lips to hers. She moaned into my mouth, and it took everything I had to not take her there on the porch.

"Where are the kids? How's Ellie?" Speaking between kisses, I didn't give her a chance to answer before kissing her again. I got a couple more in before she pulled back.

"Ellie's fine. She is actually spending the night at her friend's house. Same with the boys. They went over to Mike's house. None of them are here."

Her eyes were pools of desire. She made it clear that we were alone. I hunched down and put my shoulder into her stomach, and lifted her. She laughed, and it was a sound that I wanted to hear for the rest of my life. But for now, I would settle for moans. I got us inside, slammed the door and turned, and locked it.

"Room?"

"Third door on the left."

As soon as we were in the room, I placed her down on the bed. My body covered hers instantly. Her legs spread, welcoming me without restraint, other than our clothes. Her hands came up and gripped my hair, pulling at the strands. I moaned into her mouth. Barely breaking away, I spoke.

"I want you, baby. I want you so fucking much."

"Take me, Ken. Please, fucking take me."

My hands come up and squeeze her tits through her shirt. I wanted them out and in my mouth. Biting one nipple, squeezing the other. Bringing her slight pain while giving her even more pleasure. I pulled myself up enough to bring her shirt over her head. Her tits were covered a by lace, nude bra. It was almost like she was wearing nothing.

I growled out loud, letting her know how much I appreciated what she was wearing. I wanted to see the rest. I undo her jeans and scoot myself backward, bringing them with me. Her creamy skin is on display. The same underwear covered her pussy, and I wanted to plant my face between her legs and never get up.

I had never seen a more beautifully delicious sight.

"Get up, baby. Stand over there, let me see you."

I flopped down and laid on my back, waiting for her to do what I had asked. She smiled and got up, and turned to face me. Her tits were massive, spilling out of her barely there bra. Waiting to be devoured. I motioned with my finger for her to spin. That was where I lost all control.

She turned so delectably slow that I was able to throw myself forward and grab her ass. I couldn't fit a single cheek in my hand. Her ass was huge, round, and jiggled beyond control. I wanted to eat it until I had my fill.

"Oh my god, baby, you're fucking perfect."

I brought the sides of her thong down her legs, and she stepped out of it. My hands ran back up her legs. My left gripped her ass cheek while my right came up between her legs and stroked her cunt. She was soaking wet already. I brought my fingers to my mouth and moaned.

"You're so fucking delicious, baby. I am going to ravish you."

"Oh, fuck. Yes. Please."

She was panting, and I was the hardest I had ever been in my life. My hands continued to trail up her back and undid her bra. She let it fall to the floor, and I spun her around. I grabbed both of the massive globes and brought them together, and stuck my face between them. Sucking any inch of skin my mouth could reach.

Her hands came back into my hair, and as I sucked one pink nipple into my mouth, my fingers twisted and pulled the other.

"Oh fuck, Ken! Keep going, baby, oh shit."

"Sensitive baby?"

"Yes. Don't fucking stop. Ahhh."

Her moans turned me on more, and I was painfully strained behind my zipper. I had to let go of the one nipple I was torturing and unzip myself. I needed some form of relief. I moved to the nipple my fingers just vacated and sucked it as deep as I could.

"Ken! Oh fuck, baby, baby, I'm going to come."

I groaned as I twisted the other nipple, and she shattered in my arms. Screams of pleasure left her, and it took everything I had not to come right then and there.

"Lay down, baby. I am not done with you yet."

She laid in the middle of her bed, and I stripped myself. My cock jutting out and hitting above my belly button. If I had anything to brag about, it was the fact that I did not lack in the dick department.

"Oh my god. Put that in me, now."

"Yes, ma'am."

I brought myself up against her body and started kissing her. Rubbing my cock up and down her slit, teasing her entrance.

"Baby, how do you want me? I'm clean, but I will wrap it for you."

"I'm on the pill, and I'm clean. I trust you. I want...OH FUCK!"

I didn't let her finish. I slammed into and pounded relentlessly. Her screams turning me on, even more, telling me to continue with my assault. She wrapped her legs around my waist, and I pulled up and unwrapped them. Spreading them as far as they would go, I bent her knees and then pressed her legs to her chest.

She tightened, and I could see my dick popping the area above her cunt up and down. Hitting her sweet spot deep within over and over. Her screams continued as she orgasmed again. I could feel her tightening and her release coating my cock, dripping out of her cunt every time I pulled back.

"Baby, fuck. Fuck, you feel so good. I'm going to come."

"Come. Come. Oh fuck, Ken. Come in me. I'm coming again; come with me."

I put everything I had into pounding into her as hard as I could. I went for maybe a minute longer before the hardest orgasm of my life took over my body. I pushed in as deep as I could as I emptied everything I had in her.

Bringing my face down to hers, I kissed her deeply while bringing her legs down as I rubbed my hands up and down her body.

"Are you okay, baby?"

"More than okay. That was amazing." She giggles, and her smile is absolutely radiant.

"What is it?"

"You still owe me a date."

"You're right. I do. You wanna go now or another day?"

She laid there thinking about it for a second and gave me another smile.

"Another day. I think you need to do it right, pick me up, talk to the kids, the whole nine yards."

I laughed and pulled her closer to me, "I can do that, baby. I can definitely do that."

TEN

JUDGE

-Past-

We laid there in her bed, wrapped up close, kissing and exploring all the best parts of each other's bodies. El thought it was a good time for some food and water to re-energize to have another round. As I watched her flit around the kitchen making sandwiches in nothing but my shirt, I thought back to Theo and our conversation from before. As much as I was against it all, I think he is right.

Like fuck I am ever going to admit that to his face. His head is big enough as it is.

"El, baby." She places the sandwich in front of me and moves to get our water. "Remember the other day when that fucker showed up?" She freezes, not turning to look at me. "What we needed to talk about after that but didn't? Well, I think it's time to revisit that conversation."

I pray that this isn't going to start another war of words, but leave it to me to ruin a perfect evening. She remains still for what feels like forever. She shakes her head and retrieves our water, still not meeting my eye. Sitting down across from me, I can see the wheels turning. She is trying to figure out a way to sidetrack this conversation.

“El, I need to know. He is still a part of those kids, and he brought danger to your doorstep.” I speak softly, reaching for her hand that she quickly puts under the table. “I can’t help you, babe, if I don’t know about the trouble knocking at our door.”

Her eyes flew to mine, full of the same fire from the other day, but this time I was ready for all the shit, she was going to spit at me. All the excuses like before, but I will remind her again that I am all in this. With her, J.J., R.J., and Ellie, I claimed them all. They are mine, and I will go to the ends of the earth. I will fight the devil himself to keep them safe. She must see the look on my face, as the fire in her eyes is fading but not leaving completely.

“Ken, I just….” She lets out a sigh, pushing her food away. “There is so much to that story. I don’t have much time left to feel safe from him. I don’t want him in our happy bubble just yet.”

“Elvira, he is in the bubble because he sent the fucking mafia to knock on your door. I am not asking because I want to know if I am better than him. I *know* I am. I am not a perfect man by any means. I am asking so I know how to keep you safe, from Travis, from Artem and his hired goons.”

I am trying to remain calm, but burying your head in the sand is a surefire way to lose it. She gets up, moving to the desk she has set up in the far end of the kitchen before returning with a business card. Looking from her and back to the card, in Bold letters was the name ‘***Artem Sidorov***.’ His profession listed was investor… Ya, I bet he ‘Invested’ in a lot of things. Along the bottom, there was his personal cell number.

"He came back last night, this time alone." She told me softly. My mind starts to race. "Ken, stop overthinking and listen, he just-." I couldn't let her finish.

"Why didn't you call me? Elvira! These men are dangerous. Were the kids home? What did they see?" I was firing questions and thoughts at her left and right, not allowing her any time to answer. "I would have been here in a heartbeat, and you have to know this." I am up and pacing, begging her with my voice to know I am here. For her to see I am here, for her.

"There wasn't time!" She yells out, stopping me dead in my tracks. She is now in front of me, holding on to my forearms. "He came here last night and just dropped off the card for when I wanted and needed to get in touch with him." She flips the card over, and in neat, almost feminine writing was an address. "This is where he will be all day tomorrow. We can -." I cut her off.

"I will talk to him. I will fix this." I said, hoping my tone left no room for argument, but I knew I was wrong.

"This is my mess, and I don't need you fixing it *FOR* me."

"Actually, this is Travis' mess, and I am not fixing it for you. I am ending it, once and for all."

There was a menace in my tone that I hope she would not assume directed to her. I cut off more protest by smashing my mouth to hers.

I push her back towards the table, her ass hitting the edge. I lean down on her and use my arm to swipe everything to the floor. I know that she will be pissed at me later, but right now, I don't really care.

She lands with a loud thump onto the top of the table and lets out a breathy moan. The sound traveling down, making me even harder than I already am. I pushed down on her, bringing her hands above her head and pinning them to the table.

Breaking the kiss, I bite her neck, right where her shoulder meets. "I mean it El, I will take care of this."

"I don't need - ah!"

I silence her by slamming my fingers into her tight cunt. Her walls are gripping me immediately. I know that she is already close. I started pumping my fingers in and out of her, rough and fast. Her moans are getting louder, her body shaking.

"Come for me, baby."

"Yes. Yes. Fuck! Ken! Ahhh."

Her screams are music to my ears. She's coming down from her high, and I am pushing my pants down just enough to get my cock out. She looks at me, completely sedated but nowhere near where I want her.

I slam into her. Her body moving up, and the table itself skidding across the floor. I keep pounding, and the table keeps moving. She keeps screaming. I push down on the area that I know will push her g-spot down. Slamming into it repeatedly.

"Fuck. Fuck. Ken. I can't - Oh my god. I can't. It's too much. Too much. Ah - fuck. Don't you dare fucking stop!"

I couldn't help letting out a small chuckle before telling her, "yes, ma'am."

By the time the table hit the wall, I was ready to explode. El was screaming louder than ever before, and it was making it harder and harder for me to hold off on coming. I needed her distracted. I looked down at her, and there were a couple of tears sliding down her face.

I truly brought orgasm after orgasm out of her, and now her body was at the point of not being able to handle it. She was right where I wanted her. Right where I needed her.

"Come one more time, baby. Just once."

"No. I can't. I can't."

"You can, and you goddamn will! I will not come without you."

I slammed in as hard as I could and brought my hand to her clit. Rubbing circles and right as I was about to blow my load, I slapped her clit - hard.

"HOLY FUCKING SHIT!"

Her screaming was loud enough that I wouldn't be surprised if the neighbors called the cops. As she convulsed and covered me with her own release, I pumped as far up as I could and gave her every drop my body wanted to get rid of.

The hottest sex of my life was all so I could make her forget about the trouble her life was currently in. I could live with that. I carried her relaxed body to her room, quickly rushing to clean the mess I made before crawling back into bed, wrapping her up in my arms because that is where I knew she was safe from anything and everything out there.

A few hours later, I watched as she slept before slowly making my way out of the bed and gathering my things. I quickly get dressed, and as I am grabbing Artem's card from the table, I see a pen and paper. It felt like a dirty little secret, but we both knew the truth.

'Never doubt what I will do for you. Never doubt how I feel for you.

I will call you in the afternoon. Feel free to stop by for Tea with Yaya.

-Your Judge'

I slip the note on her pillow, kiss her head one last time and head out into the night, knowing that what I'm about to do tomorrow might have been my last night with her. Because only death or she would stop me from coming back, and I wasn't sure which would be my demise in the morning.

"This is so cool! It's like those mobster movies." Theo is bouncing up and down on his toes as he follows me into the bistro-style diner on the outskirts of Wyman proper.

"Ya, and just like those movies, the loudmouth always gets shot. So, shut the fuck up." I snap back, meeting the hostess' eye. "Please excuse my friend; he doesn't get out much and is like an excited puppy when I take him to new places." She smiles, but it doesn't quite reach her eyes. "I am hoping to speak to Mr. Artem Sidorov, if he is in, please."

The color drains from her face. Her eyes flick from left to right looking Theo and myself up and down. Trying to decide what her first move should be.

"We have business with him regarding the 'May' account." Theo fills in, and that seems to settle her enough.

"Right this way, gentlemen. Can I please get your names and a drink while you wait here?"

She escorted us to a secluded booth at the back near the kitchen doors. We both asked for coffee then she rushed through those doors. We looked around, trying to get in as many details of this place as we could before a large body slid in beside Theo, and Artem slid in beside me.

"Well, I knew you would be coming, but I was hoping you would be bringing a more attractive bargaining chip," Artem says, looking my best friend up and down.

"I will have you know that what I lack in looks I make up for by being *VERY* giving in the bedroom." He eyes Artems bodyguard up and down, licking his lips. "What I wouldn't do to this jolly green giant. Mmm." *Fucking Theo.*

"Alright, put it away." I bark at Theo. I reach into my back pocket and produce a check. "This is the full 20 grand that you are owed. Now you and your men can leave Elvira alone. Also, anything that fucker says about El from this point on is a lie, and you would be better to end his sad life right then and there."

I know it's cold. That is the father of her kids, a man she loved once, but setting the mob off on his kids and their mother shows how terrible a person he is. Artem looks at the folded check I slid in front of him and pushed it back to me.

"In this line of work, we don't deal in anything that isn't cash. But I am willing to make you a deal. Your family's land and the debt is wiped clean, and then consider Travis deleted from existence."

"Sorry, nope, I just got this land back, and I am not losing it. I will get you your cash then, and I will deal with Travis myself. Me and my MC." *Why the fuck did I say that?*

"Your MC? I have worked with MCs, and they are strangely proud of leather and bikes. I see no Leather cuts, nor a 'hog' between the two of you." Artem looks amused.

"We are new, founding, starting to spread our wings and get new members." I hold my head up, no backing down now. Fake it until you make it.

"Really?" He seems very amused. "So you have spoken to the other MCs and made sure that you aren't going to cause a 'turf war'?" He asks, and that is when I knew I fucked up. "Are you serious about starting an MC?" He asks, looking from Theo, who is nodding like a bobblehead doll, to me. "If you are, you call Detroit here, at this number," He writes Detroit and a phone number on the back of my check. "Tell him Artem sent you and set up a meeting here, in three days. We will help you, get what you need, and you can help me get what I need." He finishes and places the paper in front of me.

Detroit, Prez

Satan's Children

720-555-3354

"What about what Travis owes? I have the money to cover it. I refuse to allow you to come after Elvira just because you want cash." I state firmly. I need him to understand that I will not back down from this.

He smirks at me, and I want to wipe his face clean of it. This guy was a smug as hell asshole, and I didn't want to continue to have to deal with him.

"As I said, I want your land."

"And as I said, you ain't fucking getting it."

"You didn't let me finish. You allow me to use your land. Let me store my goods there, hide what I need hidden and when the time comes, you run for me."

"We ain't selling drugs or guns for you."

"Did I ask you to? No. I asked you to store and run. If you do that for me, I will not hold Elvira to the money that her husband owes me."

"Ex. He is her ex-husband."

"Schematics," he waves his hand, "the fact is, she will not be held responsible. Do we have a deal?"

I look over to Theo. This is something that I wanted him to be on as well. This seemed like an easy enough deal to get this danger away from Elvira. He nods his head, and I turn back to Artem.

"For how long?"

"Until I no longer need you."

"And Elvira is responsible for none of the garbage that Travis has accumulated?"

"None of it."

"You have a deal."

We shake hands, he then signaled to his goon, and they were gone. Theo rips the paper from me and starts hopping up and down in the booth. He was happier than a pig and shit, and I had a feeling we just agreed to sign a deal with the devil.

ELEVEN

ELVIRA

-Present-

I was sitting on the loveseat in our room, trying to rock to sleep sweet baby Kelsey. She and her sister, Carley, were in the worst way when they came to us about a week ago. We have had babies who couldn't be settled before, but there was something more to this. Almost like she was in pain, and she couldn't communicate with us.

"Is she still at it?" Ken asked, walking into our master suite.

"Ya, I just don't get it. It's like she is hurting more than just missing her mom." I look at this sweet girl's face. It's red and wet with both tears and sweat. She has been crying hard like this for well over an hour. Nothing can settle her. She's been off and on like this since we brought her home.

"Are you sure the Sheriff had the hospital check them out?" He asked, scooping her from my arms, which just caused her to shriek even louder. But he didn't pay it any mind and kept trying to settle her, bouncing while walking about.

"It was just the paramedics that gave them the all-clear. The social worker at the police station said that we were cleared to take them home." I knew something about the whole thing felt off.

We had been at this for many years, and our intuition was never wrong. We also had to tread on the right side of the law if we were going to keep being allowed to take in these kids. Well, as far as the world knew, we were just a club that helped kids get a fresh start. We helped kids face their abusers and give them the confidence to be better people and grow from their experiences. What happens behind closed doors at the far end of the property? No one needs to know except those involved.

"Did you call Margret?" He asked, trying to get her to retake the bottle. Which she surprisingly took and quieted down enough for me to gather a thought.

"I did, but because of the circumstances, we don't have guardianship to make medical decisions for them. That is up to the state of Colorado, and they are not returning my calls." I feel myself getting emotional.

It was hard having our hands tied, and unless it was an emergency, there was nothing we could do. She might be crying and hard to settle, but medically speaking, she was fine. She ate more than enough, had a good amount of wet and dirty diapers, which to the state did not really warrant an emergency room visit. So even if they did call me back, there was nothing we could do. Before Ken could even make a smart-ass comment about this like he always did when our hands were tied, Kelsey pushed the bottle away and projectile vomited all of the milk she just consumed.

I scooped her from him and took off to the attached bathroom. She just kept puking. So much so that there was blood streaking the bile and milk that was coming up. Ken quickly stripped his shirt and pulled on a new one while I held her over the tub while she continued. She was screaming in what can only be described as complete and total anguish. I allowed the tears to flow from my eyes, but I kept my voice calm and as soothing as I could.

I grabbed a towel, stripped her down to nothing, noticing there was a bloody stool in her diaper as well. Before I could even turn to tell Ken that we needed to go, he stormed back into the bathroom with his phone to his ear.

"Cowboy, climb off the whore and get to the main house now. There is no time to drag your ass!" Hanging up, not waiting for a reply

"Ken, I'm worried," I whisper as he is dialing another number. He nodded, giving me that look that I knew so well, the one that said, 'Don't worry baby, I've got this.' I felt myself relax and just focused on her.

"Storm, I need you to wake up the sheriff and drag his ass to the hospital. Meet us there." He barked into the receiver in that authoritative tone that made my body tingle every time, no matter the circumstance. *You would think after fifteen years, I would have a handle on that.* "Give me the baby, and you get cleaned up. Our boy will be here soon to watch over the other littles. Theo will meet us at the ER."

I hand him over Kelsey, who has stopped puking and crying, now only whimpering and shaking. Watching this mountain of a man be so tender and gentle while cleaning up her frail little body made me fall in love all over again. This man always knew who to trust and what to do to help those in his care. He is the strongest human I know, and I will do whatever I can to help him and his cause.

After Cowboy showed up, we took off quickly to the hospital. We blazed into the Emergency Department, demanding to be taken to the back, saying we needed a doctor, that the baby was sick. I handed over all the paperwork from the police and state saying we had emergency and critical care rights until the state stated otherwise. The nurses were trying to get us to wait to be triaged, not even bothering to look at the paperwork once we said we were foster parents.

"Ma'am, I know you are busy here tonight, but I have a little girl who is puking and shitting blood. She has been like this for days. She needs to be seen." Judge says, trying to stay calm, but I can see that the vein at his temple starts to pulse.

"Sir, there are a lot of sick people here tonight. We will see to you when we can." She doesn't even meet his eye, dismissing us and our concerns.

"Listen here bitch, just because we are foster parents with a child that is not biologically ours doesn't mean we are trying to shove her and her 'issues' off on your ER. So you need to listen and look at her before I climb over the desk and force *your* admittance into a room here." I snap.

Her eyes snap up to me. "I understand your concern; however, you are not her parent. You have no legal right to demand anything. Just because you say she is having trouble doesn't mean she is. Foster parents are all the same. They don't care. Don't pretend you do. Go sit down, and we will call you when we're ready for you."

"You fucking cunt!"

"El!" As I turn around, Kelsey is flailing backward from Ken's chest, seizing. "Kelsey!" I run over to her and support her head as Ken lowers her down to the ground. I look over at the twat behind the desk, "are you going to do *anything?*"

She scoffs and turns back to the computer. I'm going to fucking kill her. Here she is, thinking I am lying while my baby is seizing right in front of her.

A nurse comes out from the double doors, holding a clipboard. I only assume that it is to call another patient when she sees the scene in front of her. She runs over to the desk, "What the hell are you doing just sitting here?" She yells at the useless nurse.

"What? It's not like anything is happening."

The nurse that just arrived gets on the intercom and calls for rapid response in ER Triage.

"I don't know why you're wasting your time calling them. These people aren't even the kids' real parents."

"I'm going to pretend like I didn't hear you just dismiss a child, Brenda."

The new nurse, whose name tag says Maria, gets me out of the way and starts tending to Kelsey. I stand and set my sights on the hoe now named Brenda. She must see the anger radiating off me as she now looks slightly panicked. I can faintly hear the Sheriff talking to Ken behind me, but I am not to be stopped. This bitch is going down.

I walk around the counter, and she stands. She is smaller than I am, but I don't care. She was going to let my baby die on the floor right in front of her all because I'm not Kelsey's "real mom."

"You are a piece of shit for a human being. You should be ashamed of yourself."

Before I let her get a word in, which I was sure would be garbage anyways, I punched her in the face. The crunch of her nose is the most satisfying sound.

"Ahhh! You broke my nose! Sheriff, did you see what she did? I want to file an assault charge this instant."

Blood is streaming down her face; it's a beautiful sight. I turn to look at Sheriff Anderson, almost daring him to say something. He looks over to the nurse and starts walking towards us.

"What I see is a little one-year-old girl seizing on the floor and you just sitting there as nothing happened. That's all I see. Now, if you'll excuse me."

The sheriff follows Ken into the back of the ER. I turn back to the nurse and smirk. Giving her the best parting words. "You won't have your job by the time I leave here. Have a great day!" I say disgustingly sweet and walk to find my kid.

I see Ken and Sheriff Anderson standing outside what I assume to be Kelsey's room. As I come closer to them, they are speaking in hushed tones, but what they have to say, I can't concern myself with now as Kelsey needs me.

Getting into her room, I see that she is now hooked up to IVs and a nasal cannula on her tiny little face. The little crib she is laying in makes her look even smaller. The precious nurse from before is checking her vitals and writing information down on her chart.

"Thank you. That nurse up front was so terrible to us because she isn't ours. But the thing is, she is ours in our hearts. I wouldn't be able to live with myself if something happened to her. Thank you for doing what needed to be done."

Maria walks over to me and places a hand on my arm. I immediately felt comfortable. "She's a tough little girl. I have already taken her blood and sent it off for testing. We will get to the bottom of this. The Dr. will be in shortly."

I move over to Kelsey's side and sit down, gently rubbing her head. She was so tiny. She was already frail, and now she looked even smaller, and her skin was now almost translucently white. Her room became quiet, only the low constant beep of the machine telling me her heart was still beating. I had managed to slow my breathing and calm myself enough to hear Ken and the Sheriff's voices coming from the hall.

"I need to know, Judge, is this Artem?"

"No, Anderson, it isn't Artem. Artem may be a quote-unquote bad man, but he doesn't deal in drugs like this. The shit he deals with is pure. It's cut with nothing. That's bad business."

"Well then, we have a new player in town, Judge. Tox reports show that her dad was high as a fucking kite. Cocaine mixed with fuck all. The toxicologist confirmed that traces of PCP were cut in along with other shit that's too long to list. That baby, don't be surprised if shit comes up in her reports."

"You're telling me that they shot that baby up with drugs?"

"There is no way to know with both of them dead, Judge. I'm only telling you because if this isn't Artem, we need to figure out what the fuck we're going to do. We can't let this shit into our town."

"I'll bring it up at Church. Get me everything you know, and once I have her bloodwork, I'll call my brothers."

I hear what sounds like a smack and Sheriff Anderson telling Ken he will get the information to him as soon as possible. My husband then walks through the door.

"What was that about?"

"Club business, babe."

"Don't 'club business, babe' me Kenneth Kelley! This has to do with our little girl. What the fuck is going on?"

He shakes his head and goes to open his mouth when the Doctor comes in. Before the Doctor can say anything, I look at him and remind him that we are nowhere near done talking about this.

"Mr. and Mrs. Kelley, I'm Dr. Mills, and I have the preliminary results back from Kelsey's blood tests. We have called her social worker to join us, but she has given me the go-ahead to talk to you. It seems Kelsey is going through some pretty serious drug withdrawals. Judging by her size in accordance with her age, she has been under-nourished for quite some time. You have only had her in your care for a little under a week, is that correct?" He asked, looking from me to Judge.

"Yes, when her parents died, she and her sister came to us," I respond, floored at the life those little girls must have led before they came to our loving arms.

"I am going to assume that the mother was using and breast-feeding at the same time and giving her small doses of whatever she was taking. We are going to have to admit her. As well as run more tests. We will also put her on some pain meds to stop the shakes and start the process to wean her off again more naturally." He explains writing on her chart and handing it to a nurse that popped in for a moment to add to the fluids already pumping into her tiny body.

"I'm sorry, can you explain this to me? You tell me she is hooked on drugs and needs to be given more drugs to be taken of them? How does that make any sense?" I asked, trying to really see reason in this logic. "She hasn't had anything for a week; can't we just keep doing this?"

"Unfortunately, no. Her body is starting to shut down because, in her short life, she has always had a 'fix' for lack of a better word. This way, we can control how she comes down to avoid a reaction this severe and make her more comfortable at the same time. It's a long process, but we have almost an 80% success rate with this method. I am confident she is strong and resilient enough to pull through and live a happy, healthy life on the other side. With little to no severe defects as she grows." His smile and words should bring some peace, but he will still pump narcotics into this little girl, which hurts my heart.

"How do I know you won't make her overdose?"

"In all my years of dealing with drug and/or alcohol-addicted babies, I have never made one O.D., and I will not let your little girl be my first. I will be here every step of the way. Any questions you have, any concerns that arise, I will do everything in my power to answer or calm your fears. She is safe here. You have my word."

I nod my head yes and reach up to my short hair and start to rub it out of habit, remembering a time when I would be too scared to do so in times like this. Times of stress and heartbreak that I knew was coming my way.

TWELVE

ELVIRA

-Past-

I had never had a panic attack before, but I was sure that I was in the beginning stages of one. He wanted me to have my hair down.

Our last few dates were with the kids doing things at the ranch, so I could have my hair up in a bun, ponytail, or even hidden under a hat. Even when we fooled around, my hair was still always tied back or up in some manner. When his hands reached for more than the ends of my ponytail, I would distract him with anything I could think of. But today, he was taking me on the *proper date* I had teased him about.

Why did I have to tease him about this? I didn't care; I liked that he got along with my kids. I loved seeing him bring J.J. out of his shell and be a 'real kid' again. He never pushed R.J. to do more than he was comfortable with, and while he struggled to make that connection with him, he never let the kids know. Ellie slipped a few times and called him Dad when I had all three of the kids out at the ranch. The joy in his face was hard to hide, just as the guilt was hard to hide on hers.

I would have loved to have met Ken sooner than the POS that is my ex, the reason why I am in full panic mode looking at myself in the bathroom mirror. The reason why I can't wear my hair down, the reason why at only 34 years old, I am going bald. The hair loss was mild. First, the doctor said it was stress-induced alopecia, and when I kicked his ass to the curb and filed for divorce, I thought it would get better, but it's getting worse and worse.

I look at myself repeatedly; my dress is light green with pretty pink, red, and orange flowers on it. A sundress that comes to just above my knees and thicker straps on my shoulders. It is fun and nice enough for a higher-end place. Not that I think he would break the bank for this date, that's not the type of man he is. My makeup is done, light and natural but makes me feel beautiful. But my hair, I don't even know what to do with it. I pull the towel down, and when I look at it, I see more strands of my beautiful red locks. It's coming out in more of a clump form lately. I pick up the long locks and set them on the counter, their color a stark contrast to the faux white marble bathroom vanity.

The brush is right beside this pile, and my eyes flit back and forth between the hair and the brush. I know when I pick that up and start to use it, more and more hair is going to come out and get stuck in the tines, pulling from my already damaged and barren scalp. The gathering of hair already on the counter is enough to bring me to tears. Once I start brushing the bald spot I know is there, it's going to grow at the back of my head. It will prove that I am ugly and undeserving of a guy like Ken. Ken has a thick full head of hair that I love to run my fingers through. I think about how it felt when I last did it and then subconsciously run my fingers through my own, pulling more out. A whole handful of strands are in my hand, and I just can't.

What man wants to be with a bald woman? What man wants to be with a woman who has an ex that comes around and makes threats on her life and threatens to take her kids away daily. Because I am stuck paying for his debt, I struggle to make ends meet to fix his mistakes and survive with growing boys and a daughter who is trying not to be the poor girl in class. What man, no matter how amazing he seems on paper, would stick around for this mess?

I didn't even notice the tears until the soft, salty fluttering hit my wrist. Ken deserves a woman he can have on his arm that he can be proud to show off. I am too broken mentally, emotionally, and physically. I think tonight I am going to end this because he worked so hard for this dream. My emotional baggage and the fact that I will not want to be seen in public after tonight is too much. He needs more than I am.

I start sobbing, trying to keep it as quiet as I can. The last thing I need is J.J. rushing in here and seeing my hair like this, causing that child more worry than he should have at 15. My hands cover my face, and I cry, ruining the makeup I worked hard on. Creating a mess of this image that I have been putting out there. Frankly, I really don't care.

I knew it was too good to be true. I knew the joy I was feeling was short-lived. Because I am not worth this much, I need to work and get my kids on to the next stage, and then I will be free of my ex. Then maybe I can focus on myself. This thing with Ken, while I have loved it, has shown me I am not ready; I am still too broken. I take a few cleansing breaths and look back up at my face. My mascara is running, my lipstick is gone, and my eyeliner is smudged all over. I grab my brush, looking at it, the hair in my hand that I cried into, and the strands all over the counter.

"Might as well finish the job," I mutter to myself and bring the brush to my hair, and after one downstroke, there is a startling knock on the bathroom door.

"Mom?" J.J.s voice booms through the hollow-core door. "Ken is here. He brought flowers for Ellie, and Theo is gonna play video games with me and R.J. tonight." He sounded so excited and ready for a night to be a kid.

"Okay, baby, I'll be right out." My voice sounds rough and scratchy like it normally did after a good cry.

"Mama?" He asked. He knows me; I sounded like this way too many times in his life.

"J.J., why don't you and Theo go set up. I'll talk to your mom." I hear Ken on the other side.

My heart sinks. My hair. My face. What is he going to think? Is he going to leave as soon as he sees me? Well, I would walk away anyway, so let's get this over with sooner rather than later.

"El?" He knocks on the door softly. "Babe, can you let me in?"

My breath is in my throat. I am not ready for this; there is something in his tone that makes me want to hold on to that selfish feeling. To keep him for me, but that is not fair to anyone. I am panicking. He cannot see me like this. No man wants to be around a woman who isn't put together.

"Elvira, I am coming in babe."

He turns the knob, and before my brain tells my hand to stop him, he is already in the doorway. His huge, larger-than-life body and presence are in my small bathroom. His eyes scan my face, smudged and flushed from the tears and the self-loathing I let free and am still feeling. He looks to the counter where all my hair is sitting, no longer in the neat pile but scattered about from the rush of air caused by the opening and closing of the bathroom door. He reaches for my hairbrush and sets it on the counter, and before I can even ask, he scoops me into his embrace. I don't make a move. I don't know what is going on. His right hand is on my lower back, holding me close to him. His left is slowly going up and down my spine in a soothing and calming manner. He bends down to my level and burrows his face into the junction where my neck meets my shoulder. His warm breath caressing my neck, shoulder, and the time it hits the front of my chest is cooler and causes my skin and nipples to pebble. My arms raise and wrap around him, clinging to him and the sobs start coming. Loud and broken. Everything I kept in, tried to keep quiet, I let it go. He allowed me to be weak with no judgment, just held me close and told me he was there, and I felt it. I didn't feel alone, and I felt like he was really, truly there.

I don't know how long we stood there in my bathroom, holding one another. The sobs and tears subsided, but I still clung to him, worried that he would disappear if I let him go. He started to pull away, but I clung tighter. His left hand made its way to my hair, and he started running his fingers through it, not seeming to care that it was falling out in clumps into his hand.

"I have wanted this for months." His smooth, timbering voice vibrated from his chest to mine.

"What? Pull out my hair?" He pushes me back looking me dead in the eyes. I see emotion shining in them like this is going to be a profound moment.

"No, just running my fingers through the red curls you've always teased me with. They looked soft and wonderful. I always wondered why they were up, why you never let them be free and wild like Ellies. Because you have just as much of a wild side in you as she does, and the pinned back school marm hair never matched. Now I know why. What is going on, firecracker?" He asks, holding my face in both his hands, searching my eyes for the truth among all the lies I want to tell him.

"I have Stress-Induced Alopecia. My hair," my voice starts to crack. This is the first time I have said it out loud. "My hair is falling out, and I am going bald."

Ken, looking at me for a beat, pushes me back away from him. My heart sinks. He is going to run. He doesn't want a woman who will have no hair, need a wig to function in a normal society, and avoid the stares that I will get with no hair. He pushes me to sit on the closed toilet lid, and he starts opening the cabinet under the sink. I watched with confusion, and I was sure he was going to run. What is he doing now? What is he going to do?

He digs into the back and finds it, my old hairdressing box. It has my scissors and clippers in there with multi-length heads. He pulls the clippers and plugs them into the wall. He turns back to me, holding out his hand for me. I stand in front of him, and he picks them up; his eyes meet mine in the mirror. He is asking for permission to stop delaying the inevitable and shave it off. I give him a small nod, and when I hear it come to life, I close my eyes. Taking in a few deep breaths before I feel his feather-light touch on my head, running his fingers along my hairline. I feel the vibration on my head as he slowly starts to run them from the front of my head to the back, right down the middle.

"No turning back now," he says softly over the sharp hum while he cuts away the last of my hair.

I don't open my eyes, and I don't say anything. I keep my eyes closed and let the tears fall as my hair falls away. Brushing along my cheeks, down my shoulders, I feel the feather-light touch as it falls past the exposed skin. I feel the warmth of Ken's expansive chest at my back, like an anchor holding me steady.

After a short while, the vibrations of the hair clippers stop on my head, but I still hear them on. I slowly open my eyes and see my new reflection, and there is just a small amount of stubble along with my head. That is all that is left.

I look to meet his hot penetrative gaze in the mirror. They are still on and buzzing in his hand. I gave him a soft smile, letting him know with my face, eyes, and breathing that I was Okay. That he did good, he raises them again, only this time to his head. I spin to meet his face.

"No, Ken!" I reach for them, and he pulls them from my grasp. "What are you doing?"

"What part of we are a team do you not understand?" He says, putting his free hand on my face, holding my gaze. "You are going through this, so I am too. Because I love you, woman. I love those kids out there, and when it hits you hard, it hits me too."

He pulls his hand free and buzzes down the middle as he did me. His long wavy, chocolate brown locks fall to our feet. I watch as the hair that my daughter has braided, the hair that I ran my hands through on more than one makeout session, the hair that he has used to define him from the time he was 18 and could make decisions in his own best interest. He cut it all off for me to show me solidarity, and at that moment, I realized what he said to me that he loved me.

Ken. Loved. Me.

At this moment, watching him cut the hair that he swore he would never cut, the hair that he wanted to grow long and wild for all his days, he was shaving it to prove his love for me. At that same moment, I realized that I was in love with him too. That he didn't need to do this, that I was so in love with him there was no breaking this bond at any point. Everything I thought before this moment no longer held any bear in mind.

He shaved the front of his head. I put the clippers on the counter with his hair finished, and he pulls me in for another deep embrace. As he struggled to reach the back, I took them from his hand, and we shared the same moment that we just had.

I pull my head back from his chest and look up towards him. His eyes meet mine, and I push up on my tiptoes and give him a soft kiss on the lips. "I love you, too."

The realization hits me hard. We are a team, we are in love, and we can do anything we put our minds to.

THIRTEEN

JUDGE

-Past-

These past six months have been a blur of joy and hard work. Finding my family that had been looking for me so hard, then taking on the family Ranch and learning all the ins and outs of the operation. I loved the hard work and how tired I felt at the end of it all, and as much as I wanted just to shower and fall into bed at the end of the day, I had Sweet Elvira and her troupe of kiddos that I wanted to see as often as I could. While I was loading up the gator for the day to check the fencing around the closest pasture, my phone beeps with a text.

Unknown: *Detroit will be here in 2 hours, have a spot ready for a meeting.*

"Shit," I mumble, looking around for my shit head of a best friend. "Theo!" His head pops out of the far stall, pitchfork in hand. "Did Yaya go into town this morning for the shop?"

"Yuppers, she said she was meeting El for lunch and not to expect her anytime soon." He slowly starts making his way down to me.

"Great, make sure the guys are set, and we can drop off the supplies and set up the kitchen for a meeting. " Giving Theo a knowing smile.

"You mean…" His eyes light up like I told him we were going to Disneyland

"Yes, it's time to start our MC." I brace myself for his reaction.

He started hooting and hollering, jumping up and down, causing the biggest scene I have ever seen. The horses start whining and kicking the stall sides at the ruckus he was causing. I smacked him, and we went on to get what we needed to be done as quickly as we could.

By the time I dropped off the fencing supplies to the farmhand out there and picked up William from the easternmost pasture, I saw the clouds of dust kicking up from someone speeding their way to the main house. Our time to set up was over. Theo quickly made his way up the porch bolting into the side kitchen door while I made my way to meet the bikes and town car pulling to a stop.

"Gentleman," I say, shaking hands with Detroit and Artem. Eyeing the three other men that rode up with them. Unsure of them being here. "What do I owe the pleasure of this meeting?" Detroit looks from me to the men. "I'd like you to meet your new members."

"I'm sorry?" I look from William back to the men, unsure of how to take that.

"You wanted an MC. Well, you need more than two people. I have been in the game a long time and know-how to vet men.

These men here know how to vet potential prospects and brothers." Detroit points to a mountain of a man with wild hair and a beard to match. "This here is Bigfoot. I have known him for many years, and he is willing to help you bring up your prospects and make sure they know your club rules and charter." He points to a younger man, about mid-20s, with hair closely cropped to his head and tattoos that poked from the collar of his t-shirt. "This is Sever, he prospected with us right out of high school, and the big man in the back is Omen. He doesn't say much but is deadly with a knife. They are all willing to patch over from us to you, help found this Club and build it to what you need it to be."

"You are now responsible for these men's lives and livelihood. Are you ready for that?" Artem asks.

I look from these new faces to William and these men who are willing to help me. I started to question this, was I doing it for the right things? Will this club be enough to help police what the police can't? Can I build this to what this town needs?

"Don't overthink it, Judge!" Theo called from the house. "I got the beers all set up! Wee Willie Winky can get the guys set up in the bunkhouse while us big boys get down to the nitty-gritty of it all."

"Okay, Shit Storm!" I called back to him. "William will show you where to get settled and set up with work detail for the day."

I then escort Artem and Detroit into the main house. I see that my best friend had a cooler of beer set up, paper and pens, as well as coffee brewing. I was sure he was ready to build the brotherhood for reasons he would never fully explain to me. But seeing this and knowing there is a strong chance we can make a bigger difference in the lives of those who don't know where to turn. The thoughts of starting this because of Theo,

Elvira, for me, made me want to build this up as best I could. All those fears and doubts from earlier just faded away, and I knew with the help of a seasoned Prez and a man with the brains of know-how behind a crime syndicate, I could start this off with very little trial and error.

We talked and created a charter and rules for the brotherhood to abide by; we decided on our board that we would leave open and flexible as we got to know the men I would now see as brothers. Theo mentioned he found a nice older Harley that ran, but he would fix it up at his new shop that was doing amazing.

"Now, have you thought of a name for your MC cause your name sets a good tone for you," Detroit asks, leaning back and crossing his legs on the kitchen table. "You will also need a cleaner and a guy who is not afraid of getting dirty in the name of the club. He will be your fall guy if things don't go as planned, and that has to be known by him. This job is to make sure none of this gets back to the club in any manner. Our guy is fucking psychopath when you set him off."

The sound of the kitchen door opening and closing snapped up from the conversation as my small Yaya walked in with groceries. Theo jumped up and went to get the rest of the bags from the farm truck. He likes to see if he can haul them all in one trip. *Fucking Theo.* El walked into the house with a few bags as well, setting them on the counter before I locked my arms around her waist and pulled her into my lap, kissing her neck while she looked at the two men at the table.

"You will never guess the show that we saw at the butcher shop today!" Yaya started to say, then quick as always, smacks Detroit upside the head with the wooden spoon she produced out of thin air. "Get your dirty boots from my table. There is a rag in the sink to clean up that mess. This is my house. You want your feet on the table-the barn is out back." She turns away and starts unpacking groceries. "As I was saying, there was a sight to be seen today. He is normally such a loving man, sweet and kind to all of us, his wife as well. But they had some row in the back room. The whole shop was dead quiet while they were at each other's throats."

"Yaya, we don't need to hear the gossip from town. We were in a business meeting." I start to tell her, but the look she gives me stops any more complaints. I was thinking of dead in their tracks.

"As I was saying, we were quiet listening because what else were we to do. I needed the pork for us and set up a time for him to slaughter that cow and chickens so we could have meals for a few months. Then Ailene stops cold, and we hear Hank walk back to us, and he is soaked from head to toe in blood. And it doesn't even phase him." Theo comes running into the kitchen with all the bags in hand and starts helping Yaya out. El starts giggling on my lap, and I hide my smile on her shoulder.

Detroit, after returning with the rag to clean up his mess, looks me dead in the eye, "get him. Trust me."

Artem, who was surprisingly quiet for most of this meeting, looks around the room. "Is she alive?"

"What? Who? Oh, you mean Abilene? Oh yeah, she's fine," Yaya says, dismissing Artem's surprising concern. "That woman has Hank by the balls. She apparently got mad at him for tracking blood everywhere, and he said, and I quote, 'It's only piggy blood, not people,' and threw the rest of said blood all over him. Thinking about it now, it's fucking hilarious."

"Yaya!" Theo says with an admonishing tone.

"What?"

"You have a dirty mouth." He tries not to laugh, keeping a straight face. He loved calling her out more than she loved to whip his ass with that spoon of hers.

"Pish-posh, I say what I want. Put this all away. I'm tired." With a quick kiss to my temple, Yaya heads out of the kitchen. El, following her lead, does the same, and we are once again alone, able to continue from right where we left off.

"As I said, get him. That man will be who you need. He will be the one to dispose of bodies. I promise you. Get the butcher."

After what Yaya disclosed, I had to trust that Detroit was right.

"Now we are back to the question of the name." Artem reminds me, sipping from his beer. To me, it looked comical because he seemed to be dressed more like a martini or an old-fashioned rather than a Bud.

"Name for what?" I hear Elvira ask, coming back into the room. Detroit's eyes shot from her to me, almost giving a look of don't say anything.

"We are naming our MC!" Theo replies, bouncing up and down like the puppy I think he was in a former life. I can hear both men mumble under their breath, 'fucking Theo' before turning their eyes to me.

"What about 'The Nameless Order'?" She suggested. "I mean, you said many times that you and Theo felt nameless and faceless in the system. I have felt nameless in my life with Travis as well. I was always a name that wasn't my own, or the kid's mother, never just 'Elvira.' You guys wanted to help people like ourselves. It could be fitting." The room was deathly quiet, all eyes on my woman. My heart thumping with pride. This is why I love her. She knows what's up.

Then from across the room, where Theo is still putting the produce and canned goods away, I hear him humming 'Elvira' by the Oak Ridge Boys. *Fucking Theo.*

It's been a few days since that meeting, and surprisingly, getting along with the guys that Detroit brought. I was hesitant because they were so willing to leave their previous club, but two of them were nomads. They decided that somewhere outside of the city, with fewer people, would be an okay spot to drop that nomad status. Bigfoot said he knew what it was like to start and understood the help needed for something like this. Plus, having a member patched over from another club helps start those clubs off on an even playing ground and with no bad blood.

The guys also have no issue with doing the work that is needed on the ranch. While we have the ranch hands and the cowboys, this is an operation that everyone partakes in. There were no if, and, or buts about it. For men who grew up in the city, they work out here well.

It was about seven o'clock at night a few days later when Artem came back.

"I have something for you. Call it a gift in good faith that you will honor your part of our deal."

"I am a man of my word Artem. As long as you understand our terms of the deal and stick to them."

Artem smirks and hands me a box. "Just open that and remember our deal, yeah?"

He walks away and gets back into his car. As he is driving away, Theo comes up with the rest of the guys. The others, no longer in cuts as Detroit took them back with him.

"What was Artem here for?" Theo asks.

"He gave me this and said to remember the deal."

Placing it on the table, I opened the box, and looking up at me was El's stencil come to life. A Celtic sword with angel wings, MC to the right, and across the top 'Nameless Order' filled the rocker. The bottom rocker says 'Wyman, CO."

I pull the top cut out and turn it around. On the left, there is a patch that says 'President' and right underneath 'Judge.' I skim my fingers along the patches and turn around to show the guys.

"Well, Prez, put it on. We can't wear ours until you put yours on," Bigfoot informs me.

"Is that really a thing?" I ask.

"Technically, no. It's a matter of respect, though."

I nod in acknowledgment and put the cut on. The weight it adds to my back isn't heavy physically, but the emotional weight it gives I can feel. This patch will mean something big one day, and I will not let this club fail.

"Go on, get yours."

Theo walks up and pulls the next one out. Turning it over, he turns around, and his face is red. Not the embarrassing type red, the 'I'm going to murder someone,' red.

"Is this a fucking joke?"

"What? What does it say?"

"Vice President."

"Yeah, and?"

"Shit Storm! Fucking Shit Storm. What the actual fuck, Judge? Storm. My name is Storm. Why the hell would Artem do me dirty like this? The only one that calls me Shit Storm is…."

He storms off, and right as he gets to the front door, I hear him scream, "ELVIRA!"

I can't help but laugh. He can think it was her all he wants. I told Artem to do it as a joke, but I am not worried about him going after her. At the end of that conversation, Theo is going to be apologizing for screaming at her, blaming her, and something he hasn't even done yet.

Once everyone is in their cuts, minus Theo because he is still gone, I take a look at my men. We may not be much at this moment, but we are going to be something.

FOURTEEN

JUDGE

-Present-

El is at the hospital still. It's been almost a week, and she hasn't left. I don't blame her; she is terrified that Kelsey isn't going to make it. While she is putting her faith in the Dr., she still fears that the baby will have severe deficits after all is said and done. She tells me she is okay and knows the baby will pull through, but I know my wife. I see the fear in her eyes.

I only see her long enough for her to shower and eat. She has me come back to handle the kids, the house, the ranch, and of course, the MC. I can say I knew she did a lot. But when shit like this happens, it makes me appreciate my wife more. The woman works so hard. Now that I am juggling my responsibilities and hers, I have realized that I don't thank her nearly enough.

Thankfully today, the kids are calm, the house is clean, and the ranch is running. Storm is acting Prez while Elvira is gone. I tried to be at the front and center of everything, but it didn't take long to see that I am nothing like my wife. I can't handle the stress and the attention that this house needs, along with everything else.

I am man enough to admit that my wife is a thousand times better than me. Until she comes back, my only concerns are the kids and the house.

"PawPaw!"

I hear Marley screaming, and I run towards the back of the house and out the door. I see Marley running towards me.

"PawPaw! PawPaw quick! Caleb is going to the piggies. The BIG piggies. He says he wants a play with them in the mud. I tolded him no but hes says hes gonna."

I pick Marley up and run towards the hogs enclosure. "Caleb! Don't you dare take another step, boy."

He thankfully stops, and I can catch up to him quickly. Placing Marley down, I get down to be eye level with him. "You can not go near those hogs, Caleb. It isn't safe. Plus, those are Butcher's piggies, and he doesn't like anyone going 'round them when he ain't here."

"But they are so big, and I just wanted to see them. They look like they're having so much fun in the mud. I wanna play in the mud."

He gives me the puppy dog eyes that I know Theo taught him, and I almost want to crack. I am certain that he knows exactly what he is doing.

"Buddy, I know. If you want to play in the mud, Dizz would be more than happy to make a puddle and play in it with you. But the animals, you can't just go in there and mess around near them. It isn't safe. I have seen those hogs bite the fingers of a ranch hand that got too close," *among other things,* "and I don't want that happening to you. So, if you want to look at the animals, let me or one of the guys know. If you want to play in the mud, get Dizz. He loves it. Mud baths are his favorite."

"OKAY!"

Caleb runs off towards the house, and I pick Marley back up. "PawPaw, I wanna plays in the muds too."

"You got it, baby girl. Run off and get Dizz. He'll take ya."

I set her down, and she took off. "Caleb, wait for me!" Her little pigtails flapping in the wind behind her. Marley has stolen our hearts, especially Cowboy's. That little girl has brought so much light to this house. It's such a shame that her life is what it is in such a short amount of time.

As I walk back into the house, my cell phone goes off, and I throw myself onto the couch before I answer. I don't need to look. The ringtone is specific to one man.

"The fuck do you want? It isn't a good time."

"That is no way to greet a friend or a business partner, Judge."

I sigh, "Artem, look, this isn't the time. El is still in the hospital with the baby. What do you need?"

"That's why I was calling. I know who you need to go visit to get this shit out of our town."

I sit straight up. We haven't had any leads on this new drug that almost killed Kelsey, and no matter who we asked, all were staying tight-lipped.

"How the hell did you find out?"

"Do you forget who I am? How I found out doesn't matter, the point is, I found out. Now, are you going to do something about it, or am I?"

"You know I am never one to back down from getting my hands dirty. Send me the address, and I will get my guys on it." I groan, getting up from my spot on the couch. "I am getting too old for this shit." I hear Artem laugh before the line disconnects, and it beeps with a text notification.

MAFIA GUY: 1254 Alpine Drive, Wyman, CO

Fuckers name is Carson Maypole.

I call Sever and have him gather Cowboy and Turd and tell them to bring the truck because it's gonna be a hard haul. Before I can call Butcher, I hear Manda start calling for me from outside.

"Jesus Christ, so much for a decent day," I mumble, making my way to the side door. "What?"

Before she can even reply, I see Butcher's big old white pedo van screaming down the drive. I rush the kids to the side out of his way as he goes to a screeching halt in front of the barn. He jumps out, slinging his cut over his shoulder. Well, at least he isn't covered in mud.

"Let me guess, Artem called you before he called me?" I ask, crossing my arms.

"He just knows I like-." He stops seeing all the little eyes and ears on him, waiting to see what he will say. "To have a new friend to play with. I like teaching my trade to more than one willing soul at a time."

"Nice. Manda, I know you needed help, but right now, I could really use some. Would you mind taking these kids to Dizz? He's playing out behind the house in the mud with Caleb and Marley. I promise we will talk later."

"Yeah, that's fine. Come on, guys. I make the best mud pies you've ever tasted."

They all scream, and it's a mix of yeahs, yays, and gross as they run to the house. I can only hope and pray that she doesn't actually let them eat the mud.

He has a grin on his face that I know to be terrifying when in this context. We don't call him the Butcher just because it is his day job. He knows his way around a knife and is a stone-cold killer when crossed or tasked with a job.

"How are my little piggies doing?" He asks in a baby voice, walking to the far pen housing our big boar males.

This man is a walking contradiction, and he looks like he is crazy and would gut you if you looked at him wrong. Still, he also is soft and great with all the kids and a huge animal lover who is also another contradiction given his chosen profession of slaughtering those creatures he loves.

Sever comes riding in the Gator with Cowboy and Turd riding close behind on my horse, and if they didn't have places to be, I would tear into him for that. My horse is like my bike and my woman. No other man's hands are allowed to touch.

"Nice of you to join us! Let's get this show on the road." I call to them as they offload in the barn.

"Sorry, but we don't answer to you right now *Judge,* Storm is *OUR* current Prez." There is a reason why his road name is Turd.

He thinks he's got the upper hand on me and walks past with that confident swagger. He thinks he really has won this round, but he doesn't even have half a point to go along with his half a brain. I kick my steel toe-out, catching him in the back of the knee. He stumbles forward. I catch a mit full of his hair wrenching his neck back, putting him on his knees in front of me. Like Yaya, and that magic wooden spoon, we now have framed in our kitchen, I produce my knife and hold it tight to his neck.

"This is your only warning. You disrespect your Prez again, I will give you to Butcher, and you will be his piggies next meal." I hear a cruel, almost giddy laugh coming from the man himself. "You were going to get a pass for being on my horse, but now, you are on diaper duty and door duty at the bar until I see fit. Get this job done, and head to the bar."

I pull my knife away from his neck and toss him down to the ground, giving him one kick to his side. I may be pretty lenient with many things, but blatant disrespect does not fly, not in my house. Cowboy scoops him up, shaking his head and tossing him in the back of Butcher's van.

"Awe, man, when was the last time you wiped up back here?" Turd cries.

I can only assume how much blood is in the back there, and I am almost certainly not all of it is animal. They all load up and ship out, knowing to take our 'new friend' to the far end of the property, by Cowboys house and the original homestead home. I turn back to the house to see what kind of trouble the kids are getting into.

A few hours later, I got the call that Artem's intel was fruitful, and the shithead in question is now sitting in the abandoned root cellar. I gave Butcher the go-ahead to start without me; being the responsible adult I needed to be, I had to wait for the babysitter to show up before I could go out and 'play.' I had called our head waitress because she was off tonight.

I know it was a dick move as she has a kid of her own, but she is free to bring him, and I will pay her for her time.

Natasha knows that she works for the MC more than the bar, and we are fair when it comes to what she needs in the form of child care. Her mom is normally her go-to, but life and plans never go as expected.

About a half-hour, after I sent Butcher, Natasha and her son showed up.

"Judge, I am so sorry. I got here as fast as I could."

"It's fine. Listen, I am sorry, I have to run, but I promise it's fine. Help yourself. The kids are all in the basement watching a movie. They know it's lights out when it's over. Billy can sleep with you or with Caleb in the boy's bunk. I'll be back tomorrow."

"Okay. Be careful."

Natasha isn't dumb. We don't tell her what goes on behind the scenes, but she understands what this club does and is about. She also knows not to question anything or say anything. The fact that I can trust her with the kids is a huge plus.

I make my way to the cellar where we have the piece of shit responsible for the drugs that are starting to mess up my town and almost killed my kid. Opening the doors, my boots slam down on the steps, letting them all know that I am here.

"Nice of you to show up!" I hear Cowboy call to me. As I pass him, he gets a cuff upside his head.

"What have we learned?"

"Nothing, he said he was waiting for the Big Man in charge," Butcher said, giving one last deep slice to the piece of shits bicep.

They had him strung up from the reinforced rafters, chains wrapped tight around his wrists, his hands almost blue from the lack of blood running to them. His toes barely skitted the ground, but still, there was nothing useful coming from his mouth—screams, and blubbering.

"Well, here I am, and unless he means Jesus, well, he will be confessing his sins to him soon enough," I said, grabbing the metal chair and taking a seat in front of this broken and bleeding excuse for a human being. "You gonna tell me why you picked this town to pettle your trash?"

"Fuck your mama." He spits out at me.

"Well, aren't we a gracious guest? If you want to fuck my momma, I'm sure we can get ya shovel. Ya can dig up her bones. It'll be really fucking romantic." I stood and gave an uppercut to his gut. "Now, I am going to ask you again. Why. The Fuck. Did. You. Pick. Wyman?"

I could hear him gurgle, unsure if it was blood or bile that was going to be coming from his face, I took a step back. His eyes stayed on me; I gave him no sign that I was backing down, nor that I was going to let him walk out of here.

"It was easy, and you have a lot of underground shit going on here. It was easy to blend in for a while. Then that stupid fucker had to get greedy and take more than his share." He finished spitting out a mouthful of blood, nearly hitting my boot.

"We keep this town clean and in order, ain't nothing shady going down that I don't know, or who has their hands in it." I flick my eyes to Butcher, giving him a slight nod to give him another deep cut.

Instead of screaming like he did the last time, he laughs at me. Laughing as if he knew the secret that I was never going to be let in on. I could feel unease churning in my gut, but I kept my face strong and hard. My eyes lasered focused on this waste of skin, who was soon going to fill my hogs bellies.

He stopped laughing and reined his features in as much as he could, "it's funny that you think that, but you're wrong. There is a lot that you don't know, and you are never going to find out. That I can promise."

"Seems to me like you aren't in a position to be making any promises."

"Wrong again. You ain't getting shit from me. It doesn't matter what you do. I'll take it to my grave."

"We'll see," I turn to Butcher, "have fun but make sure you leave enough for Artem."

I head up the stairs, followed closely by Cowboy and Sever. They can handle some shit, but when Butcher gets to really play, we all tend to let him be. Getting out the door, I pull out my phone and hit 'Mafia Guy.' *God damn fucking Theo.* He answers on the second ring.

"We've got a problem."

FIFTEEN

ELVIRA

-Past-

I was looking forward to a nice, easy night with just my boys. It seemed like forever since I got time with J.J. and R.J. Ellie was over at the Ranch with Yaya, working on some secret surprise for Ken and his birthday. These past months have been amazing; how quickly we were taken into the Faulkner/Kelley household was beautiful.

The boys are getting in less and less trouble outside of school. Ken and his Club Brothers are always picking them up and putting them to work. J.J. is loving learning the ways of the Ranch. The guys brought in some big old hogs at the barn's far end, so the smell doesn't waft into the house. He is learning all about them along with the guys, and with insemination of the cow's time coming close, he is learning more of the technical ins and outs of what bull can go with what cows, all the first time mothers, and what to expect there.

R.J. is more interested in the business end of it all with Theo and the mechanic's shop, learning the invoicing process and getting his hands dirty building a bike from the ground up. His analytical mind is growing every day, the mathematics and planning that goes into it all with very little variation.

Ellie and Yaya have become thick as thieves, always in the kitchen cooking or baking something. I feel that Yaya needed that companionship just as much as my Ellie baby did. Her migraines are coming in less. The specialist said that they are induced more often when she is stressed and under extreme duress. Which I could have told him! I mean, when Travis and I were together, they were weekly, whereas now, if she gets one a month, it's a bad time.

I put the pizzas in the oven for our movie night, and the boys talked me into watching Batman Begins. But really, getting to watch Christian Bale in a tight leather suit, I can't say I put up much of a fight.

"Boys, get the movie in the DVD player; the pizzas will be ready in fifteen!" I called towards the living room.

I was met with a groan; I can assume it was from J.J. as he complained that his feet and back hurt from fixing the barbed wire fencing the bulls ran through trying to get a heifer in heat. I just smile and am happy at fifteen and fourteen; these boys are working hard and learning skills that they can use later in life. I was shaken from my thoughts by a pounding at my front door. I knew I wasn't expecting anyone. Ken was meeting with a man about acquiring the bar in town and making it one of the first club owned and operated businesses in town.

"R.J., come in the kitchen and watch the timer on the pizza," I asked, tapping his head walking by the couch to the door.

I should have looked through the peephole before opening the door, things had been way too settled, and the other shoe was about to drop. When I unlocked the deadbolt reaching for the doorknob before I could turn it, the door broke open, causing me to stumble backward, and there in front of me was the other shoe, dropping to the ground at a rapid pace.

"Travis, you need to leave," I say, trying to keep the waiver out of my voice. I am very aware of where the boys are in proximity to my wild-eyed ex.

"I won't be leaving. This is my house." He starts stalking towards me, and I meet every step forward with a step back of my own until I am backed against a corner.

There is a sour tinge to his breath, one that tells me he has been drinking heavily for days on end. The smell makes my stomach churn with memories of the last time I was in the presence of it. The very thought of what Ellie had walked in on all that time ago broke down all the self-confidence I had been building all these months out of his presence. I could see movement from the corner of my eye and saw J.J. My sweet, strong oldest boy make a move to come to save me. I gave him a slight shake of my head, hoping he would leave and go to his brother. Travis seemed unaware that the boys were even home, and I felt some sort of relief in that. J.J. slinks off to the kitchen, and I can focus on the issue at hand.

"This isn't your home Travis. You need to leave." I try to push him away from me, but he is not moving.

"My hard-earned money went into buying this place and supporting those kids. It's just as much mine as it is yours." He huffs another rank breath in my face.

I am trying with everything in me not to throw back that this place costs more than the $300.00 a month he *should* be sending me, but hasn't for some time. I try to think of a way to defuse this situation without it coming to blows. But as he cages me against the wall, hands on either side of my head, my flight and fight instincts are getting harder and harder to suppress to remain level-headed.

"Travis, you have never lived here with us." I try to talk softly, keeping the condescension from my tone. "This is not our family home. You still live there; that is your home now. You should go there, sleep this off and we can talk in the morning. Where clearer heads will prevail." I try to push him back to escape to the kitchen, hoping the boys bailed out the back to get some help.

"You are my wife. I don't care what some piece of paper from some crackpot judge says. In the eyes of the lord, we are still man and wife. You, flaunting your new man around town, for all my friends and family to see, well that doesn't sit well with the lord or me." He smooths my hair down while trying to lower his voice, thinking he can draw me in. "Baby, we had some good times. We have these kids that need a father's love and a man in the home. We can make it work. I can take you back; even though you pushed me away and cheated on me with that biker bitch, I will always forgive you and take you back."

He tried to lean in and kiss me, but I turned my head. He continued the follow-through, and his forehead landed on the junction where my neck meets my shoulder. He punches my wall with the hand still by my head, cracking the drywall and causing me to jump. There are tears and flashbacks of those fists coming in contact with me, cracking my face. Making me bleed, all because I said no, or laughed at the wrong part of his story. Or because I took the kids' side over his in one of the many custody hearings we had, that is when we were given the order of protection, and supervised visitation started.

"Why are you pushing me away? All I have ever done was love you." His head shakes from side to side, unmoving from my body. "I tried to correct your actions that were not suitable for any wife of mine, and you fought me on everything. You tried to take my kids from me. You POISONED them against me!"

He yelled, punching the wall again, this time putting a hole through the drywall. I jumped and tried and flee from him, needing the distance. My hands were shaking, my heart was pounding, and I didn't know how volatile he would get with me or if the boys came back into the room. He was quick, and the hand that was on my head looped around my waist, pulling him into me. I can't help the yelp of fear that came from me. I am praying so hard my boys aren't here to see this.

"You are going to learn your place in this world, you are my wife, and those are my kids. Because of that, this is my home!" He yells, spinning me around and then backhanding me once, causing me to lose my balance and fall.

"Don't touch my mom!" I heard a voice yell from the hall.

I looked up in time to see R.J. standing there, with the small pistol I had in my nightstand. His hands were shaking, but the determination and the laser focus on his father scared me. He had just turned fourteen, and he didn't need to see this. He shouldn't have to defend his mom from his dad.

"What the hell do you think you are doing? Pointing a gun at your own father!" The incredulous tone in his voice caused RJs arm to twitch. "You think you are man enough to take me?"

"I think even Ellie is man enough to take you. You are a small worm who has hurt our family for the last time!" R.J. yells the last few words, taking a charging step forward.

"Well, well, look at this, Elvira. Our baby boy thinks himself a man now, with a joke and everything." There was humor in his tone but not in his face.

"Robert Joseph, please put that gun away and run," I say, trying to get Travis to focus back on me from our son.

"No, mom, he isn't going to hurt you again. He isn't going to put you back in the hospital. I sat by the last few times, but now.... Now I know I need to protect you as you did us." My heart broke watching my baby take another step towards Travis, who had his hands up. RJs arms stopped shaking, and his resolve had strengthened.

"Well, stop talking about it and take your shot, boy. If you are going to shoot, then shoot me. SHOOT ME!" He yells, and before I can react, three loud shots ring through our small living room.

Travis drops to the floor, blood pouring from his chest and life fading from his eyes. I look at the site only a foot away from me for a moment more before scrambling to my feet and taking the gun from RJs hands, and tossing it to the ground. I wrap my boy in my arms just as the sobs start wracking his body. We fall to the ground, hold on to one another. I am not sure how much time passes when another body comes in through the front door. Ken, J.J. following closely behind him, looks over the scene and sees us on the floor, I can see the wheels turning in his head.

"J.J., help me gather your brother and you and take him to the truck where Theo is. Tell him to take you back to the Ranch and get cleaned up, both of you. You hear me?" He tells him, scooping up R.J. from my grasp, pulling him into a big bear hug. "I am proud of you, son." He whispers before pushing my boys out the door.

"What are we going to do about this?" I ask as he pulls me close, my whole body shaking from shock.

"The neighbors have called the police already. They will be here soon. I heard the scanner as I pulled up. We are going to say you shot him after he broke in here. The boys went to find me, and I came in after the fact. There is more than enough evidence to prove you acted in self-defense. No Jury would convict you, and with his track record, the world is a better place without him." He kisses me all over his face. "You are strong, and it's over. Okay, El, it's all over." He says, holding my face to look him in the eyes.

Then it all hits me at once, and I crumble into him, sobbing. I can't understand the amount of relief that is hitting me, all this with my ex's bloody body hidden behind the man that I love more than anything. It's over. The kids and I are really safe. I don't hear the sirens pull up or remember much from the police interview that happened, they escort me to the back of the cop car, and Ken follows in my car.

I was in there for what seemed like days, but I am sure it was only a few hours. Ken was there when Sheriff Anderson escorted me out to the main waiting area. I told them everything Ken told me to say, that I shot Travis, that my boys went to get Ken for help while I fought with Travis. Normally, lies taste like ashes on my tongue, but I was saving my child. There were records of him beating me and abusing me. None of the kids, I was a safe bet. I heard the Sheriff talking to Ken, I am sure about things that I needed to know, but I was broke and numb and unsure what to think. My baby boy killed someone for me.

"El, baby?" Ken touched my arm, and out of reflex, I flinched away.

I could see the hurt in his eyes that I did that, thinking that I was scared of him. But it wasn't him. He needed to know that my body was still high on everything. I quickly wrapped my arms around his waist and embraced the warmth of him, and I started to cry again. I am not sure why this time, but I am sure there would be more than once in the next few days where I burst into tears for no reason.

"Let's get you home." He murmurs into what is left of my hair. My body goes rigid at the thought of stepping foot in that house. "No, baby." He says, reading my thoughts. "You are coming home with me, and you aren't leaving again. We are going to build you and those kids back up, and we are going to be a family."

He always knows what words to say and when to say them. This is why I love this man, I may be broken and battered, but he has never treated me that way. He still is a caveman in so many ways, telling his brothers that I am his, and I have a cut in my closet that states I am his Property. But he always treated me like an equal partner, like we truly are a team.

He guides me to my car, folding himself into the driver's seat. I see in the back seat there are several bags and baskets of clothing. A mixture of the kids and my own, as well as all the stuffed animals from Ellie's bed and the cowboy hats and boots Ken, bought all three kids. I lean back into my seat and relish in the fact that I am going home, and for the first time in such a long time, it doesn't feel like just a place. It's not just words. There is love and a feeling that goes along with it.

I watch out the window as the quiet town passes by, going on the highway to the Ranch. Ken has his hand on my thigh, grounding me to him. I think he is scared I will pull away from him again, but I cannot see that happening any time soon.

We arrived at the Ranch, and there to greet us were all the Brothers, Yaya, and my kids. J.J., R.J., and Ellie rush to me, crushing me in a solid tight liberating hug. It hits harder now, knowing we are free of Travis; there is no more nagging fear that he will show up and ruin everything. We are free!

I hear Ken shoo everyone away and start to guide us into the house. We all pass Yaya, the kids all hug and kiss the small woman. When it's my turn, she holds me close and lets the new wave of tears fall.

"Welcome home, baby girl." She whispers in my ear, and I know I am finally here.

Home.

SIXTEEN

JUDGE

-Past-

I was sitting in my office going over the books. Something wasn't adding up. The work wasn't getting done, yet the time was being clocked. The workers were getting paid for shit they hadn't done, and I couldn't figure out where it was all taking place. Maybe I'd been looking at these spreadsheets for too long. Maybe I didn't know what the fuck I was doing. Fuck! What am I missing?

I took a deep breath, held it for as long as I could, then exhaled slowly. I did this about two or three more times, and I lost count before I finally calmed down and took a minute to reassure myself.

I would figure this out. I just needed to step away for a moment, clear my head, and then have Elvira look at it because the woman could figure anything and everything out before I could explain what the hell was happening.

I had made up my mind that she would yet again be my saving grace, and before I could even get up, the door to my office opened. It was J.J., and he looked completely distraught. What happened? It had only been a week since they moved in here, and they had seemed happier than ever, but you never really know with teenagers.

"Dad…I, I mean, Ken -Kenneth…sir?"

I knew I couldn't hide the smile that graced my face at this slip-up. Ellie had been calling me Dad for a while now, and I can tell this boy wanted to as well, and I was more than okay with it. I had told him that repeatedly. He normally did, unless something was wrong. Then he stuttered through names like he just did. That was his tell.

"Son, I told you, you can call me dad. You can call me whatever you're most comfortable with. I promise it's okay."

"I…I know. I just - I need, no, not me. Not me. My fr-fr-friend Michael - Mike. He needs, I need….forget it." He turns to leave, but not very quickly. He wants me to stop him.

"Jonathan," I said sternly. Something was wrong. I wasn't about to just let him walk away. "Tell me what's wrong with Mike."

He looked away from me and let his eyes roam. His hands twisted. For a fifteen-year-old boy, he looked five at the moment. Something is seriously wrong with his friend. He let out a breath and finally continued.

"Please don't be mad at me. Or Mike. He, he made me promise that I wouldn't tell but I just - I can't do it anymore. I can't!" Tears were welling up in his eyes. For a child who has looked death in the face and didn't bat an eye, this really got my senses in overdrive.

I walk over to him, and I pull him into my embrace. He sobs against my chest as I try my hardest to soothe him. I'm obviously failing because he's still fucking crying, harder and harder as we stood there. His hands clawing at my back like he cannot get close enough to me. He needs it, though, but I need to know why he's acting this way.

"Jonathan, what happened?" I ask, trying to keep the worry and tenseness I felt out of my voice.

"It's his father. Well, his foster father. He beats Michael. But this time, he almost killed him." He sniffs, pulling away, wiping his nose on his sleeve.

Pure, unfiltered rage is coursing through my veins. I can feel my heart hammering through my chest. I wouldn't be surprised if Jonathan could see it. Through gritted teeth, I ask, "where is Michael?"

"He's in the last horse stall in the barn. He didn't know what to do or where to go. He rode his bike here and just collapsed. I dragged him in there when he begged that none of the hands or brothers should see him."

"Fuck!" I push past him and start hauling ass out of the office.

"Dad, I'm sorry! Please. Please don't hurt him. Please!" J.J. called out after me, the anguish in his voice that he betrayed his best friend very evidently. I whip around so fast; I'm surprised I'm still standing straight.

"You think I'd hurt him? Do you think I'd hurt you for telling me? No. Never! I'm going to get him, so he doesn't get an infection. I'm going to make sure he's still breathing. And then, I'm going to kill that son of a bitch who calls himself a father. Mike's family blood or not, he's a goddamn deadman."

"Dad, what about Mike, though?" New waves of emotion filter through his eyes.

"We WILL get him better, and he will stay here. I'll figure it out. Thank you for telling me, son." I pulled J.J. into me by the back of his head, planting a loving kiss on his forehead. I let him go and rush out of the house and head towards the barn. Sliding open the door, I look around, but I don't see him right away. I remember he is in the stall, hiding from all adults. I start walking down the aisle when I hear the groaning.

"J.J.? J.J., is that you?. Fuck. It hurts." The strain in his voice breaks me before I even lay eyes on him.

I find him in the last stall on the right. At least he is in one that hasn't had a horse in it in months. It's fairly clean for a barn. His eyes are closed. Well, one is swollen shut; the other is close to it. His whole fucking face is black and purple. His lip and eye socket both split, blood leaving a trail down his face and neck.

His neck has a goddamn handprint on it, as well as his arm. His breathing is labored, and I wouldn't be surprised if he has either cracked, fractured, bruised or all fucking three ribs.

I start walking into the stall, and he barely sees me before he starts begging and pleading with me. My soul bleeds for this boy, this amazing best friend to my son.

"Please don't. Please don't take me back. Ahh. Fuck. It hurts. It hurts so much. I can't - I can't breathe. Ahhhhh!"

The agonizing scream that leaves his body has me scooping him up into my arms and rushing to my truck. He is crying and begging me to stop. To put him down, let him die.

"I can't do that, Mike. Don't worry, son, I've got you."

Tears somehow manage to escape his eyes, but he nuzzles into me further. I don't know if it's because he finally feels a sense of comfort or if it helps with the pain. Hell, it could be both. I don't care. What I care about is that he knows I'm not the bad guy. He knows I'm getting him help. And after I do, the man who did this is a dead man.

After I speed through town and thankfully don't get caught, I get him to the ER. Nurses and doctors rush me and take Mike away from me. I tell them what I know before they've all disappeared through the doors to what I am positive leads to operating rooms.

Please, don't let this kid die. He's my kid's best friend. He's a goddamn joy. He watches Disney channel or Disney movies all day. This isn't his time. This. Is. Not. His. Time.

What feels like hours later, and the Dr is coming out of the doors. I can tell he is looking me over to see if I did this. I realize I didn't think of a lie to say how I'm related without coming off as the abuser. Fuck! And now I'm out of time. Not that it would matter. This small ass town, they know I'm not.

"Doc, how is he?" Trying to keep my voice level and calm.

"Are you family? His father?" To which I can see the hatred in his eyes. His facial muscles may not move, but his eyes say it all.

Okay, I guess this Dr doesn't know who I am. But was quick to judge me with the cut on my back.

"I'm not his father, no." *But I want to be.*

"Then I can't….." I cut him off, trying to think quickly on my feet.

"I'm his brother. Our parents had him late in life, but when they died, he had no one else; I was away on assignment in

Afghanistan. Special Ops and couldn't leave. They awarded him to the state. I had just gotten back and found him like that." The lie came so fucking easy off my tongue, I was amazed at myself. I put a little more emotion into my voice and continued, "please. Please tell me what's wrong and that he's still breathing. Please."

"He ended up needing surgery. His left ribs were broken, and one stabbed and tore through his spleen. We had to remove it as it was not salvageable. His left eye socket is broken, while his right is fractured. He has multiple lacerations and contusions along with minor swelling of his brain. He.."

"Is he still breathing?" I cut in because I have seen grown men die from less severe injuries.

"Technically, no. The machines are doing it for him. However, it's because we had to put him into a medically induced coma so he could heal. Everything was too severe. But in the scheme of things, yes, he is breathing. I truly believe he can make a full recovery. He just needs time."

"Please, can I see him? Just for a minute. Please." I am not above begging to see him with my own two eyes.

"Normally, I'd say no. But given the circumstances, five minutes." He jerks his head for me to follow him down the hall.

"Thank you."

We walk down the hall of the ICU, and once we get to his room, I can see him through the windows. Tubes and wires are sticking out from every part of his body.

"Five minutes." He reminds me before turning to walk away to the nurses' station.

I only nod and walk into the room. I walk straight up to Mike and grab his hand. Giving it a little squeeze, I whisper the promise I will keep no matter the cost.

"I'm gonna find him, Mike. I'm gonna find him, and I'm gonna kill him. You're coming home with me, son. You will be safe, loved and you will never be in this position again. I promise, son. I promise."

With one final squeeze, I walk out. I give the nurse my information, and she promises to call me with all updates. I leave the hospital and head back to the ranch. J.J. knows who this fucker is and where I can find him. When I do, he will wish he never got on my radar.

At this very moment, I'm grateful for my brother, and the hogs that I know will love this little snack I have planned for them.

"What the fuck do you mean there is nothing they can do?" Elvira angrily whispers to me.

"Just what I said. There is nothing the cops can do because in his file, he is listed as the problem child, and there have been other homes that stated they have had to administer corporal punishment to get him to comply." The words felt dirty in my mouth.

El and I sat and watched through the nurses' window as J.J. and Mike talked quietly in his hospital room. My whole body aches just looking at the bruises and cuts all over him, and there was so much that we couldn't see. Watching how those two boys interacted made me thankful that I had Theo when we went through times like this. It makes me love J.J. more and more like my own because he was helping his friend the same way we helped Theo.

"There has to be some sort of good news, something we can go in there and tell those boys." She was desperate to help that sweet kid.

"I talked to the so-called foster parents." I cross my arms across my chest in remembrance of that meeting. "Their Social Worker was there and happened to be a really nice lady. We all talked about how you had to be investigated by CPS during your custody battle and recent events, and my life is public knowledge in the system because I grew up there and mentored troubled kids in the system. We also talked about how Mike's foster parents are overwhelmed with their bio kids and the three other fosters. All four of us agreed because you and I have that news we have not shared with anyone yet, we would be the perfect fit for Mike to recover and stay with." I said, casting her a side-eyed glance.

"Wh-. What… What news haven't we shared?" She asked, paling.

"The one where you agree to be not only my Ol' Lady and treasurer of this Motorcycle Club you had a hand in creating," I said, pulling the ring Yaya handed me on my way here. "What do you say, Firecracker? You wanna see me every morning for the rest of your life?"

She didn't even get a word out before her eyes rolled to the back of her head, and she was on her way to the ground. Christ! I scoop her up and start calling for a nurse or a doctor, thanking god we were in a hospital.

"Dad?" J.J. calls out to me as the nurses put El onto the stretcher. I turn and pull him to me; nurses and doctors yell that they need things while rolling her down the hall further and further away from us. "What happened to my mom? Where are they taking my mom!?"

He yells over and over again, trying to pull away from me to follow them. A nurse was here trying to calm him and get answers from me about what happened just now and if she had any health issues that I knew about.

"John! Johnny!" I call out to him, turning him to face me. "I need you to go back with Mike and call Theo to bring your siblings and Yaya here. Okay? I will talk to the doctors and nurses and figure out what is going on with your mom, Okay? Trust me. We may not be married yet, but your mama is part of my whole world, Okay? You need to be the man I know you are and take care of your siblings while I take care of your mom. We are a team, and we will always have each other's back. I love you; we got this." I pull him in for a deep hard hug, pressing my lips to the top of his ebony hair, then pushing him back into the room.

I turned to follow the nurse telling her what I knew about her feeling off this morning, but we thought it was just stress from everything that happened recently and Mike's current situation. I told them about how I proposed to her and told her that we were getting a new mouth to feed and care for. When we reached the end of the hall, she called up to the Doctor. My whole body was tingling. It was on fire with the need to be where Elvira was, with the need to be with the kids. I was torn, but I needed to keep myself together as best I could.

"They have taken her to surgery. They did an ultrasound, and there was so much free fluid in the abdomen. They cannot find the source, and they need to open her up. I need you to come with me to the surgical floor and sign some paperwork." The nurse pulls me towards the elevator.

I follow that broken feeling is gone, everything is gone, she was in surgery with a belly full of blood. She has made me watch enough of those medical dramas to know this is not good, I just found her, and I am going to lose her. I lost everyone close to me, my parents, I lost my grandpa before I even met him, I met Yaya so late in life that I will soon lose her. Now I am losing the love of my life, the one woman I saw everything with. The one I wanted to protect with my life, I felt helpless. There was nothing I could do. I was stuck and had to trust these people knew what they were doing to bring her back to me. I was so lost in my own self-pity about losing her that I didn't notice we arrived. I was only snapped from my reverie when a new nurse handed me a clipboard and pointed to a waiting area.

SEVENTEEN

ELVIRA

-Present-

We have been here for, going on, three weeks, and they have only decreased her twice in that time. Both of those times she was in and out of consciousness, it was terrifying. One minute she is awake and laying in my arms, enjoying a bottle; next, she is floppy and languid. None of her vitals changed; it was almost like she was passing out in my arms. I have barely been home. Ken tells me he has this. That Cowboy, my boy, is taking care of the ranch, Natasha has a handle on the bar, Theo minds the MC and the shop while Judge is holding down the house.

I am scared to see what kinds of meals he has been making or what the state of the kitchen is in. He has been stopping in and sitting with Kelsey so I can shower, change and get real meals as opposed to the hospital food. However, I am over the burgers and fries at the same time. I dream of all the homemade meals that I want to make when all this is over, but I am soon snapped from my reverie by a knock on the door.

"There's my Ducky and wee one." Abilene's voice carried through the small room, never failing to bring a smile to my face.

"Hey, Abilene." She comes up to me and engulfs me in a hug. As she pulls back, her hands rub up and down my shoulders, "how are you feeling?"

"Honestly? Like shit but better at the same time. It's so rough being here. Seeing her like this. It's been so long already, and I am just ready to take her home and let her grow up. Then on top of that, I am so over being in the hospital. She's lucky in the sense that she doesn't know any better yet and doesn't get how devastating they are."

"Yeah, I know what you mean. The last time I was here I…." She pauses. I can see the tears welling in her eyes. Heartbreak is clear across her face. I realize then that I really don't know much about her other than what I see when we're at the club. While we get along, and she is a wonderful woman to have in your life, we haven't taken the time to know more about each other on a more personal level.

I can tell that the topic is a rough one, and I now decide a better time than any to breach the subject.

"Hey, you can tell me. I can see that you are upset and if you wanna talk about it, what better time to do so? No little ears, no crazy men, just us girls."

"You know what," she sniffles before continuing, "I would like that."

She takes a couple of deep breaths, and I allow her all the time she needs to gather her bearings before diving into a story that I am sure is going to break me apart. I want her to know that we can be more than the "Ol' Ladies." We can be friends. Real friends. I know a lot of it is on me too. I know that I don't try as hard as I should, but I put everything I have into the home with the kids to make sure that they always feel loved.

I grab her hand and give her a slight squeeze. She takes a deep breath and begins.

"You know that we have our daughter, A.J. well, what you probably don't know is that we also had a son, Bennett Gunner."

She stops and takes a long pause. I go over what she just told me and realize that she said she *had. She had a son.*

"Had? What happened? I am so sorry, you're right, I didn't know."

"It's okay. Not a lot of people do. It wasn't an easy time for us. In fact, the time that we lost Bennett was when Hank became....Butcher. It wasn't easy at first, losing our son. Over time, the emotions weren't as powerful, but some things stayed. Hank, bless his soul, took it the hardest.

He and Bennett were so close. They did everything they could together. B.G. looked up to his daddy and thought that he held the world at his fingertips. He was about ten when we moved to Alabama from Georgia. Opportunities and all that.

Well, the house we moved in was cute and quaint and fit us perfectly. The neighborhood was quiet, and neighbors that came out and helped you with your yard gave you sugar, milk, eggs, anything you needed.

It was perfect. Until it wasn't."

I can tell that she is going to fight to continue. I pull her into my embrace, letting her know it's okay and to take her time. It isn't long before she shatters me.

"Our neighbor was the typical blue-collar American man. Kind as all get out and coach the kids' baseball team. Bennett hadn't been into sports before, but all of his new friends were on the team. The coach told him that he could try out if he wanted since he was the new kid.

If you can imagine, this lanky little boy has never thrown a ball in his life or ran more than twenty feet, playing ball; that was Bennett. Bennett was a homebody. He loved staying in and working in the shop with Hank. That was what he was good at. He was terrible at baseball." She chuckles slightly, and I know it's from the description she gave me of her son attempting to play sports for the first time.

"The coach said he could come over, and he would help him out more. He lived right next door. I didn't see the harm. My mistake, misguided trust, killed my son."

"No. You can't blame yourself. You did nothing wrong."

"I did. I gave him the trust he didn't deserve. I let that man fool me into thinking he wasn't a horrible human. I let him take my son away from me. B.G. came home that night, and he said, 'I don't want to play anymore, mom. He said that I would be the best catcher. He pitched for hours, and I caught it, but it hurt. I don't like that position.' Do you know how long it took me to figure out he wasn't talking about the game!

That man raped my son, repeatedly and because I didn't realize what he was trying to tell me, I lost him. I asked about other positions, and he yelled no and wouldn't talk about the game ever again. I ask the man. Do you know what he said? 'Unfortunately, some kids just don't mesh well with the sport. His height, he may be great at track and field, maybe basketball, if he really wants to continue to play.' Like he did nothing wrong.

Hank used to do a lot of manual labor. But a back injury took him out of commission and led him to what he does now. He would sometimes have a flair up, though, and he would need to take the meds for pain. He went to get a pill one day, and the bottle was gone. He went looking through the house and found Bennetts door open, him slumped on the floor, bottle empty.

We got him to the hospital, he overdosed, they pumped his stomach, but we were too late. He couldn't breathe on his own. His brain was barely functioning. Hank refused to believe that he wouldn't pull through. He held on until the bitter end. The second we powered off life support, he flatlined.

It broke me, but I had A.J at home that I had to be strong for. It killed Hank. Hank broke. He spiraled out of control and went on a rampage. He found our son's suicide letter and took the coach to the shop. I will never know how he got away with everything he did to that man, but I will always be grateful for it.

It took a while for Hank to get it under control. Moving here was the biggest catalyst for him reigning it in. So when the MC approached him, he said yes instantly because of what we went through. I don't know all the details. I don't want to know all the details. All I know is I will be forever grateful to you and Judge for bringing my husband back to me."

I couldn't speak. I just hugged her close, and we cried together. They both went through so much. A lot more than I would be able to handle. She was the epitome of strength.

"I am so sorry. I know that nothing I can ever say will ever help with the pain. I wish I could take it all from you."

"I know, thank you. I know you would, but really, it's okay. It helped me open my eyes to things. See things for what they really are. It may have caused a bumpy as hell road for us for a while, but Hank is who he is supposed to be now. We are where we are supposed to be now. And A.J. is thriving. Doing things we never dreamed of. I would give anything to have my son back, but I can't complain about what we have been given and blessed with since. Losing him put us all on the paths we needed to be on.

I admired her more and more with each word she spoke. She was able to take something so awful and depressing and see the light that it has since brought. It makes me think of times back in my life and how I need to look at them from different angles, see the good, see the light and find the happiness when certain topics are brought up.

"I know that it is nowhere near the same; please don't think I am trying to compare because I am not. R.J. killed his father when he was fourteen. I took the blame for it. I needed to protect my son, but sometimes I think that it hurt him.

Anytime Judge and I argued, he would panic. He became closed off and worried about everything. Anytime I got hurt, even if stubbing my toe, he would look around to see who did something to me. I very well believe that he had, has, PTSD.

But as he got older, his reactions stopped. He hid what was bothering him and just closed off even more. He turned eighteen about a month before he graduated. I had no idea the day of his birthday, he went to a Marine recruiters office and signed up.

The day after graduation, I woke up and found the note on the counter that he was gone, that he enlisted and he won't be back. And since that day, he hasn't been back. It took a while, but I was finally able to get phone calls out of him, but those are few and far between.

All I know at this moment, right now, is he is alive. I haven't physically seen him in eleven years."

At least he is alive. I keep telling myself that, but I miss my son. My son was my world. He saved my life, but it took a toll on him that I didn't understand. He wouldn't talk about it, and I couldn't force him. Ken, Theo, Willie, Yaya, everyone tried. Everyone failed. He was so enclosed within himself that I wasn't sure what I would wake up to each morning. But, he is still alive.

"That must be hard. I'm sorry. I hope that he soon realizes that he has a mother that loves him and misses him something fierce. That she would do anything for him."

"Me too. But I also know that I can only hope at this point."

At that moment, a nurse came in to check Kelsey's vitals. Once again, nothing changed. She tries to reassure me that that is a good thing, but I don't get how she is getting better if nothing is changing. I need to get her out of here. I need to get her home.

"I don't know how much more I can take Abilene."

"Don't worry, Ducky. It's going to be over before you know it. One day, Kelsey's mind and body are going to go 'fuck this place,' and she will come home. Trust me."

She seemed so confident that I had to believe her. I needed to start telling myself that Kelsey would be okay. It may take a little time, but she would get there, and I would be here waiting for her when those pretty eyes opened again.

EIGHTEEN

ELVIRA

-Past-

I had woken up with a start. I looked forward towards the window of my hospital room and closed my eyes again. Maybe, just maybe, when I open them, this won't be my reality. I opened my eyes, and the truth hit me like a semi. I was still here, I was still in this bed, I still lost my tubes, but worst of all - I lost the baby.

I started sobbing again. How could I do this? How could I not do the one thing I am supposed to, keep my baby safe? I failed my baby. I failed Ken, the baby's siblings, myself. I failed. One of my jobs as a woman is to bring life into this world. I didn't do that. I couldn't keep that baby alive.

I ignored the pain before when cramps didn't feel like cramps. When I looked at Ken and said, "my ovaries hurt," I should have listened to my body. Maybe then they could have saved my baby. There had to have been something they could have done, right? Or was I always doomed to fail this child? To fail Ken.

How will Ken ever forgive me? I killed his only biological child, and now, I can't give him anymore. The baby ruptured my right tube, and my left tube and ovary were so covered in cysts that they couldn't save it. There was so much damage on my left tube that even if they could get the cysts off without a problem, the tube wouldn't function anyway. My right ovary was also cyst bound that if they even tried to remove them I would be in a worse off state.

This way I still got my hormone production, but I was now sterile.

I wasn't worth anything to Ken now that I couldn't have his children. Add on the fact that I lost his baby. My body rejected the one job that it was supposed to do without a problem. I had three other kids with no issue. Why, all of a sudden, did I fail? With the one man that deserved everything in the world. The one-man that deserved his own kids, why did this have to happen to him? To us. He isn't going to want me anymore. Why would he?

He only tolerates you now that you're bald. You just ruined what feelings he had left.

That couldn't be true, though, could it? He said that we were doing this together. That yes, he loved my hair, but my hair didn't make me. He wasn't in love with my hair, and he was in love with me. He can still be, right?

I sit myself up, tears still streaming from my eyes, and look around. He isn't here. No one is here. I am alone. The steady stream of tears has now become a river. Ken isn't here. My kids aren't here. No *one is here*. How can no one be here? Am I really not that important to anyone?

My body racks with sobs. My chest heaving, and I closed my eyes. I can't do this. I failed, and everyone makes it clear that they know that I did by not being here. By not being here, they are speaking loud and clear. *"You're a failure. You killed your baby. You're garbage."*

"I am. I am. I know I am."

"You're what, baby girl?"

I open my eyes, and Yaya is standing next to the curtain that blocks the door. What is she doing here? Doesn't she know what I did?

"I'm a failure."

She rushes over to me and sits down on the bed, gripping my hand in hers as tightly as she possibly can. I look at her face, and I don't see judgment. I don't see pity. I see pain. Pain as if she knows what I am feeling. But how can she?

"You listen to me, and you listen to me good. You get those horseshit ideas outta that pretty little head of yours. Those thoughts are trash. You are not a failure. You didn't do anything wrong. This had nothing to do with you. Unfortunately, these things happen."

I just shook my head and continued to cry. She didn't know. She didn't know what I was feeling and what I was going through. I knew that she was just trying to make me feel better, but I also knew that she was lying. I am a failure.

"I am. I am. My baby is gone. I didn't keep it safe."

"Stop it!" Her tone was harsh. The shock of it stopped my tears. Yaya had never spoken to me with this much ferocity within her voice. "Listen to me. I am going to tell you something, and I need you to really listen. You can't do that if you continue to let the negative thoughts control your mind right now. Take a breath, and just listen. Can you do that?"

I nodded my head up and down and took a few deep breaths as she had asked. Her face was stern. She wanted me to know she meant business. Whatever Yaya wanted me to hear, I knew I needed to.

"Okay, Yaya. Tell me."

"Ken and I got married when I was barely eighteen years old. That man, boy, did he sink those claws into me the first time I laid eyes on him. You probably know how I feel. Kenny is the spitting image of his grandfather. Anyways, we tried from the moment we got married to have babies.

It was short-lived, though, when Uncle Sam called him to the line ten days after we got married. I didn't see that man for two and a half years - give or take a few days. But when he came home, boy, did he make up for the lost time." She winks at me, letting me know that she and her husband couldn't get enough of each other. She smiled and then continued.

"Every month, my cycle came and went. I wasn't getting pregnant.

Back then, we didn't have the options that people have now. Sure, adoption was there but, back then, it was also not an easy process. A lot more secretive about where the baby came from because, more often than not, the mother was unmarried and that, that was a big no-no.

Anyways, I finally got pregnant with Kenny's mom when I was a little bit younger than you are now. We were over the moon. Almost eleven years of trying, and we were finally having a baby. Things were going smoothly. I was growing the baby was growing, Ken did anything to make sure I stayed healthy. I didn't have to lift a finger. That man took "spoil your wife" to a new extreme."

She laughed, and I gave a slight smile. If Ken is anything like his grandson, I can absolutely believe what Yaya is saying.

"We get to the end, and the due date is near. Everything was great until one day, and I felt faint. I couldn't stand. I went to find Ken, I needed his help, his support, and that's when I felt the gush. The only problem was that when my waters broke, blood also came out. I didn't know much, but I knew that shouldn't involve that blood.

I screamed; Ken came rushing in. He saw the mess, and he wasted no time. He got me into the car and broke every traffic law known to man, and got me to the ER. I was rushed into surgery. It wasn't long after that Kenny's momma was born.

Because of the drugs they put me on to help with my sickness, she was born missing some fingers and toes. Otherwise, she was healthy and perfect, but me? The doctors couldn't stop the bleeding. To save my life, my way of giving life was taken. I had one child before I could never have any more. I had an emergency hysterectomy. One baby. That was it.

Ken and I wanted a house full of kids. I would have been over the moon if I could have had six or seven kids, if not more. That many mouths didn't scare me. It thrilled me. All I wanted to do was have babies and give them every ounce of love that I had. Ken as well. A family that would grow and grow and grow. So many of our own kids that when the time came, we'd have an abundance of grandchildren and great-grandchildren.

All I wanted was that large, joyous, completely insane family, and it was never going to happen. Because of me, my family was always going to be a family of three. It would never get any bigger.

When I woke from surgery, I couldn't even hold the one healthy baby the Lord blessed me with. I, too, felt like the biggest failure. I did everything right. I ate right. I took care of myself. I was careful. I did nothing wrong, yet my body betrayed me.

Ken tried to get me to hold our daughter. He tried really hard, but I couldn't. How could I hold her knowing that I would never give her siblings? She would grow up alone because I couldn't keep my body healthy. My own body. Mine. What I had been in control of for almost 30 years at the time, I couldn't control it when it mattered most.

I laid in my bed at the hospital, and I cried. I cried for all the children I would never have. For all the grandbabies I would never have. For all the siblings Melanie would never have. For Ken. I would never give him a son.

My body failed. What good was I?"

I was crying again. I couldn't believe what Yaya was telling me. How could she think that this was her fault? Hemorrhaging is uncontrollable. Anything can cause it. There wasn't anything that she could do.

"Yaya, that wasn't your fault. Your body didn't fail you. There was nothing that you could do."

"Exactly."

"What?"

"There was nothing that I could do. Just like there was nothing that you could do. Your body didn't fail you. Your egg was on its way to your uterus. Kenny's sperm," I know I shouldn't, but the way she said it, made me cringe, "was just too fast. They met too soon. There is literally nothing that you can do to prevent that. You didn't even know it happened. You can't blame yourself for this, just like I couldn't."

"But I..."

"No buts. I mean it. I know this is hard. Believe me, I know. But you have to remind yourself that you couldn't have done anything. This baby was meant to be your Angel. You have three others, and from the sounds of it, one more that needs you. Had this not happened, you could be gone. I know it isn't what you want to hear, but losing the baby prevented your kids from losing you.

It's rough, but it's life. Until there are sure-fire ways to stop ectopic pregnancies from happening, they are going to happen. This isn't the end for you. So what if you can't have babies anymore. That doesn't define you. Your worth is not measured by how many kids you pop out. Your worth is measured by how you act. It's measured by how you treat others and how you love.

You love in stupid amounts. It's almost embarrassing." That made me smile, and I knew she knew what she was doing. The shocking thing was that it was working.

"You will have some time where this is sad, and you are allowed that. What you are not allowed to tell yourself is that you failed. You did not. Bad things sometimes happen to great people. What you need to remember, though, is that you are not alone. This isn't the end for you. I won't let you bring yourself down. Neither will your kids, and neither will Kenny."

"Kenny isn't even here, though."

"You're right. He isn't. He's with your children. I told him to go. This was something that you and I needed to speak about. Kenny doesn't know the story about what happened to me after his mom was born. Knowing that man, he'd somehow tie to himself.

You and I are a lot alike in a lot of ways. This is probably one of the biggest ways. The darkness you are feeling will fade. I promise you. However, it won't go away until you stop feeding yourself lies."

Yaya stood and gave me a tight hug. "You will be okay. I'm going to step out and call Kenny."

"Thanks, Yaya."

"You're welcome, baby girl."

Yaya stepped out of the room, and when I heard the door click, I took a deep breath. Tears still came, but they were nowhere near the levels that they were at before. What Yaya said made sense. I knew it did. Now that I have taken the time to breathe and really listen to what she told me, I knew deep down that this wasn't my fault.

My body didn't fail me. Everything just ended up in the wrong place. As she put it, his *sperm* were too excited and wanted to get busy. *But if my slow ass eggs didn't...NO.* No. No more thinking like that. Yaya was right. How the hell would I have changed the outcome? There was just no way.

The biggest thing that stuck with me, though, *"you losing the baby prevented your kids from losing you."* This hit harder than anything else, she said to me. This pregnancy was only six to eight weeks. It wasn't conclusive at the time but, had this not happened, I could be dead—my kids without a mother. Legally, without a father. My kids needed me. Yes, I wanted Ken's babies, but I wanted to be with the ones I already had more.

Yaya's speech was already helping me see the truth. I am not a failure. My body didn't fail. I didn't murder my baby. An unfortunate event that I had ZERO control over happened to me. Yes, I can't have any more biological kids, but, as Yaya pointed out, I have three of my own, as well as the one I inherited just before all of this happened.

My life may have changed now slightly, but I wasn't going to let it break me down. I have done enough of that to myself already. Right here and now, the choice was made. I will allow myself to be sad here in the hospital, but when I get home, I will be the mom that I am still able to be. My Angel will forever be watching over me.

Yaya had stayed for a little while after her shocking heart to heart. Once she left, I stuck with my plan of letting myself feel the sorrow I currently feel until I go home. Lost in my thoughts, I almost didn't notice when the nurse came in to check my vitals and ask how I was doing. She also informed me that food would be coming soon as well.

As she cleaned my surprisingly small surgery sites, she let me know that I also had a visitor waiting for me. After finishing up what she needed to do, I let her know to let my visitor in. I could only hope that it was Ken and the kids. After a slight knock on the door, it opens, and in walks Ken. His eyes land on me, and he rushes forward.

His hands encase my head, and his lips crash down to mine. I can feel the emotion he is pouring into the kiss, how much I missed him, and the truth that I need to tell him weighs heavy.

"Baby," he pulls back, giving me feather-light kisses across my face between words, "I was so scared. They wouldn't tell me anything. What happened? Are you okay?"

"Yes, I'm okay. But I - I am scared."

"Why are you scared, baby?"

"Because after what I tell you, I don't know how you will be able to look at me. How you will be able to love me."

"Baby, let me make this clear right now. Nothing that you say will make me love you any less. Nothing that you say will make me not want to look at you. I promise I am always here. Tell me, please. I need to know that you are okay."

"I am okay, but," I take a deep breath, it was now or never, with my eyes cast down, I tell him everything. "I was pregnant, and I lost the baby. It was ectopic, and there was no saving it. The baby ruptured my tube; that's why I passed out. Then I had so many cysts on my other tube that they couldn't save it. I can no longer have kids. I can't give you children."

I can't look at him. I don't want to see the anger in his eyes. I don't want to see the grief I know is there. I feel his finger come up under my chin, and he lifts my head.

"Baby, open your eyes and look at me."

I open my eyes, and I see tears coming down his face, but I don't see anger.

"You've already given me three kids. Those kids, waiting to know what happened to their momma, those are *MY* kids. Yeah, I didn't make them, they have nothing of me, but they have every ounce of love I can give.

I would have loved to have a baby with you. Seeing you round, feeling those kicks, but I don't need that to feel complete. Everything you have given me so far makes me feel complete. You are what I need. I wish I could have been here. I wish I could have done something to make the outcome different, but you are who I need in this world to survive. You are my whole world, and you have my whole heart.

Had I lost you, I would have lost every bit of myself."

He chooses that moment to kiss me, and with every word he spoke, I can feel the truth in his kiss. This man loves me, no matter what.

I am sailing high, knowing that he is still okay while sad because he has me and has my kids. This man loves my kids as much as I do. He's claimed them, and he means it when he says he claims them. He has given my kids everything their father never could. In a short amount of time, he has shown them what a real father is, and he has shown me that being loved is something that I am worthy of.

NINETEEN

JUDGE

-Present-

I have been on the phone with Artem and the Sheriff for what seems like 3 days straight. None of our underground connections and sources have found out what that piece of shit was talking about. There was something going on in this town, and it affected my kids, not just the sweet baby girl we have in the hospital. But I have teenagers here, troubled teenagers on top of that. While having eyes and ears all over the place does help with teenagers, it seems to have made the town itself weak to this new danger that is lurking behind the scenes.

"Butcher could have left me a little more to work with than the shell of a man I retrieved." Artem bitched over the phone.

"You are the one who waited two days to come and get him. You are lucky he was even alive." I gripe back. I am in no mood. I haven't shared a bed with my wife in weeks. Now, this. I don't have the patience for all his bellyaching.

"Well, he wasn't instrumental in the information department for either of us. So I am assuming he is lower on the totem pole than it was suggested." You can tell that Artem is displeased his sources have been failing like the rest of us.

Truly though, if Artem can't get to the bottom of it all, then you know these guys are deep underground. I can't figure out why though, I know the cartel isn't here because we are too far north, and any real gang activity would read quickly. Those guys are far from subtle.

"This has to be bigger than drugs," I mumble my thoughts into my cell.

"That is my conclusion as well. I mean, I deal in drugs, but that is to fund a different side of my business. Sides that help fund you and your Clubs requirements as well. But with how deep they are, it's dark."

I don't know all of Artem's dealings. I know that there were some things his father was involved in that he stopped almost immediately when he took over. I know that he was invested in many different business dealings, varied from legal to unbelievably illegal. But there was never a drop of judgment from us. We helped hold some of his dealings and shipments here. We also did the runs that were needed as well into other MC territories.

"Have you talked to Detroit?" I asked, trying to see how far this stretched.

"Yes, the drugs have not yet made it that far south, which means it could be our friends from the North."

"The Canadians? Really?" I was kind of skeptical of that idea.

"Where do you think Butcher got the idea for the pigs as a means for body disposal? Don't underestimate a culture that apologizes for everything. They are hiding some deep dark secrets."

Before I could even entertain his comment with an answer, the kids started calling for me outside. I paid him a good night and went to see what the commotion was. There was a white SUV creeping down the main drive. I called for Manda to get the young ones in the house. Turd and a prospect were quick to pop out of the barn at the sound of my voice. Joining me as I walk to meet the visitor. I really need to invest in a main gate now that all this is going on.

"Expecting anyone, Prez?" The young prospect pipes up when they are at my side.

"Nope, be ready just in case." I never have my gun on me when the kids are around, but the boys are always packing. I am who the kids see on a constant basis. While we will teach them gun safety, I won't risk it. The men that aren't around the kids twenty-four-seven will never be without. It also gives me a way to grab quickly when needed.

The SUV came to a slow halt, and we approached slowly. The window rolled down, and there was Bonnie… PTA President, I did not have enough energy or coffee to deal with the pep coming my way.

"Kenny!" She calls out the window, trying to give me a cutesy wave.

"Hi…. Bonnie. We don't see you around these parts much." I try and wave off the men back, but Turd has his sights set on the blonde ditz. I wasn't sure what he saw, though. I also couldn't be sure if he was watching her because he wanted to fuck her, because he didn't trust her, or both. Turd may live up to his namesake completely, but he was an excellent judge of character as well. While I would never admit it to his face, there have been times his judgment was more spot-on than mine. Now, if he could stop acting like a jackass most of the time.

"Yes, I know it's just so far out here. But I had heard you guys got a few new mouths to feed and figured I could stop by and see if Sweet Elvira needed any help. I have a back seat FULL of casseroles from the PTA moms." She seemed all sweet and innocent, but this woman annoyed me. Then the fact that small-town living made word travel through the grapevine incredibly quick. There were definitely times I wish we lived in a more populated area so people wouldn't know who we had and when we got them. Granted, it didn't happen all the time. We have cases where the child in our care is secret. I wish they all were.

She reminded me of those Stepford wives, always in dresses and heels. She was the president of the PTA, local MADD Chapter; she was a certified lifeguard and made sure she taught all the local teenagers their babysitting courses and first aid. She also organized all the school and town fundraisers. She ran for town council but backed down; for some reason, I think she said she already had so much on the go and didn't want to give the people of Wyman less than 110%, like everything else in her life. She was also a mother of 5, all of whom are closing in on graduating, and she goes to all their sporting, dance, and drama events. She is insane. I don't understand how women do this, we have a team helping us out here, and I can't get into bed fast enough at night when it's all said and done.

"Ya, I am sure she will thank you when she sees you. She is up at the hospital right now with the youngest of the two. Hasn't been home long enough for anything but a shower and a hug from the kids." I explain as Bonnie hops out of the car and opens the back showing us all the meals that are prepared.

"Holy Shit! Free food!" I hear Dizz call from the porch as Turd loads up the prospect's arms with a few dishes at a time.

"Get down here and help them if you want any," I called back up to him, but he was already there. Arms open, ready to take food. The kid can eat us all out of house and home, and you would never know it looking at him. I don't think I have ever seen abs on abs before until Dizz. It's trippy as hell, but I respect the dedication and care he now has for himself.

"Oh, El isn't here holding down the fort?" She asks, almost a slight tinge of judgment in her tone. I see Turd's ears turn red, his tell that he is holding his tongue.

"Well, that's why we have a team here, Bonnie. We men are capable of taking care of the house and the ranch's needs while she is away caring for the baby." I am trying to play nice, but I don't want to at the same time.

"I meant no disrespect by that. I am sorry if that's how it came across. I know how my husband is, and here she is, the only woman with kids, ranchers, and, uhm, well, bikers all around her. I imagine she would want to be here to keep you lot in line." She reaches out to pat my arm, but I take a step back. Her correction did nothing but dig herself into a deeper hole with me.

"I will be sure to let her know that you stopped by. I will get Cowboy to drop off the dishes back at your place. As you said, there are a lot of growing kids and grown men here to feed. I am sure we will polish off these meals in no time. Thank you, Bonnie. Turd, can you please see our visitor out." I turn before I have to listen to that voice a moment longer.

Pulling out my phone, I make my way to the kitchen to see Dizz sitting at the counter, elbows deep in the lasagna already, getting it all over his Hercules shirt. That Man-Child is never without a Disney-themed t-shirt or sweater under his Cut, and he is the one who is ready to play princesses with the girls. I roll my eyes and look at all the food laid about, stopping only to see a cat sitting on the kitchen table.

We have farm cats, they are good at keeping the mice down outside, but they are not allowed in the house. We have too many kids coming and going here that we cannot risk allergens inside the home. It's hard enough when you run a foster home on a Ranch with every animal under the sun outside.

"Dizz?" I ask. He looks at me, wiping the sauce from his face with a paper towel. "Why the fuck is there a cat in my house?"

"Caleb said she looked sad and cold and would only keep her in for a few days. But I guess she thinks she got a free ride to come in whenever." He replies, walking over to scratch the affectionate animal's head.

I take a deep breath. This is a later problem; I need to deal with the now problem.

"Get the cat out. I will talk to Caleb later." I push the speed dial, and he answers quickly. "Artem? Who did the security fencing around Cowboy's place? I need some put up at the main house."

Too many people stop by and do not call first.

Having Artem as an ally was paying off. It took two days after that phone call to get the gate installed. I ain't gonna lie, it's impressive as hell. The gate is solid and tall as fuck. There is no getting in without its opening and no climbing over it. He understands how important safety and security here at the ranch is.

I can't help but marvel at it as it slides open. Once the gate is finally open, I drive over the hidden compartment he had installed in the road. Should someone not invited be successful in gaining entry, all we have to do is press a button for spikes to be shot out of the ground and pop the tires of any moving vehicle.

"Better have it and not need it than not have it and need it." He had told me and can't say that I disagree with him.

Turning left on the main drive, I kick my bike into gear and let loose. This part of the drive is ours. There is no traffic. I can go as fast as I want to. I hit the throttle and take advantage of the speed that my bike can achieve.

It doesn't take long after that for me to get through town and get to Artem's mansion in the mountains. The guy has impeccable taste when it comes to homes. I will give him that. His house is rustic, covered in stones and dark wood. It's large as fuck, but it isn't goddy as you would assume most people in his stature would live.

I should kill him and take his place for myself.

Shaking my head of the thought that I have every time I come here, I park my bike and head inside. I know my way around this house like the back of my hand. Our partnership has blossomed into a friendship, though neither of us will ever admit it.

Reputations to uphold and all that shit.

I get to the office and step inside. I see Artem immediately and the back of Sheriff Anderson's head. Shutting the door behind me, I make my way to my chair right next to him.

"Glad you could finally make it," Artem says.

"You know me. I always like to be fashionably late or what-the-fuck-ever."

He smiles and shakes his head. Out of the corner of my eye, I can see Anderson doing the same. This is the least likely trio someone would slap together, but it works for us. Ironic when you think about it.

A biker, a cop, and a mob boss walk into a bar.

"Alright," Anderson says, taking me out of the joke I was about to tell myself, "we need to figure out what the fuck is going on. We have an unknown player out there, and the fact that you don't know anything about it scares me. I can only handle one crime lord slash drug kingpin. Plus, I like you. Who the fuck is this guy?"

"Aw, you like me? That's so fucking sweet." Artem says in a mocking sugar tone. "As for who the fuck it is, I wish I knew. This is completely new to me. They are somehow pushing it underground and in plain sight. I haven't seen any merchandise or heard a word. I only hear of anything when someone pops up dead."

"We only know of two dead."

"Exactly! How the hell am I supposed to do something about this when it's just now here? With how quiet it is, I wouldn't be surprised if it is a local. Someone who knows their way around Wyman. Someone who has been here for a long time and knows how to make drugs."

"You can Google anything. They don't need to know how or understand it. They need to be able to read. Someone local makes sense, but we don't even know where to look. We have to find a way to get word on the street. Do we even have a name for the drug yet?" I turn towards Anderson.

He sighs loudly and shakes his head. He and I came to an agreement years ago. We have an understanding. It didn't take long for Artem to be brought into that fold. The rules have always been simple.

Keep it away from you, and you're fine. Evidence points to you, and you go down.

So when this new drug pops up, and the only known drug lord is sitting in this room, it makes it harder when you don't have anything to go on. I wouldn't be surprised if he hoped it was Artem so he could clear it out and get this solved. He would never dare threaten Artem with that, though, unless he had the proof.

"Alright," I pull my hand down across my face, "I think what we need is to get people on the ground. I'll get the prospects to go out without their cuts and have them ask around. If they get picked up by any of your undercovers, fill them in then. I don't want anyone else knowing what we're doing. With the possibility of this being local, we can't trust the entire force.

Artem, if you have anyone you can spare or bring in to do the same, I suggest you do it. Especially if you can bring people in. People, no one here knows but doesn't scream, "I'm in the Mafia."

Anderson, anyone that you can fully trust scoping out is all we need. Too many right now, whoever this is, will figure us out, and it will become harder to find. The easiest right now may be having the prospects looking to score. Fuck, this is all a goddamn shit show."

"Yes, but I like that plan. I can bring people in. That won't be an issue. Have them look around, ask around, plant cameras, the works. We need to try and narrow down the search of who we would be looking for."

"Any rich quick shitbags come across for either of you? The most the precinct is seeing lately is drunks and men getting a little too handsy for someone's liking."

"No, I haven't seen any but, only time will tell. Look. I want to stay and plot more, but I need to get to the hospital. This little girl has stolen my wife's heart, and something tells me adoption papers will be put in front of my face shortly. Let me know what the final plan is. You know you have us wherever you need us."

I nod at both of them and make my way out. Working together would be the only way to get this stopped. There was something fucking gigantic coming our way, and I wasn't sure how any of us were going to prepare.

TWENTY

JUDGE

-Past-

It was a nice night; it had been a good quiet day, the first in a long time. My Elvira was home and in my arms every night. She still has yet to answer my proposal verbally, but I also have not asked again. But Yaya's engagement ring from Grandpa is on her finger, so it's safe to say that it is a done deal, and she will be my wife.

I know that I was assuming a lot given what had happened to her before my asking. I hoped she still understood that I was here for her for the long haul. I felt that she did, but I wasn't going to push her. She needed her time, and I was going to give all the time I had to her.

Sitting with Yaya, it was easy to think about what life had to offer me. Where life was going to take me. As long as it included Elvira, I was okay with it; however, it turned out. Sighing, I gave in to the complete moment of bliss.

Just then, the dogs start going nuts, barking at the dust being kicked up, coming down the drive. *I need a gate.* It wasn't until I saw the cherries on the top that I knew it was the Sheriff.

"What is he doing out here?" Yaya asks from her spot on the swing. Giving me that look. The one that says, "what did you do?" but for once, I didn't do anything. I don't think.

"You can see him, but you can't see your glasses on the counter?" Theo asks, while a valid question, he should have known better than to ask; he will pay for that. If there is one thing Yaya loves, it's beating Theo's ass with that wooden spoon. I've told him that he should carry a spare with him to make it easier on her.

"Evening, folks," Anderson said, tipping his hat at us.

"Sheriff." I greet him, making no move from my spot on the porch. While I didn't go out of my way to be an asshole to him, I also didn't go out of my way to be his best fucking friend. That role was already filled. Although at times, I questioned my pick. Walking up the steps, Anderson stops on the porch and takes his hat off his head, holding it in front of him.

I swear that's the pose all cops give when they're about to tell you the worse fucking news. I take a quick mental inventory of who is here and try and think if anyone would be hurt or dead. Coming up empty, I start to worry about what it is that he is here for.

"Ken, I need to talk to you about something, something sensitive." He looks from Yaya and El to Theo and me. Almost like the womenfolk need not hear what he is about to ask me. There are things that I would share with El no matter what. She is a part of Yaya and me, but the look in his eyes tells me that this isn't something that they need to hear. He almost looks scared.

"El, love, I think it's time for us to start dinner for the men before they come in from the field," Yaya stated, reaching out for help from her to stand. It seems that I wasn't the only one that saw the concern on Anderson's face.

El helped her from her perch on the swing as they passed me, both leaning in to kiss the side of my head. As they passed Theo, he received a smack upside the head from both ladies. *I knew they would get him back.* My attention never wavered from the Sheriff, who was shuffling from foot to foot, looking very uncomfortable being here.

"Let's head to the barn." I stand, leading the two men to the office.

"I know that you two started an MC here to help Elvira as well as young Mike Berlusconi

and the issues he was having with his foster family." Sheriff Anderson started. Part of me wanted to be mad that he knew, but the bigger part of me was proud to know that word has gotten 'round, and our MC is already starting to make a name for itself.

"We didn't start it for him. We started it because we like to ride, and kids like Mike need someone tough looking in their corner. Nothing more." Theo started. I could tell he was on edge. Having to tread lightly on how much he gives away.

"Understood." Anderson throws one of the file folders on the desk in front of me. "But I know, personally speaking, I know you had something to do with him disappearing. I don't care if you did or didn't. I am not here on police business. I am here as a father." He cuts Theo off quickly before he can refuse our involvement. "I am going to leave this here." He tosses the rest of the folders on the desk. "And what you do or don't do with them is up to you. The station's hands are tied even with all this evidence." His voice starts to crack, and his face starts to get more and more flushed the longer he stares at the files. "Don't let it lead back to you or me."

I look at him and raise an eyebrow, "You expect me to believe that it's that easy, Anderson?"

Letting out a large sigh, he shakes his head. "No, I don't. If I were you, I wouldn't trust me either. But I can't do shit about this. There are too many politics and a whole bunch of other shit that puts me between a rock and a hard place. As I said, I am not here as a cop. But as a cop and a hopeful ally, let me be clear. The rule is fucking simple."

I give him a look, letting him know that he is close to crossing the line with the way he is speaking to me. But I also stick to the line he just said, a hopeful ally. After all, he said he isn't here as a cop. So I let him continue without threatening his life.

"Whatever you do, you don't let it come back to you, your club, or me. You don't leave any evidence behind. If you do, and you get caught, you're on your own. I will do my part unless you fuck up. If it is obvious, it was you or your men. I won't save you."

"So, what does this mean for us?"

"It means that from this moment on, we are a team, and I will get you the names you need. You do the rest, and we all sleep better at night. Deal?"

He holds out his hand and waits for me to grab it. Taking a quick moment to look over at Theo, he nods his head, yes, and I turn my attention back to Anderson.

"Deal. But if we do what I think you want us to do and you screw us, I will kill you."

"Fair enough. Have a good night, fellas."

With that, he leaves Theo and me standing there, watching him make his way back to his cruiser and spinning out of the yard.

"Do you think that we can trust him?"

"I want to, Theo. Whatever he just gave us, it's bigger than him." His face said everything before he even made the deal.

I take a seat and start flipping through the stack of files, trying to make heads or tails of what he said, as well as the files, dropped off. I look at the names, and these are all kids not much younger than J.J. and R.J… These kids range from 10 to 12 years old. All boys, then a name jumps out at me.

"Fuck." I mumble, pulling it out and opening it up. " 'Jacob Anderson, age 11 years old. Accuser. Murray Martin, Age 62 years old, Accused.' Fuck, what the fuck?" What the fuck am I reading? "Charges, Molestation, and Child abuse." Theo quickly grabs another file and starts reading out loud.

"Kyle Keats, age 10 years old. Accuser. Murray Martin, Age 62 years old, accused.' same charges. Are these all the same thing but different kids?" Theo starts shuffling and reading the same line over and over again different kids, same dirt old fucker. "How are the department's hands tied? There are 10 kids here! We know there are more! When one comes forward 10 more, stay silent!"

"Look at his profession, that is why. It's politics." I state, pointing to Jacob's file. "He's the former Sheriff, now running for County Commission."

"Judge," he starts using the newly appointed road name. "We need to call Church and take care of this."

"Agreed. Get them all here. We're going to fix this Storm. One way or another."

I slap the picture of the rapist up on the wall. Stabbing it with a knife to hold it up. I don't let go of the hilt of the knife at first. The anger within me is boiling my skin. It is breaking me apart from the inside out. This man has raped multiple boys, and no one can get a charge to stick. This asshole is sixty-something fucking years old. Who knows how long this has been going on.

I turn my body towards my men. All of them are questioning why I just did what I did.

"That piece of shit is Murray Martin," I throw the case files onto the table. They spread out on their own, and the guys reach for them.

"He has been charged with multiple counts of rape against boys age ranges from ten to twelve. None of the charges have stuck. It doesn't fucking matter that he has been accused multiple times or what these boys say. He walks every time."

The men are furious. I can see the same level of rage across each of their faces. For a moment, I can't even make out what they are saying as they are all speaking at once. They need to get it out. This disgusting human being needs to be taken out, and I know they are itching to get their hands on him, especially Butcher.

"How was this brought to our attention in the first place?" Willie asks. It was a fair question. We're a new club. We don't have the connections we need or people in our pockets yet.

Yeah, we may have an alliance with the Mafia here, but that doesn't get us this.

"Sheriff Anderson ca-"

"ARE YOU SERIOUS?!" Willie stands and shouts at me. "You made a deal with the pigs?'

"Given the situation, I will give you that ONE outburst Willie but disrespect me again, and you won't live to regret it."

He nods at me and sits down. I am still standing but now at the end of the table. My knuckles on both hands are against the table, and I drop my head between my arms.

"Look, I know having Anderson give us these names is a huge risk, but he isn't going to do anything."

"How do you know for sure?"

"Because his son was a victim. When they couldn't even get justice for his own fucking son, his eleven-year-old child killed himself. We do this; Anderson will not come after us. We officially have an agreement."

I take a moment to look around at all of them. Letting them look into my eyes to see that this is serious. That I believe that this is a good idea.

"The only rule is anything we do with the information that Anderson provides us CAN NOT come back to us. If any of you leave *any* evidence that clearly puts you there, you are on your own. He will not save you. You do it quick and clean, and you will never see the inside of a cell. Can you live with that?"

They all mumble and look around at one another. Butcher is the first to speak.

"So you're telling me that I can go gut this man, feed him to my piggies, and as long as I don't leave no prints, no hairs, no nothin' I ain't gotta worry 'bout leaving my wife alone?"

"Yes. You think that you can do that?"

"Oh, I can do that and then some. Where is he? My babies are hungry."

"Chill the fuck out, Butcher. We ain't killing him yet. We need to go in with a plan. This has to be clean. We can not get caught. Give me any ideas about how to get in and out without any being the wiser."

"And why can't we just roll right up to his house and take his ass?" Willie asks.

"I am not against it if We. Don't. Get. Caught. We can't go in there half-cocked. This needs to be a solid fucking plan!"

"Alright, y'all. We can figure this out. We need to start with someone tailing him. Learn his patterns. Please find the most opportune time to take him. I can take that role. I'm sneaky as hell." Theo exclaims proudly. The others snicker but what they don't know is that it is true. Growing up the way we did, he has a scary as fuck ability to blend in with the shadows and the surrounding areas.

"That's a good start. After Storm gets back to us from his recon, we will plan it out and officially go hunting. Butcher, can your piggies last a couple more days?"

"Oh yeah, they'll be fine. It's not like all I feed them is human parts." He turns and looks at Sever, his face morphing into something sinister, "or do I?"

“Fuck off, man.” Sever pushes him away. Butcher laughs, but I know that Sever is freaked out. Butcher is a scary motherfucker and even keeps all of us on our toes.

“Alright fuckers. That’s it for now. Adjourned.”

“Ya know, you should get a gavel or something, *Judge.*”

“Fuck off, Theo.”

He laughs and walks out of the barn. I hate that he has a point.

TWENTY-ONE

ELVIRA

-Past-

I was in the garden with Yaya one afternoon; we harvested what we could from it for dinner and maybe a few snacks for the kids to take to school. She kept looking over at the barn. When all the men had filed out for the day, both Ranch hands and MC brothers alike, she got up and made her way over slowly across the drive. I hopped up as quickly as my tired still healing body would allow me and followed her. She slowly climbed up those steps to what I know as 'Church,' and I am only allowed in when it's time to talk dollars and cents.

I watch her make her way around the room, gently touching the parts of the wall that looked well worn. She got to the far corner and sighed loudly. I hear boots coming up the steps behind my spot, leaning on the door jam just watching. I knew before he even wrapped me up in his strong arms that it was Ken. He pushed his face into my neck, kissing me, letting his warm breath sweep over me.

"What is she doing?" He asked softly, both of us just watching her.

"I am not sure. We were in the garden, then she just wandered up here and was touching and looking at things." We just stand and watch, knowing she will share when she is good and ready to.

It was a good while later that her eyes met ours, and she called us over to take a seat at the makeshift table the boys put together up here for their meetings. Ken, ever the gentleman, pulled out a chair for both Yaya and me before taking a seat.

"This place holds so many memories." She said softly, her eyes still looking around. "Some good, some bad, and almost all of them revolve around your Grandfather."

I feel Ken start to tense a little beside me, like he wants to know more but doesn't want to pressure her into sharing things that will upset her. He loves his grandmother more than himself, he will never say it, but you can see it in everything that he does for her and this ranch.

"Do you want to talk about it?" I ask her, knowing that she does have a lot to share just doesn't know how to approach it with Ken. They were apart his whole life and had those thirty-five years of his life to make up for. But not only that, she has eighty-plus years of her life to share with him as well.

"Your Grandfather left me ten days after we were married. We were living with my parents at the time, the war was on, and his number got called. While he was away, your great Granddaddies got together and helped me build this barn on our land. We turned this loft into our home, and it's where I stayed for just over two years until he came home to me." She has a small smile on her face as she thinks back.

"That had to have been hard being away from him for so long. And so quickly after you got married." I mention. Ken is still sitting and watching his Grandmother talk, the dreamy look on her face, thinking about Kenny.

"Not very many things in our relationship were done slowly. We fell in love fast and furious. He told me all the time how the second he saw the fire in my eyes, that's when he knew I was going to be his wife, his partner in life. We were married forty-five days after our first date—something small at the county courthouse with just his two brothers and our parents. Then ten days after that, he was ripped from me by a stupid war. I was worried that was all the time we would have had together. Fifty-five glorious days filled with love, laughter, and planning, we wanted so much for this place. This barn was the first thing built, and the only building put up until he came home.

I had refused to build the house until he was back. That was our home. It was something that we were determined to build together. Your great Grand-daddies wanted to get it started, said I shouldn't wait, but I couldn't do it. Not without him.

When he finally came home, we got started right away. This barn, this is where we lived during that time. Seeing it again, for what it's used, for now, I know good is going to come out of it. Just like it did with him and me."

"What do you mean? What good?" Ken asks.

"Well, we made your momma right over there." She points to a random spot in the barn. Ken gags, and she just looks at me and winks. She doesn't talk about her sex life very often, but I love it when she does. Purely for the reaction from Ken. He turns into a giant child, all of a sudden disgusted about what sex entails.

I know that he is going to complain about it later to me, and that's when I will remind him about how he likes to do worse to me. Then he will do worse to me. It's a win-win for me.

"Yaya, please. I don't need to know this. Really. That's my momma. Your sex life, as far as I am concerned, is nonexistent."

She waves her hand and gets a gleam in her eye. I know Ken is about to regret those words.

"Boy, you see that sink? He bent me over that. Multiple times. See that workbench; he did things between my legs that had me screaming so loud, the animals went crazy. And that bed that's over there in pieces wanna guess how it broke?"

"OH MY GOD, STOP!" Ken screams and runs down the stairs and out of the barn. I am dying of laughter when Yaya just looks at me, "you'd think he never heard of sex before. I wonder if I need to feel sorry for you."

"Oh, trust me, you don't."

Yaya shudders and pushes her chair back, "okay, I can see why he hates me talking about it. I asked for it, and it's still terrible to hear. Walk with me back outside. I guess I should apologize to him."

"Naw, don't worry about it. He knows you had a life before him. He's just making up for the lost time. The overreaction towards your parents, or in his case - grandparents - having sex is just a step in life. He missed it in his teen years, so he's having it now."

I wink at her, and she just smiles. We get outside, and Ken is nowhere to be found. I start moving my head back and forth to try and find him when I hear retching coming from behind the barn. Oh my God, what a baby.

Present

There was a knock on the door that jolted me out of my thoughts. I found myself thinking of the past a lot while sitting here with Kelsey. I look up, and a beautiful redhead comes walking in. She isn't a nurse, which I can only deduce due to her not wearing scrubs. She must see that I don't recognize her as she holds out her hand. Her smile is bright but nothing compared to the bright blue eyes she has.

"Hi, my name is Audrina. I am a social worker for the state. I was called in by the hospital. I was informed that you are Miss Kelsey's current guardian."

I shake her hand, and I nod. Too shocked to speak as to why the hospital would have called her in. I haven't done a thing wrong. All I have done is sit with this baby and make sure she is getting the care that she should.

The look on her face tells me that she is expecting an answer. I shake my head to clear my thoughts. I know that I am okay; I shouldn't worry. Easier said than done.

"Um, hi. Hi. Why are you here? I mean, what can I help you with?" I was stammering, and that is something that I never do. I am usually put together. How is it that right now, I'm not? The time that I most definitely should be at the top of my game.

She just smiles.

"No need to panic. I am here because she is hopefully going to be released soon. We have paperwork to get in order as she will be leaving with you."

I let out a gigantic breath, and we sat down at the small table that is in the room. About forty-five minutes later, we have everything situated, and she packs up, getting ready to leave.

"El, one, more thing." She pauses. Even after the great conversation we just had, this makes me nervous. "When was the last time you went home?"

"Home? Oh, umm, I don't know—the other day. I went and showered. I said hi to the kids and came back. Why do you ask?"

"Have you spent any real time away from the hospital?"

"No. I am too worried about Kelsey. What if she needs me? I need to be here for her."

"I understand that completely, and we are concerned for her too. But you are the mama, and moms need to be on their game too. You need to look after yourself as well." She starts to explain to me.

"I will when she is home. I will be better and more myself when she is home. You guys are not the babysitters here; you are the health care professionals. I am supposed to take care of the day-to-day needs, like diapers and feeding, and comfort. That is what moms do." I start to feel my anxiety levels rise. This woman is going to think that I am controlling and crazy.

"Elvira, we get that. The nurses love you and all that you do for Kelsey, but they are worried about you. You are not getting enough sleep. You are barely eating, and they have expressed concerns about your stress levels each time they need to make changes to Kelsey's medications and doses. They want what is best for Kelsey, and what is best for her is a happy, healthy mama to come home to. Let's try and explain this when you are at home. Who is there to help you?" She asks, leaning in a bit towards me.

"I have my husband, our kids, the farmhands, and the MC brothers." When I say it out loud, I didn't realize that I do have a lot of help at home.

"And they help you as you need it? Like if you need a shower, to run to the store, or even to ravage that husband of yours, right?" I know she is making light for me to see the point, but I was in no mood for anyone to talk about my man.

"Right." I snap shortly.

"What I am saying is, here, we are that team. You need to set a schedule here as you have at home. When it's her 'nap time' at home, that is when you shower, do dishes, read, or eat, right?"

"Yes."

"Okay, so when it's her nap time here, go home, take a break. Go Shopping, take a nap in your own bed. The same goes for bedtime. We will handle bedtime here and overnights, so you can go home and be refreshed for what she needs the next day. Maybe on the weekends, send your husband to sit, or one of her other support members to sit with her." She reaches and takes my hand from the table, trying to get me to see reason. "It takes a village, and you have a great one at home. It's time to see them, too, and let us help with Kelsey. We will still call you when we need anything. But, my advice, go home for the night. Hug your kids and relax. We have everything under control here. I promise."

"I'm scared," I tell her truthfully. I was afraid that if I left, something would go wrong, and I wouldn't get here in time. If that were to happen, I wouldn't be able to live with myself.

"I know. But she is safe here. Her numbers are good, her vitals are great, and you have the most amazing nurses and Dr.'s surrounding her. She will be okay. Go. Plus, you have a man you need to see." She winks at me.

This time, my smile is genuine. I know that she means well, and she is right. The staff here taking care of Kelsey are some of the best I have ever dealt with. I stand, give her a hug, and my thanks. I walk over to Kelsey, who is sleeping peacefully in the crib.

Giving her a kiss and rubbing her hair, I let her know, "I love you, baby girl. I'll be back later. You stay put, don't give your nurse any trouble, and you get better. See you soon."

With one last kiss to her head, I leave the hospital and make my way home.

"What the fuck is this shit?"

I finally decide to come home, and I can't even get there due to the massive fucking gate blocking my way. This is the last thing I needed. I didn't even want to leave the hospital in the first place, and now this, it's a fucking sign. I should just turn around and go back.

No. You need to go home. See your kids, your husband.

Sighing, I know that my bitch-ass self is right. I get out and look around. There has to be a way to communicate that I am here. I'd call, but of course, my phone is dead, and I don't have a charger in the car. Fucking winning.

"UGHHHH!" I yell out with my face towards the clouds. Bringing my head back down, I look to my left. There is a box with a number pad and a speaker. On closer inspection, I also see a call button. I hit it and impatiently waited.

"Yeah?"

"Theo. Open this goddamn monstrosity and let me in my fucking house!"

"Hey, El. I didn't know you were coming-"

"Theo! The gate."

"Uh, yeah. There ya go."

The next thing I hear is a loud buzz, and the gate starts to open. I walk back to the car and get back in. It is finally open enough that I can drive through. The tail end of my car passes over the threshold when I see Ken's bike racing down the drive. I stop the car and get out. Might as well let him come to me.

He pulls up, and I am hit with how sexy he is. It's been weeks since we've been together, and I've seen him longer than twenty minutes. All of my time has been spent at the hospital with Kelsey. He is, without a doubt, the most gorgeous man I have ever seen. And right now, coming up on his bike, hair blowing in the wind, tattoos covering his right arm. His pants are tight, but even more so from the position, he is in. I know what he is hiding in those pants, and the anticipation of him getting to me burns brighter.

I turn around quickly and pull the girls up to attention and my shirt down. Turning back around to face him, I lean myself against the hood of my car and popped my hip out. I know how to accentuate the parts of me he loves the most.

He stops his bike, and he looks like a feral beast, ready to attack his prey. He swings his leg over his bike, and he stalks towards me. He doesn't even speak. One hand grips the back of my head while the other wraps around my waist, crushing my body and my mouth to his.

He lets out a deep growl as he pushes me flat onto the hood of my car, my head hitting it hard. Thankfully, the hood gives out a little, and it doesn't hurt that badly. Even if it had, though, I wouldn't have cared. All I care about right now is this man pressed up against me.

His hands travel up my body, gripping my tits. He pushes them together and brings his mouth down, and bites the top of them. He pulls back just enough to take my shirt off of me and then goes back to them. He pulls the cups down and takes a nipple into his mouth. He sucks it to the point of pain and then licks it to soothe it. He then repeats the process on the other side.

"Fuck, baby."

"I missed you so much," he states as he travels down my body. He kisses and sucks on my soft stomach as he undoes the button of my jeans. I hear the zipper and then feel his hand go inside. It takes no time for him to find my soaking wet clit, and he starts pulling an orgasm out of me.

I am making all the noise in the world, knowing that no one can hear me. Letting him know that I am about to bust from what he is doing. He had brought his mouth back up my body and was sucking on my neck. That sweet spot that I have at the base of my ear.

"You gonna come for me, baby?"

"Yes…yes. Oh fuck, don't stop. Don't stop."

"Oh baby, I have no plans on stopping. I missed you so fucking much. Come all over my hand. Let me feel you."

It wasn't long after that I was doing exactly what he wanted. The shockwaves I felt didn't diminish as he pulled my pants down and off. I was breathing heavily. He stood up and stepped back, starting to take off his clothes. He places his cut on his bike seat while the rest just falls to the ground.

I am still watching him take each piece off. This man, you'd never think he is as old as he is. The only thing that gives a hint to his age is the gray in his hair. His body is on a scale all of its own. Broad shoulders that equal out to a massive chest. A six-pack that is also soft at the same time. Thighs that are basically tree trunks, and let's not forget the part in the middle that always has me screaming his name.

That cock is my downfall every time. He knows that all he has to do to get out of trouble is promise me that it will be put into one of my holes, and he wins. He may think he has the upper hand when it comes to that, but I'm the one getting the multiple orgasms out of it.

As he kicks off his pants, he comes back up to me. He pushes me back down onto the hood as he drops to the ground. He takes my legs and throws them over his shoulder, and his face is buried deep within my cunt. Eating me out like he has never had a meal before in his life.

My screams echo in the fields, and I am now certain they can hear me at the ranch. I don't even care. He bites down on my clit before sucking it deep into his mouth. All while shoving two fingers deep within me. Curling them just so to hit my g-spot repeatedly.

My orgasm shakes me to my core, and I squirt all over his face. He laps it's up like it's honey, and he's a starved bee. I can feel my clit pulsating as he stands and lines himself up with me. Bringing his face down to mine, kissing me deeply.

In between moans, he breathes out, "I can't be away from you for this long ever again." Slamming into me, balls deep, as he says again.

My body arches off the car, and I crane my neck back. My mouth opens with a silent scream. Not having him deep inside of me for this long should be considered a crime.

"Fuck, Ken. Move baby. Fuck."

He pulls out and slams back into me again. The motion is making the car shake. Each thrust feels deeper, harder, thicker. Almost like I can feel his cock getting harder than it already was.

"Shit. Shit. Shit. Yes. Right there. Right there. Oh fuck, I'm gonna come. I'm gonna...."

"Come, baby. Come all over my cock."

His lips are back on mine, stifling my screams as I come again. As I'm coming down from my high, he puts more of his weight on top of me and thrusts harder.

"Fuck El. You feel so fucking good. So. Fucking. Tight."

He empathizes each word with each thrust. He bites down on my neck, right at the base where it meets my shoulder, and I moan. I've always enjoyed him leaving marks on me. This is no exception.

I yank his hair hard, and it pulls his head back while using my other to scratch down his back. He lets out a hiss before pulling back. He then grabs my legs, and my knees come up by my ears with my calves over his shoulders. His right hand comes around my leg and gives my clit a smack. He then pinches it before rubbing it in circles.

I'm screaming his name and every word I can manage to put together. The damn is about to break, literally. I can hear the sounds from the river that's already flowing. The change in position has only made it worse. He's a moment away from an ocean.

"Ken!! Oh, my fucking, fuck! I'm about to come everywhere. Ahhh!"

He pulls out. I squirt out my come everywhere. I learned a while ago I can do what women in porn do, and Ken loves it. He lets it cover him completely before bringing his face to my center and drinking it down.

He isn't there long before he's back inside me, thrusting harder than before.

"You know how much I love that baby. Are you ready for my come? You gonna milk this cock dry?"

"Yes. Fuck yes. Give it to me. I fucking want it."

"Fuck baby. El! Fuck!"

His hand slams down on the hood of the car as he pushes as far as he can within me, pumping weeks' worth of cum into me. When he pulls out, I can feel it come out with him. He takes his hands and smears it all over my pussy. He then brings his hand up and puts his fingers in my mouth. Sucking him clean, he closes his eyes and moans deep.

Once done, he sits me up and wraps me up in his arms.

"Baby. I missed you so much. I meant what I said. I can't be away from you for this long. Call me a selfish man, but I need you here with me."

"I missed you too. I'm going to manage my time better and be home more."

"Really?" He raises a brow, challenging me. He knows me better than anyone, so I know he is shocked to find out that I'll be spending less time at the hospital.

"Yes. The social worker, Audrina, talked some sense into me today."

"Well, make sure I remember to send her a thank you card. I've needed you so much. I love you, baby."

"I love you, too."

He kisses me again, but this time is different. The kisses he always gives me after sex is the same one he gave me all those years ago. So full of passion, love, and trust. He gives me his whole soul in these kisses. Kisses that I love more than any other.

He places his forehead against mine and just breathes me in for a moment. His eyes closed. It's almost like he is in pain from our distance recently. "How did you know that I was out here? Theo had just barely opened the gate when you were coming barreling down the drive."

"I saw you on the camera. We have TVs set up in our room, the office, the kitchen, and the living room so we can see anyone at the gate as well."

"Are you telling me that anyone could have just watched us fuck? Kenneth Kelley!"

"Baby, I would never let anyone watch you soak my chest with your come and then me slop it up with my tongue." He growls before his mouth connects again with mine. Breaking away, he continues, "it's only on the other side of the gate to see the driver."

"You would have been kissing my ass for the next month had there been a camera on this side."

"Oh baby, I'd do more than kiss it."

I smack his arm and wrap myself back around him. Giving him another kiss. I love this man with all that I am.

When we part, we start to dress. That's when I see the giant monstrosity out of the corner of my eye.

"Want to tell me what that fucking thing is doing in my yard?"

Ken shakes his head and chuckles. I bet the pain knew I'd hate the damn thing.

"We kept getting unwanted visitors up at the ranch. It was time to keep 'em out."

"And who was it, after fifteen years, that made you finally crack?"

"Bonnie."

"Bonnie? What the hell did she want?"

"Give us food, claim to help, and piss me off."

"She is annoying. I'll give you that."

I smile and wink at him before getting in my car. He's back on his bike and working on turning it around to head home. Looking in the rearview mirror, I look at the gate again. I guess it isn't that bad. Although Bonnie really is annoying as hell, so keeping her away, I ain't mad at it.

TWENTY-TWO

ELVIRA

-Present-

I didn't want Audrina to be right, but she was. The men did a great job of keeping this house going while I spent all my time at the hospital. Coming home and putting myself on a schedule was the best thing for me mentally and the best thing for my family.

On the days that I am not there, I call in the morning and get an update on Kelsey's previous night and how they are looking for the current day. Then I follow up at night to get a rundown of how she did for the day. I am sure the nurses are tired of my calling, but they don't let on if they are.

I really did get lucky with who is taking care of my little girl.

Speaking of little girls. My, not so little anymore, Manda. Something has been going on with that girl, and I am determined to get to the bottom of it. I tried to be sly with it at first. I asked Ken. He said that there was a time where she needed to talk to him, and something had come up. The amount of guilt radiating off him when he realized he never went back to ask her what was wrong was strong.

He went out right then and there and tried to talk to her. She played it off like it wasn't a big deal, but he still took her out for lunch to have some time together and say sorry. He is always trying to do special things for the kids like that. I know Manda appreciated the gesture, but she still hasn't said what's going on.

Well, today, that's going to change. Watching her for the past week, give or take a few days, I have noticed something that I had to do a double-take on.

"Hey, Manda," I say as I walk up to her at the kitchen counter. "Can you come with me? I saw something that I wanted to get your opinion on for Ken's birthday."

She smiles brightly at me, and I instantly feel like a jackass. I do everything in my power not to lie to these kids. To always be forward with them. After the things they have gone through, they deserve it. I tell myself it's fine in this case because I didn't want to bring attention to her. I needed her to come willingly and not try to come up with an excuse before I can even ask.

We start walking towards the office, and she starts rattling off ideas for the party. I can tell that she is excited to get to celebrate and be a part of the planning. I will have to make at least a few of the ideas she's rattling off a reality if she doesn't shut down completely in the next twenty minutes.

Once we are in my office, I shut the door, and we have a seat on the couch that I have in here.

"And then I thought that maybe we could get him a blueberry cake because he told me how much he loves blueberries. He said that he didn't get to have them a lot when he was growing up, so now that he can get them whenever he wants, he does. I think he would really like that. Right?"

"You're right, sweetheart. He definitely would. Hey, listen. While I love all the ideas, especially the cake, there is something that I need to talk to you about."

"You. I thought. But. Do you not want to talk to me about the party?"

"I do, sweetie, I promise, but there is something else. I know that I was gone a lot with Kelsey, and I am sorry. I should have been here for you as well."

"It's okay, Momma El. I know how much Kelsey needs you right now. I have Poppa Ken, Funcle Theo, Dizz. Plus, I have all my siblings. I wasn't alone."

"I know you weren't alone. But I still should have been here. If I had been, I would have been able to see the signs sooner." At this, her eyes almost pop out of her head. She looks down and starts fidgeting with her fingers. "sweetie, look at me." Her head raises, and her eyes are red-rimmed. "You say that you have everyone here, but I can see it. More and more, you are distancing yourself from them. You are spending all your time with the little ones, and if any of the guys come around, you go out of your way to get away from them."

I grab her hands, and I pull her closer to me. I grip her hands tightly and look her in the eyes. "I need you to tell me right now, I promise, nothing that you say will get *you* in trouble, okay? Have any of the men done something to you? Anything that you are not completely comfortable with?"

She looks away from me and just shakes her head, but I can see the tears that have escaped her eyes.

"sweetie, I promise. Nothing you say will be held against you. You know that anything that someone has done to you is not your fault. You can trust me to take care of you, but to do so, I need you to tell me."

I know that I shouldn't push, but I know that something happened. If one of my guys did something to her, I will cut his dick off and make him eat it before I feed him to the pigs while he is still alive. The others won't get to touch him. I can feel my momma bear starting to rage beneath my skin.

"I…They…None of the guys here have done anything to me. I love them all. I love it here."

"Okay. So how come you are pulling away?"

"I'm scared."

"Of them? If someone is scaring you, you have to let me know. I can handle it. You feeling safe is number one."

"It's not that. I am afraid of what will happen to…."

"You?"

She just shakes her head. She lets out a shaky breath and opens and closes her mouth. I know that she is trying to tell me. I am not going to push her any harder. She wants to tell me, I can see it. So I am going to let her do so on her own time.

"I….I'm late."

It takes about two point five seconds to register what she means before I am standing up and running to the supply closet. While not something I have ever thought to need in abundance, I am prepared. We take teenage girls in, and unfortunately, this is a risk that they are faced with.

I walk back out to her and sit down. She is crying into her hands. Her sobs making her body shake.

"Sweetheart, look at me. It's okay. Stop crying. I need you to take this into the bathroom that's attached and take this test." I hand over the pregnancy test, her hand barely able to grip it. "You just take the cap off, hold it down, and pee on it for a few seconds. Or, if you would like, you can pee into one of the mouthwash cups and stick it in for a few seconds."

"I can't. I can't do this. What happens if it says yes. I don't want to do it. Please don't make me."

"Hey. Pee in the cup, and I'll do it for you, okay. But this is something that we need to know. If you are pregnant, we have to get you the care that you need to keep you and the baby healthy."

"But I don't want this baby! I don't want to be reminded of him!"

"Hey, hey, hey," I pull her into an embrace. "If that's what you want, that's what we will look into. I won't tell you no. But, it all starts with confirming that you are pregnant, okay?"

She nods and gets up, and goes to the bathroom. About a minute later, she comes back and sits down. I walk into the bathroom, and there on the counter is a little cup that will help me determine how much more her life will change.

Sticking the test in the cup, I count to three and pull it out. I go to cap it and wait two minutes, but there is no need. The test lights up like a Christmas tree with the double lines telling me that my sweet girl is definitely pregnant.

I walk back out of the bathroom, and my face must say it all as she bursts into tears. She runs to me and smashes into me, wrapping her arms around me, and that's when I feel it.

"What am I going to do, Momma El? I don't want his baby."

"I know. I know. Hey," I pull her back and turn her face to mine, "who is he?"

She shakes her head, "I don't know. He came into my room one night. His voice sounded familiar, like one of their friends. I tried to scream, but he was so much stronger than me. He was able to stop me from screaming, and still…still…."

"You don't have to say, honey."

She nods and continues, "I told my foster parents what happened. That I thought it was one of their friends. They called me a liar. They wouldn't call the cops. Later the next day, the social worker was taking me and bringing me to you because I'm *a problem.*"

Doing the math in my head would mean that she is at least five or six months pregnant. It may have been the next day for her, but I know that that isn't how fast the system works. I pull myself back and really look at her. She is wearing a black baggy sweater. She always wears it. I never thought anything of it. I thought it was more of a security blanket.

"I know I am going to ask a lot right now, but…I need you to please lift your sweater."

With trembling hands, she does as I ask, and right there in front of me is the cutest baby bump I have ever seen. It also tells me that no matter what, this baby will have to be born. Once born, we can look into whatever she wants to do. Keep it or put it up for adoption. The choice is hers.

"Okay. Looking at your size and doing the math in my head, you're probably five months at the bare minimum and almost seven months at the maximum. We will need to take you to the doctor to find out for sure."

I smile and bring her in for a hug again. I need her to know that I am here for her and I support her.

"Is this why you were shying away from the men?"

"Yes. I didn't want them to see."

"Sweetie, I love all of them, so much but they're dumb as rocks. They wouldn't have noticed."

This gets a smile out of her, and I start to go over everything that now has to be done. The first thing, tell my husband. He needs to get to the boys at her former foster house and fast.

"Alright, here's what we're going to do. You need to go upstairs and lay down. Relax, get off your feet and calm down. I am going to talk to Poppa Ken. I see your eyes bugging out, and they don't need to be. This. Is. Not. Your. Fault. He will not be mad at you. You are not in trouble, okay? But he needs to know as well , okay?"

She shakes her head up and down and heads out of the office. "Hey, I love you. We'll get through this together."

"I know, Momma El. I love you too."

And with that, she shuts the door.

"MOTHER FUCKER!" Ken screams, pulling his fist out of the drywall. Crumbs of the wall are falling to his feet. He hits the wall again, and another hole the size of Texas appears.

"Ken, you need to calm down."

"I AM CALM." As he continues to destroy my bedroom wall.

"Ken. Really? Look, I am just as pissed off as you. I want to kill the family she was with. They did nothing to help her. We need to get her the care she needs for this baby. We need to help her get through the birth and whatever it is that she wants to do after the fact. She didn't tell us because she was terrified we would blame her. We would kick her out. Of what you're doing right now."

That gets him to stop immediately. He looks at all the holes he's punched and then down to his hand. His knuckles are swollen and bleeding. His chest is rising and falling, and I don't miss the tears streaming down his face.

"Did we fail her?" He croaked, voice full of unshed emotion.

"How?"

"Because we didn't know. We didn't see it. How could we have not seen it?"

"Baby, I know how you feel, and I get it. But, this isn't something that we could have seen. And the girl has had an appetite since she got here. While she is far along, she's slight. So she's hiding it and eating. She wasn't throwing up, and if she was, she hid that too. What we need to do right now is let her know that it's okay and that we are here for her. That no matter what, she is a part of this family."

"You're right."

He pulls my head to his and kisses my forehead. "I am going to go talk to her."

"Ken…"

"El, please. I need to do this. Trust me."

"Without question. Just….nevermind. Go. Do what you need to do."

And with that, my husband leaves. I glance around the room again and think of how this is going to get fixed. Right at that moment, there is a knock, and Theo walks in.

"Hey, I need to talk to Judge about what the fuck happened in here?"

"Your boyfriend."

"Why did he-?"

"He can talk to you about it later," I cut him off, "can you see if we have what is needed to fix this? I need to go get dinner ready."

"You got it, El."

We may tease him a lot, but even I wouldn't be able to do this thing called life without Theo.

TWENTY-THREE

JUDGE

-Present-

Fifty, holy fuck, I am *not* fifty fucking years old, am I?

I look around the long table of everyone that I count as important in my life, less one person. I saw the sadness in Elvira's eyes when R.J. said that he wouldn't be able to make it. Neither of us has seen him in a few years. But he never forgets a birthday or our anniversary; I will give that boy that much. I miss him as much as his mama does, but I know he is still fighting whatever demons are keeping him away from home.

I see to the right of me, Manda, still in oversized shirts because she thinks the rest of the boys don't know, and they don't just yet, but they need to know. We are going to try and make it right for her in any way we can. The look of terror in her eyes when I walked into the room to talk to her broke something in me. Something deep that I didn't even know was there. I have had kids fear me when they first get here, but this was something new, something I didn't like and sure as shit did not want to see in her eyes again.

"Manda, can you talk to me?" I asked, knocking on the girls' room. I don't dare just let myself in there. That is their safe place and will always be their safe space.

"Come in, Poppa." She says softly. I almost missed it.

Opening the door seeing her huddled under the blankets in the far back corner of her bunk. She looked like a cornered dog. I wasn't sure if she was going to attack or try to run. I wheeled the desk chair to the middle of the room, giving her space but trying to let her know that I am here.

"Momma El told me what's going on. I wanted to see how you were feeling." I tried to keep my emotions tamed and my voice even, no sense scaring her more than she already is.

"I'm scared, Poppa. Please don't send me away! It was all an accident! I never wanted this! Honest-." I stop her with a soft tilt of my head and leaning forward, my elbows resting on my knees.

"I, we, *were never going to send you away. As far as we are concerned, you are our little girl, and you never turn away family when they are in need. We are here for you. I am here for you whatever you need. I will do everything in my power to take care of you and that little one should you choose. We are playing by new rules and a new game plan, baby girl. You are the boss, and we will do what you need." She starts to visibly relax the more I talk to her. Her knees come down, and she starts to inch forward.*

"I don't know what I want, Poppa. I don't want to remember him or what he did. But I have been feeling the baby move, I think, I'm not sure. Google said it was the baby. After talking to Momma El and feeling those things, it makes me want to hold it close and not let anything bad happen. But I am not ready to be a momma!" She burst into tears and rushes me, causing the chair to roll back slightly on impact.

"You just worry about the Doctors in a few days. From there, we will all sit and make a plan. We will protect you and that baby." I rub her back, holding her close, and I feel the bump El mentioned.

Thinking back to that conversation, it's nice to see a genuine smile on Manda's face, like she feels okay, that we lifted a weight. I am not sure how I kept repeating the same thing over and over again, in different wording. But, that could be all she needed, to know she did have a family to fall back on and that she was not all alone.

El' reported it to her social worker, who said she would be in touch with that former family, but what she doesn't know is that we plan to make that follow-up visit for her.

"Make a wish, Poppa!" Marley calls out from her spot on Cowboy's knee.

I smile at her, looking at this blue and purple monstrosity in front of me with an ungodly amount of candles. I know that El and the girls made it for me more than anyone. Manda picked the flavor while Ellie, Kathy-Rae, and Karma did the baking. I know Miss Marley and Karley were responsible for the decoration. I have never felt more love than I do right now.

"Should I say my wish out loud to Marley?"

"NOO POPPAS! That means it won't come the truth!" She says back to me. I can see all the grownups turning away, trying to hide the smiles.

"Well, alright then, boss lady, here I go!" I take a deep breath in getting ready to blow when Theo has to pipe up.

"Fifty bucks says he has enough hot air in him to blow them all out in one shot! Any takers?"

Elvira, the love of my life always having my back, smokes him good upside the head for me. "The only one full of hot air in here is you. Shut up!"

As I release my breath, blowing out the candles, I hear Miss Marley giving her Momma heck for using her hands and not her words, as well as not playing nice with Funkle Fee-Oh. God, that kid kills me.

We were getting ready to go out to the bar. The party all day had been with the whole family, but now, the kids were in bed, and it was time for the adults to have fun. One of my favorite things was to get a few drinks in El. She didn't do it very often, but when she did, I was always in for a wild night.

I had just grabbed my keys and was about to call for my wife when I heard the ear-piercing scream.

"MOM!"

Elviria appeared out of nowhere and was rushing up the stairs. Myself, Theo, and probably every other brother by the stampeding sound behind me followed her. I had just gotten to the top of the stairs when I heard El.

"Ken, get in here now."

El was trying to calm Manda down but what was more concerning was the blood between her legs. I didn't think twice. I scooped Manda up and walked her out of her room and down the stairs. We hadn't told the guys yet that she's pregnant, but I'm sure they could figure it out given she's crying in pain, clutching her bulging stomach, and the blood.

"What the hell?"

"Not now. We need to get her to the hospital."

Like deja vu, I hop in the backseat with her on my lap and El in the driver's seat. We peel out of the drive to get our girl to the hospital. It isn't long before I hear the roar of motorcycle engines surrounding the car. I look up, and sure enough, same as always, Theo is on my right and Sever on my left.

Manda is crying, and I am doing everything I can to soothe her, but I know it isn't working.

"I know, baby, I know. We're almost there." El tells her from the front seat.

"It hurts so much. What's happening? Ahhh."

Her screams and cries gut me. I would give anything to take the pain away. I can feel my leg getting wetter. I look down, and I see more blood. Looking at her, she is becoming paler by the second. She looks down, and I tilt her head back up.

"Look at me. Keep your eyes on me. We're almost there. We're going to get you to the Doctor. You will be okay. I need you to try and calm down just a bit, breathe. Come on, breathe with me—deep breath in, deep breath out. You're doing good. Keep going."

My hand was holding her head up so she wouldn't see the blood below. I could feel her heart pounding on my forearm. As she breathed, it started to slow a fraction. It was better than nothing.

"Good. Good. We're…" My words were cut off by El slamming on the breaks. One of the guys rode ahead and had the nurses out in the bay waiting for us. The door is yanked open, and the nurses reach in and take her from my arms. I instinctively hold on tighter.

"Sir, let her go."

As soon as I let her go, she is taken through the double doors with El running in after them. I turn to see the guys walking up. I toss the car keys that El left in the ignition as I shout for them to park it. I don't know if anyone even caught the damn things. I don't care. I just want to know if my kid is Okay.

Fucking deja vu.

I see El sitting outside of the Emergency Room doors. Her head in her hands. I sit down right next to her and put my arm around her, bringing her close to me.

"She needs to be okay, Ken. I know she isn't sure about the baby, but I don't think she will be okay if that baby dies."

"I think she wants the baby. When we spoke, it came across that way at least."

"I just, I need her to be okay."

"She will, baby, she will." I kiss her head and turn my head towards the doors. Storm and Cowboy are leading the pack. "El, I'm going to fill the guys in. I'll be right back." She just nods, and I get up and walk towards them.

I see their eyes widen at the sight of me. Looking down, I see that I am covered in a lot more blood than I realized.

"Dad, what the fuck is going on?"

"This is why you punched holes in your walls?"

J.J. and Theo ask at the same time. I just sigh and fill them in on everything I learned only a short few weeks ago.

We had been sitting there for a few hours, no real updates other than the blood the boys donated for Manda was accepted after the initial testing. They pulled Theo into a room an hour after that, and he hasn't been back since. I am getting worried.

"Think they are telling him he has ball cancer or something?" Butcher leans over and whispers to me, and I use the term whisper very lightly with this man.

"Naw, it's probably tittie cancer." Willie piped up across the way. See, the man can't whisper.

"I think they are going to tell him that his personality is fatal and he needs a transplant." Cowboy chips in.

"Personality? How about his whole fucking brain!" Dizz had to be a part of anything Cowboy is.

"Naw, you are all wrong; he is being told that he took too much up the ass, and he now needs a whole new asshole," Sever says, not even looking up from his phone.

"What the fuck is wrong with you all? Shut the fuck up!" Elvira is red in the face; she stands up and tries to give them all an admonishing glare. "Plus, he is probably just fucking the nurse."

All the guys start laughing and agreeing with her, and then the doors burst open with both Theo and the doctor. Theo looks like he has been put through the wringer, and it didn't go his way. He's pale, his eyes red-rimmed, and he just falls into me. His body is shaking. I am not sure from shock or sobs. I look to El to go talk to the doctor while I deal with him.

"I was right, and it's probably his balls. No man cries like that over nothing." Butcher 'whispers' again as I lead Theo outside to talk.

"Buddy, hey. You gotta talk to me. You are really starting to freak me out. When the fuck do you cry? I am the emotional one, not you." I am trying to get him to look at me.

When we get outside, he starts pacing back and forth, this look of complete broken determination on it. I have never seen him this rattled in at least forty years, not since he first came to the Foster home. I am worried; I cannot take any more bad news.

"Theo? Dude!" I snap that finally gets his attention.

"She's mine." he rasps out. He sounds like he had been smoking nothing but menthols and gargling with glass for the past three hours.

"What do you mean?"

"Manda, Amanda Euguniea Flemming is my daughter." His face starts to crack again, like saying it out loud made it even more real.

"Okay, you need to rewind here and start from the beginning. Because I am so far behind the eight balls on this one." My mind is racing; Theo, a dad?

"Manda needed blood, but because her mom died and no father was listed, they have this new thing where they take the kids' blood and put it up for familial matches every so often. So when they ran our blood to see if it was a match, they flagged mine as being a close match. They reran it, and she is my little girl. I have a little girl who had a worse life than we ever did. I couldn't save her." He is breaking down, and I pull him into me. Trying to hold the pieces of this broken man together.

Then his words hit me, 'he couldn't save her.'

TWENTY-FOUR

JUDGE

-Past-

"AHHHHHHHHH!"

"Keep screaming, you son of a bitch. It's music to my ears." Bigfoot tells the piece of shit we have strapped to a chair we have in the root cellar. He stabs a wine corkscrew through his left hand and twists.

"Oh, that's disgusting." Theo mumbles. The man will do whatever he needs to do to get the job done, but a corkscrew through the hand is disgusting—such a damn baby.

"That's nothing. Is it my turn?" Butcher jumps up and down on his toes. The excitement radiating off him is almost contagious. He has been dying to get his hands on this man since Anderson gave us the files. It took a lot of us talking him down so he wouldn't go off and grab him.

His anger was almost uncontrollable. I could tell that the issue was personal for him, but he wasn't ready to share why. However, I couldn't risk him going out before we were ready and getting sent to prison on a murder charge. So, I brought out the big guns. In not so many words, I got his wife, Abilene, to tell him if he doesn't listen to me, she won't do that thing he likes.

Apparently, he likes it a whole fucking lot because that put him in his place in an instant. I am kind of afraid to know what 'it' is.

"Soon. We all get a turn."

"But why do I have to go last!" He whines like a damn child.

"Dude, are you asking a serious question right now or what?" Sever asks him. When Butcher turns and growls at him, the fucker actually jumps back. I smile and shake my head. Sever was one of the most brutal men that were in this club. The fact that he was afraid of Butcher, I found hilarious. I gave him shit for it once, and during his pout about not being afraid of him, Butcher scared the shit out of him, *literally,* so now he never denies the fear he feels for the man.

"Why are you doing this to me? Why? I haven't done anything!" He cries out. He pretends like he doesn't know why we took him. I can see it in his eyes, though. He knows. He knows exactly what he has gotten away with and what he thinks he can convince us he isn't guilty of. Like he doesn't know that we know how much of a fucking disgusting monster he is. Thinking of all the boys that he has ruined over the years, I feel my anger start to morph into something bigger than I can handle. And I only know of a handful. This sick fuck has so many other bodies under his belt that I want to kill him for. I don't need to know the exact number. He became a monster the minute he went from zero to one.

"You know why," I say, "but in case you need reminding." I pull out the photos of all his victims that we know of and place them in front of him. His eyes give away his recognition while he speaks more lies.

"Nothing that they say is true. They were all conspiring against me. I sentenced one to juvy."

"I'm gonna stop you right there, Mr. I've never been a judge before in my life. Try again."

"Please. You want money. I can pay you."

"You think we want money? No. I don't want your disgusting, child rapist dollar bills. I want your dick shoved down your throat, your blood coating this floor, and my man's pigs' bellies full. I want your death."

The smell of piss fills the air, and he starts crying harder. That's when Sever walks right up to him and does what gave him his namesake, severs his hand right off his body.

"What the fuck! Ahhhhhhhh. Why would you do that? I DID NOTHING WRONG."

"You touched multiple little boys with those disgusting hands. Should you be so lucky to get out of here," Sever pauses and then leans down and looks him directly in the eyes, "which you won't. You won't need this one either." He says as he slices the other hand from his body. Blood is everywhere, and Sever stands up and wipes his blades off on his pants. Chuckling as he turns around.

"It wasn't my fault. They tempted me. They wanted it. They liked it. They came. I did nothing wrong! Please." He sobs.

Sever turns back around so quickly and slams his blade through his shoulder. Which only makes Marty scream even more.

"Don't you dare blame them for your sick, perverted ways. No ten-year-old child would look at you and ask for it. I can't wait to watch you drain your blood completely. Looking a little pale already." Smacking him on the cheek. Sever straightens and walks back towards myself and Butcher.

"Nice. High five." Butcher says with the enthusiasm of a child who just won a game with their team. Sever looks at him with a terrified expression but gives him the high five that Butcher wanted. I'm sure he only did it in fear of Butcher killing him.

Willie has stepped up and cauterized his stubs with a heated-up hatchet head. Not completely, but just enough that he doesn't fully bleed out. I don't understand how he hasn't passed out from the pain, but it's more fun for us. The more this hurts, the better. The fucker deserves every ounce of pain he's getting.

He keeps screaming, and now I am getting bored. I didn't want to keep going with this back and forth of his bullshit of 'I didn't do it.' I glance over at Butcher, and his hands are twitching. I am not going to be able to keep him back much longer.

"You may have gotten everyone to side with you, you disgusting piece of shit, but we know the truth. Part of that truth is that this kid, right here, killed himself because you took what doesn't belong to you. You may have had those cops, judges, juries in your pocket, but you don't have me."

"Who are you?" He says, barely in a whisper. He isn't going to last much longer with all the blood he's lost. I am sure that's just going to piss Butcher off more because his playtime will be cut short.

"I'm the real Judge, and he," I point to Butcher, "is your executioner." I turn around and look Butcher dead in the eye. "Have at him."

He lets out a maniacal laugh that is soon drowned out by the screams of Murray Martin, *former* child rapist. The sweet sounds of justice are soon gone as I walk out of the cellar and shut the door.

I needed to let him know I did it. He deserved to know that his son got the justice he needed and was denied all those years ago. No kid should have to live through that, and no person should have that done to them. But to add the fact that the law was against the victim instead of with them made me sick. It also solidified my resolve that we were doing the right thing, the brothers and I, we were going to help those the law couldn't, or just plain refused to.

Don't let it lead back to you or me.

Those words played in my head, and I knew I needed to make this quick and simple. So under cover of night, I pull my bike up on the half-circle drive in front of Anderson's house. It takes no time at all for him to come out his front door. As soon as he makes eye contact with me, I nod my head. Letting him know the job is done.

He knew what he asked of us, and he knew that we would deliver. While staying with him and comforting him like a friend is something that I should do, it's something that I can't do. This mutual understanding is going to grow, but for this to work, appearances mean something. Even when it's dark out, you never know where someone else's eyes are. For now, this unspoken word between us is all we can have.

I see the intake of breath and the slight step back he takes before I kick my bike into gear and head home. It feels like no time at all until I am stripping down to crawl into bed with my Sweet Elvira. Coming home to her after cleansing the world of another evil person makes it all that much better.

"Did you do good, baby?" She sleepily asks, rolling over to face me.

"You know it. I will always do good if it means making life better for you and the kids." I lower my body into the bed, pulling her up close. "The kids okay for you tonight?"

"J.J. tried to pull the attitude that he was grown enough for a bike like you and Theo. But Yaya smacked him down right quick. You would think I missed the days when I had to discipline my own children, but really… I love this help." She sighs, pressing soft kisses to my chest.

She moves over to my nipple and sucks it into her mouth. Something that I never thought I would like now drives me wild. I let out a slight moan, and she continues her torture. Her hand travels down the length of my stomach and wraps onto my stiffening cock. It gets hard almost instantly.

She grips my cock tight in an almost painful grip. She sits up and uses her other hand to push me down onto my back.

"Baby, fuck, what are you doing?" I gasp, watching her start to work me over good, the way I like.

"Rewarding you for doing such a good job today."

"Ungh fuck, ah, keep going. Grip me harder. Yes, just like that."

"Yeah, baby, you like my hand wrapped around your cock?"

I nod my head yes. She keeps moving up and down. Adjusting her grip while twisting her hand around the head. It feels so damn good. If she keeps this up, I know I won't last long.

"You know what else you like wrapped around your cock?"

Before I can even respond, her mouth is wrapped around me, and she is sucking me back. The angle allows her to take the whole thing in her mouth, and once her nose hits my pubes, she swallows, and I jerk up.

"Fuck! Baby, I'm going to come if you keep that up. Shit."

She hums, and the vibrations are killing me. She pulls back and continues to move up and down my cock. This goes on for a few moments before she pops off me, loud pop sound included, and looks up at me. "Stand up, baby. Get to the end of the bed."

"Oh, you the boss now?"

She doesn't respond. She lifts a brow at me, and I know that if I want to come, I'm going to do exactly what she says. I stand at the end of the bed, and she lays down on her back, bringing her head to the edge, slightly hanging off the bed.

"Fuck my face, baby."

"Oh, fuck yes."

I stick my cock between her lips and push in. She moans, and I go all the way to the back of her throat. It feels so fucking good. So incredibly wet and warm.

I keep a slow momentum going, enjoying the feeling of her wrapped around me. When I pull back, she adjusts to pop off again.

"I said fuck my face, Ken. Stop with this, whatever this is, and fuck. My. Face."

She positions herself again, and I do what she says. I start to piston into her mouth. My balls hitting the top of her head, and her moans getting louder with each thrust. I lean forward and tweak her nipples with my hands, tugging on them hard. Her hand travels down, and she starts circling her clit.

Spit is coming out the sides of her mouth and that, along with her touching herself, is one of the sexiest things I have ever seen.

"Fuck baby. Yeah. Oh. Take that fucking cock. You like that?"

She moans in response, and I push myself harder. She gags occasionally but not enough to warrant me stopping. I can tell she is close as her hand moves faster, and her moans are getting louder. Mouth full of cock be damned. The sounds escaping her are pure heaven to my ears.

"I'm gonna come, baby. Are you ready? Fuck."

I explode down her throat, and she swallows all of it. Once I am down, she sucks on me hard, and it makes my body arch forward from the sensitivity. I force myself out of her mouth, and she sits herself up. Her smirk says it all.

"I love you, baby."

"I love you too. Now get over here and eat me out. I'm not done yet."

"Yes, ma'am."

I continued to work her all night long until she was begging me to stop. I need to make sure I do these 'good deeds' more often if I get in return.

TWENTY-FIVE

ELVIRA

-Present-

I watched as Ken followed Theo out of the hospital. He was off to deal with his boyfriend's meltdown while I was here to talk to the doctor about Manda. This is why we are the team that we are. Words don't need to be said, and we know what is expected of the other.

"The family of Amanda Euguniea Flemming?" The well-dressed man called out. If not for the white coat, you would assume he was a businessman, not a doctor.

"We're all here," I said, taking tentative steps towards him.

I could see judgment pass over his face seeing the large group of men in leather and tattoos scattered among the waiting area. I didn't have time for his stereotypical bull shit. I needed to know what the fuck was going on with my kids and, well, her kid.

"Hmm," was all he got out before looking down at his chart again. Not even sparing me a second glance.

"Look here, you stuffed suit, that is my fucking kid in there. So can you push aside your preconceived notions of what we look like and tell me what the fuck is going on and if they are Okay!" I snapped. I felt an arm come around my waist, holding me back. I knew from the size it was Willie. The teddy bear that he was knew I would kill the doctor for assuming the worst about them, they are my family, and I will fight to the death for them all.

"You need to calm down. As it states here, she is a ward of the state, and you are her primary caregivers. That is-." He stares at me with condescension in his voice and mannerisms.

"No, I am not her caregiver. I am her Momma, and that is my little girl and my grandbaby. These are her uncles and brothers, so you better start talking, or I am going up the official food chain." I feel Willie adjust his grip, and tensing knowing I am about to literally jump down this fuckers throat. "This here is the Nameless Order MC, and we have done charity runs for this hospital that has created donations worth more than your worthless life. So, what is going on with my kid?"

His eyes shift and look at Willies Cut, then to J.J., who I felt come up alongside us during this whole thing. I wish Ken and Theo would hurry up and get their big boy panties on and come back and help me. The Prez and VP would add more ammo to this fire.

"Alright then. Amanda had what is called Placental Abruption. Where the Placenta completely detached from the uterine wall, which caused a hemorrhage as well as put the baby into distress. We had to perform an emergency c-section. There is no prior information on the pregnancy, so I am assuming that-."

"We didn't know. She hid it from us. We had a call with our caseworker as well as the doctor for appointments." I explained before he could get smart with me again.

"Calm yourself, Missus; this man knows the information you seek," Willie whispers in my ear. That earned him an elbow to the gut from me, which does nothing to him as the man is a damn beast.

"Right, well, from his size, we assumed he was about 25 to 28 weeks, but we have determined he is 31 weeks gestation and in our Neonatal Intensive Care Unit for the time being. The Neonatologist will give you all the information you need in regards to him." She had a little boy. Good Lord, he better be mighty like his momma. "As for Amanda, she lost a lot of blood. The units that you and your… family… donated were greatly appreciated as we didn't have to dip into the hospital's already depleted supply." I saw Cowboy take a threatening step forward but get pulled back. This guy really thought he was better than us. He did have a death wish. "She will be Okay, but we have to watch her very closely for the next little while. While she is stable now, there is no saying what the next 24 hours hold." With that, he walked away, not waiting to see if we had any questions.

I looked around for Ken or Theo to see if they were back from whatever crawled up Theo's ass. Nothing, I needed someone to take care of this fucker and show him that he is no better than us, that he is nothing without us 'little people.' That's when I look over and see Sever just as upset as me.

"Sever, call Mafia Man. I want this guy ruined." I whisper as I pass him. I needed to talk to my man. "J.J. Please call home and check on the littles. Dizz, go see if you can get information about the baby from the NICU. Willie, I need you to try and find out anything and everything you can about Manda and where she is. Bigfoot, Zombie, Turd, and Gears...... Keep doing what you are doing." They all look at me like I have grown three heads. Here I am, a woman barking orders at them. I knew that is not the way things work in the MC, but here in this hospital, when it involves the kids and their wellbeing, I am the MC Queen. "Don't look at me like that. Get your rears in gear, shit heads. We have work to do."

I walked out of the waiting area to look for my man and his man. It didn't take long to find them, Theo was pacing, and Ken was just looking at him in stunned silence. What the hell is going on here?

"I couldn't save her" Was all I heard Theo say as I walked up.

"Couldn't save who?" I asked, causing both men to jump and look in my direction.

Theos eyes were bloodshot, his face stained with tears, and his hands were shaking worse than a tweaker. I looked at Ken, who seemed to have the world placed back on his shoulders. I don't know what has happened here, but I need to know now.

"What is going on, guys? Theo, darling, come here." I say, walking to him, pulling his oversized frame down to me, hugging him close, feeling the sobs start from his body. He was mumbling things into my shoulder that I couldn't make out, I looked over to Ken for some clarification, but he was still looking at Theo with a glazed look on his face. "Okay, ladies, snap out of it and spill the beans."

"Manda was Theos," Ken says softly. My eyes flew to him, not completely sure if I heard the words he said completely accurate.

"I'm sorry. What did you just say?"

"Manda was Theo's daughter." Was? Why is he saying was? But, what the fuck?

"Hold on. Why are you? Do you not know?"

Theo's head pops up, and the tears are still falling. This man is so heartbroken, and it is killing me. Not only to find out you have a kid, which I am still trying to process, but not knowing if she is alive.

"Theo, Manda is alive. She lost a lot of blood, but they were able to save her."

He falls to the ground, and his knees hit hard. It doesn't phase him, though, as he just sobs uncontrollably. Ken has placed himself right next to Theo and wrapped his arms around him. The bond that they share, it's unbelievable at times. It's so strong and so intense. It makes moments like this a little better knowing you have someone who understands you so completely.

"The baby," Theo says, looking back up at me. "How is the baby? Did the baby make it?"

"Yes, he made it. He's going to be in the NICU for a while, but he is okay. Dizz is working on getting more information about how he is doing now."

"He? I have a grandson?"

I walked over to him and knelt down on the ground with him. I grabbed his face in my hands and wiped his tears with my thumbs. I may not love him the way I love Ken but, I love this man too.

"You have a grandson, and you have a daughter. Both are okay. Both are upstairs. So what do you say that we all get inside and you go see them?"

"I...what am I supposed to say to her? Look at how she lived. She shouldn't be having some fucking rapists kid! This isn't right, this...."

"Isn't your fault. I mean this with love, Theo but, you're a whore. My guess is a one-night stand got pregnant and didn't know how to find you. Because I know you, had she found you, you would have been there for Manda. You would have been in her life. There's no way of knowing the truth at this moment, but that's also what you tell Manda. The truth. She deserves that."

"What if she doesn't want me in her life now? What if because I wasn't a dad to her all this time, she won't want me to be now?"

"You can't expect her to call you dad the second you tell her. It's okay if she doesn't accept it right away. But she will. The good thing is she already knows you. She already loves you. You've been her Funcle Theo since she's gotten here. I think that she will come to terms with you being her dad. But, you have to respect her, and the time it takes for her to do so."

Theo just nods in agreement, and Ken and I help him up. We walk back into the waiting room and see the guys that I didn't give a task to. Turd stands up and makes his way over to us.

"Willie called. He said that we could go up to the maternity ward, but only two at a time can see her. She's in room 223. He is sitting outside her room. No one has gone in to see her yet. We figured that was something that you would want to do first. Dizz hasn't gotten back from the NICU yet."

"Thanks, Turd. I'll keep you all updated." Ken tells him.

The three of us make our way to the elevator to get to the maternity ward. Fuck them if they think the three of us aren't going in together. Once we are on the floor, it doesn't take long to find her room as it is the only one with a mammoth of a man sitting outside the door.

“El, you and Theo go first. Something tells me that they are both going to need you once this bomb is dropped.” Ken kisses my forehead and hugs Theo once more. I look to Theo, “you ready?”

“Honestly, no, but I’m not turning back.”

We walk in, Manda asleep in the bed, looking frail and so tiny. My - Theo’s - poor little girl. I still couldn’t believe that he was her father. The fact that he didn’t know about her, my heart hurts for him.

I look at him, and I can tell that he is looking at her in a completely new light. He is trying to see his features on her face. Or trying to remember the woman that she looks like. However, I don’t know if he would be able to. Manda is sixteen years old; what I would give for him to remember her mother, though. To get these unanswered questions answered.

“Theo, are you okay?”

“Just looking at her now, and I am trying to figure out where I met her momma. Trying to remember who it could have been. I look at her, and I don’t see anyone familiar. I don’t see myself. This is so fucked, El. How could I not recognize my own daughter?”

“Who is your daughter?”

We both turn and look at Manda. She is awake, but she is groggy. I can see the pain on her face as she tries to adjust herself in the bed.

“Hey, sweetie. Here, let me help you.”

“Everything hurts, Momma,” she brings her hand to her stomach, and her eyes get bigger, “what? Where? Where’s the baby? What happened?”

She is starting to panic, and I need to get her calmed down. I can’t bask in the glow I feel from her calling me momma. Right now, she needs everything I have. I notice that Theo has come to her other side. Looking at her but not knowing what to do.

“Sweetie, it’s okay. Your son is safe. He’s in the NICU. He was born a little early, but he’s okay. Dizz is up there with him now. Once he has an update, he will give me a call, and I’ll let you know, okay? You had to have an emergency c-section. You had something called placental abruption. That’s what caused the bleeding. You lost a lot of blood and.”

I swallowed. I wasn’t sure how to continue with the news that she needed to be given. This was going to change her life completely. I looked to Theo, and he just nodded to me.

“Manda,” he started. She looked over to him, and he grabbed her hand before he continued. “You lost a lot of blood, and so we all donated in the hopes of being a match for your blood type. When they tested mine, it was a match, but there was something else.”

“Okay. What was it? You guys are scaring me.”

“I’m not trying to, I swear. This is just; it’s hard for me to get out. Okay. I’m. Ugh. Fuck.”

I want to give him a look. I want to say something about language, but this isn’t the time. He needs to get this out on his own, and I can’t imagine how hard it is. He gets a pass—this time.

"Okay. I'm just gonna go for it. I am sorry I don't have a better way to do this. When they tested my blood, they found a familial match."

"I don't know what that means," Manda says. Looking more confused than worried, but the worry was still evident on her face.

"It means that I'm your dad."

Manda jerked her hand back and brought both of them to her mouth. She started crying instantly and shaking her head back and forth. Theo looked completely broken, and I could tell that he wanted to comfort her but didn't know-how. I wanted him to have this, but she needed someone, and right now, I thought that the safe bet would be me. No matter how much I wanted it to be between them.

I stand and sit on the bed next to her and wrap my arms around her. She tilts towards me, and I wish I could take the pain away. All the emotional and physical pain that she shouldn't have to go through.

"I know, sweetie. I know this is a lot to take in. We just wanted you to know. We felt that you needed to know."

"Manda. The last thing I wanted to do was upset you. I understand if you don't want me here."

"No. No. Please don't leave. It's a lot to take in, and I have so many questions but, I just, please don't leave."

"Okay. I can stay with you."

Manda just looks over at him and gives her hand back to him. It's a moment that I feel lucky to be a part of, but I also feel that I shouldn't.

"Hey," They both turn to me, and I see it. For the first time ever, I can see traits from Theo in Manda's face. "Wow. I never noticed before, but Manda, your eyes are the exact same color as Theo's. You both have those ice blue eyes with dark blue rings."

I am captivated by them. They both turn towards each other, and once they see what I see, they both break down. Manda throws her arms around him, and he stands to bring himself closer. This moment isn't something that I should be a part of. I silently make my way out of the room to find Ken and Willie sitting and waiting.

"How are they?"

"It's going to take a little bit of time but, I think they are going to be okay."

"I'm going to let everyone know the little lady is alright and give ya a moment," Willie says just before he walks away.

I wrap myself in Ken's arms, taking a deep breath. With Manda being Theo's, I already know he is going to do everything he can to get her officially out of the system and into his care. The fact that he is a grandfather as well, I also feel he will try to keep that baby.

I am worried that if Manda doesn't want the baby, he will take the baby for himself to stay in his life. Not wanting to miss a moment of his grandchild's life.

"Ken, what are we going to do? This is becoming too much, too quickly. Theo won't let Manda or that baby go."

"I know, babe. He will do everything to keep them both. We have to be ready to support Manda if she isn't ready to be a mom. Theo has rights as the baby's grandfather."

"I don't want this to cause a strain with them should she choose not to keep the baby."

"Sweetheart. We will cross that bridge when we get there. But for now, they need their time. They will figure it out, and we will be here for both of them. Nothing will tear us apart. This family just became a whole lot stronger. That girl is part Theo. She has a fight in her, even if she doesn't know it yet."

He was right. This would all work out one way or another. This MC family just gained two more souls to cherish forever.

TWENTY-SIX

JUDGE

-Present-

I look over the empty seat to the right of me in Church, playing with the gavel as the men slowly start to file in, leaving phones and other shit in the locker at the bottom of the barn stairs. Theo wasn't going to be in here for a while; he had a lot of personal stuff that he needed to work through. A lot that he would need El and me on a personal level rather than a boss and MC prez level. He has only been a funny Uncle, not in the olden day terms, but he has never had to be accountable to anyone but himself since the day he turned eighteen. I am struggling to be the best friend I know he needs right now, with my obligations to the Foster Home, the ranch, the MC, and its affiliated businesses. I am spread thin. Now being pulled in more directions.

I am deep in thought when I hear the door close with a loud bang and notice almost everyone is seated watching me with a meaningful gaze. It was time to talk about everything we had discovered, everything about Manda, Theo, and what we have yet to discover about the underground problem we know nothing about.

"Alright, guys, I know we are worried, but I have some information to share." I start and bang the gavel, a joke gift from Anderson many years ago when he learned my road name. "Manda and her little boy are doing okay currently. Manda will be home in a few days; she needs to get a few things looked after then she will be back here. Her little guy," I take a deep breath and remember the look on Manda and El's face when the baby doc came down to talk to them. "He has a lot of issues, he was small for his age, and along with the complications of what happened to Manda, he is in for a long stay. That brings us to slightly better news. Storm is a dad and a grandpa." I would stop and let that sink in when all the boys started clamoring at me for more information. Questions being hurled left and right.

"Who the fuck would let that guy reproduce?" Zombie called out, earning him a beer bottle tossed at his head from Cowboy.

"Time and place fucker, can't you see where this is going?" J.J., Cowboy, always had a special place for Theo and would back that man to the end of time.

"Alright, shut the fuck up and let me finish. Bunch of assholes." I mutter the last part. "Yes, Storm didn't do the world a favor and wrap his cock up. But that's in the past. This is the now. Manda and her little boy are now officially MC family and founding royalty. We treat them like gold. Storm is in for a lot of personal issues, and we need to have his back. We also need to dig more into Mandas' past. Knuckles, I need you to talk to your people and see what information you can find."

"What am I looking for?" He asked, pulling out a small notepad.

"Everything, anything you can, because when she was conceived, we were still living in California. How the fuck did she make her way to the middle of nowhere Colorado?" This question has been bugging me, but with Manda needing to remain as stress-free as possible, I cannot get the answers I need from her. "I also need you to find her former foster fuckers. Butcher, get your piggies ready. They will feast on his flesh. If we can… alive." The giggle that came from him set literal chills up my spine.

"Now, why did you have to make him do that? Imma have more nightmares." Sever whines, looking from the maniacal look on Butcher to me.

"Oh now, sugar, you know you love me," Butcher says, blowing him a kiss.

"Alright, I am on all that. What is going on with her former family?" Knuckles asks, moving to the computer set up in the far corner.

"Because they let the fucker into the home that did this to Manda." I knew my features went dark as I said this. "They told her that she was lying, that the man they allowed into their home wouldn't touch her, and the system then labeled her a problem child."

"Those are our bread and butter here," Turd says, with pride in his voice.

I knew why; he was a foster son we had. He was here from seventeen till he turned eighteen. After that, he thought we would turn him to the streets when we gave him a choice. Prospect with the MC, but to do that and live here at the ranch, he needed to work and go to school. The Government paid for the first year of school for foster kids; he would take that and work on a skill. Something he could fall back on no matter what happened here. That's what we did with all of our kids that wanted to be prospects. Not everyone made it here, but they all left with a skill, a trade they can use and better themselves in the outside world.

We want all kids to leave with the confidence and skills that will make them better people. Cowboy, Dizz, and Turd all took Animal Sciences so they could help here at the ranch. Gears got an engineering degree and works at the mech shop with Theo. His skills help them build custom bikes from the ground up. We have had well around a hundred kids or more come through our ranch once we were given group home designation, and each of those left here at 18 left with a skill to be a better version of them.

"Ya, but she wasn't trouble," I said. "She was told she was a liar, and the system kicked her out of there and to us. They never reported the situation. She hid it all from us until El put it all together a little under 2 weeks ago. We made a call to the caseworker, but *shockingly* she did not call us back until after Manda was admitted to the hospital."

"We need new Social Case Workers. El said there was a good one at the hospital; maybe we can talk her into switching and helping us." Dizz said I knew his former caseworker is Manda's current. There is no love lost there.

"We can't get people to switch jobs to make our life easier." Cowboy said. "But we have skills and resources to make the fuckers pay for this shit. We need to get a prospect watching them when we get the information."

"Here you go!" Knuckles said, tossing a paper wad at the back of his head.

"You could have walked the three fucking feet to hand it to me, asshole." Cowboy mutters, rubbing the back of his head while retrieving the paper. "Did you really need to put a rock in there too?"

"Made it get to you faster Peaches, you know you love me?" Knuckles winks and goes back to typing away.

"Okay, Cowboy, you get Prospects 1 and 2 on the tail and report back as soon as they get there and every move they make to you. You are overseeing this since it was your idea." I gave the order, and Cowboy hopped up to follow through.

When he stomped down the steps, the idea I had been toying with for a few weeks now seemed like a good time to bring it to the table. But I knew I needed my boy out of the room before I could do that. Before I made this change, I know I am only fifty, but I have worked hard since I was three, and I needed to be a rancher, a father, and a husband more than a business and MC leader.

"I have another important issue to bring to the table." I start, clearing my throat, waiting for all eyes on me. "I want to step down and become just an MC member. I need to be with Storm during this time. I need to be the Ranch owner, and I need to be there for El during all this time, with more babies coming through, more issues with teenagers. I need to make sure the MC gets a new vision and someone to run it the way it needs to be. So we can get all the scum we can off the streets. More so now with the new drugs and us not knowing who is running them." That part killed me, and it also solidified more why I needed to step back. "I am pulled too far and too thin that I let a threat come into our town and poison our people. You need someone who can give the MC what it needs, solid dedication."

"Who can do that? We all have side things, and us older folk are in no state to do what you do." Bigfoot asks, he was our Enforcer until Cowboy came up the ranks, proved his place more than once.

"Cowboy," I state. "He is my boy; he is strong and smart as a whip. He has repeatedly proven that he knows what we need to do to get the job done right and clean. We all respect what he has to say." The boys nod in agreement. "I have not done right by you or Wyman, and I think we need to get a fresh face and eyes on this."

"Is that why you sent him to talk to prospects?" Dizz asked.

"No, but he came up with a Prez Idea; I let him follow through so I can bring this to the table for you all to think and vote on. I have all the faith in the world that he can do this and not put his head up his own ass."

"What about Storm? I know he is taking a break to be with his kid but, shouldn't he be the next Prez?" Bigfoot states. It's a fair question and, thankfully, one I already have an answer to.

"Fair enough. I already spoke to Storm. He doesn't want to be Prez. He wants to keep his role as VP. He's never had the desire to be Prez. Plus, being VP gives him the availability to take care of his daughter and grandson. In the meantime, Sever will serve as acting VP when needed."

"You gonna pay me twice as much?" Sever asks.

"I'm gonna stick my foot up your ass." Sever just laughs and shakes his head. I knew he wasn't serious, but I was. I'll stick my foot up his ass if he thinks I'm going to pay his ass more for doing jack shit.

"I would follow Cowboy in this." Sever said, which was shocking cause he really didn't like people in general.

"As would I." Zombie chipped in.

"I will be his Road Cap." Willie pipped up.

"Alright, let's bring it to the table. All in favor of Cowboy as the new Prez?" I ask. There was a resounding roar on table knocks for the affirmative. "There you have it, new Prez, Cowboy. I am a founding member and will still be here as needed."

"New Business, now that we require a new Enforcer, I nominate Dizz." Gears calls out.

"Da Fuck?" Dizz's head snaps to the left of him, in clear shock of this.

"You have worked your ass off to be better than your past. You are strong, devoted, and one crazy mother fucker when pissed off. Maybe not Butcher crazy, but pretty damn close." Gears explained. "I think you would do us all proud as Enforcer. Plus, you are Cowboys' life mate."

"Fucking stop calling us that!" Dizz whines, his head dropping back on the chair.

"What? I'm not implying you guys are fucking or anything, but if you are, that's cool too, but you guys are in this as ride or dies. Like Judge and Storm are lifemates and ride or dies. It's a compliment!" I shake my head at Gears and his stupid fucking *completely accurate* explanation.

"Dizz, Gears is right. You would make a great Enforcer. You and Cowboy always do everything together when it comes to what he was required to handle when Enforcer. You know how it works, and you really are damn crazy. In a good way." Butcher pipes up.

"Doesn't feel like a good way." He mumbles.

"Ah, boy, don't be sad. Being crazy is fun. Watch," Butcher turns to Sever, and before Sever can prepare, Butcher is barking like a dog and flailing himself over the table to attack him.

"GAH! Goddammit, Butcher! What the fuck!"

Butcher is laughing like a maniac while Sever isn't moving because I am pretty damn sure he peed himself. At least a little.

"Okay, children, knock it the fuck off. Sever, you need to change your pants?" I ask, trying to hide the smile on my lips

"Fuck off." He's pouting again, so that is a definite maybe.

"I'm still your Prez until Cowboy takes the role. Don't push your damn luck."

"Sorry, Prez." He bows his head.

"Forgiven. This time," I wink at Dizz. "Dizz, this is something that you would be great at. I second Gears' nomination for Dizz as Enforcer."

The same boisterous noise from before was once again filling the room. "They all agree, Dizz, but it's your call. You don't have to make a decision now, but I expect one when we announce Cowboy as Prez in a few days."

I could see the worry on Dizz's face. I didn't understand why it was there, though. That man was scary as fuck. He tortured right up there with Butcher. He didn't shy from anything. I know him, though. He will sit and tell himself why he can't do this, and then he is going to go watch Mulan sing *"Make a Man Out of You"* and realize he is meant for this, that he was always made for this. It's what he always does.

TWENTY-SEVEN

ELVIRA

-Present-

It feels like I am back to where I started, in the hospital every day, watching out for our babies. Kelsey was doing so much better, and they think that if she stays on this trend, we can bring her home in the next two weeks. Manda is a day away from discharge, but we have one who is just starting his rough journey in the hospital.

Mandas' baby boy, whom she still has not given a name, has developed some lung complications to go along with being early, underweight, and dealing with the trauma of which he was brought into this world. Theo is here every single day talking with Manda but has not seen his grandson yet. He still has not been allowed. While he is Manda's father, the state is taking its sweet time with the paperwork in everything to get the ball rolling there. Because of all that, the only ones who can see Baby Boy are Ken, Manda, and myself. Ken has refused to see the baby until his best friend can. He doesn't feel it's fair. I have taken pictures and shown Theo, but they are hard for him to look at. He is broken because of all the tubes and wires he is hooked up to. But he did love the 'cool dude' shades that they put on him while he is under the UV light for bilirubin.

"I think you need to talk to a lawyer," I tell him as we sit in Manda's room.

"Why? We have the DNA proof that I am her dad, they know my record is clean, and I work with you all in the group home. I don't have anything to fear." He is sprawled on the small pumping chair at her bedside.

"I think we need to prepare for the worst, plus do you have a home that will pass inspection? Because if you gain custody, she will be in your care, and you will need to have a safe place not only for her but for Baby Boy when he is discharged. There are a lot of factors in play here, Theo. You need to look at all things. Just because you have the same DNA doesn't mean they will run for you to take her. You haven't been in her life." I feel awful for having to say this, but it's the truth.

"I don't understand this, bull.... Uh.... Plop. I mean, look at the crappy situation with Marley; her mom is in and out of rehab, in and out of prison. Yet as soon as she is clean or out of jail, we have to give her back to her. Here I am, on my own, with an actual support system, working, don't do drugs, clean record, and I have to practically sell my soul to have her in my life." I understand his issue. Every time we have to hand Marley back, I see my son's heartbreak more and more, right along with mine.

"I know Theo, I know. But we have to do this right."

"Why? She was in the system, in their care, and look what happened? I was in the system. I know these things, but I had Ken." He gets up and starts pacing.

Manda and I watched him, not sure what he was going to do next. I love this crazy fucker, but I was not going to let him scheme this one. He needed to do it the right way. There are ways to work with the system, but I know he is jaded from his time in there. So is Ken. That is why I am the go-between because he will get frustrated, and that will put us further behind rather than ahead. While I want to fight this for Theo, I can't.

"There is a way you can possibly speed this up," I say. He stops short. "You will have to play nice if we do this."

"Okay, I will do anything." He sits on the edge of the bed. I look at Manda. We seem to be making a lot of plans *for* her instead of *with* her.

"You want this too, right, baby girl?" I take her hand in mine, trying to be that calming presence.

"Yes, I want to be with my family. Theo is my dad, and you are his family, which makes you my family. I want to stay with you all." She squeezes my hand, reaching out for Theos as well.

In a short time, they have bonded more and more. He is here every waking minute while Ken and the boys are dealing with everything else.

"Okay, well, I think we should move Theo back into the farmhouse. The big main house with us. That way, we are there to help. That will help the caseworker, too, because she knows us and knows we will help. We can move Gears to the apartment over the shop for now. Then when you all feel safe and comfortable, and all this crap is behind us, you can move out." I suggest they don't have to take the help, but I think it might help them speed through this faster. They will only be watched by CPS for a year after final placement, and then they are free to be who they need to be.

"I am okay with that because we are going to need some maternal help when Baby Boy comes home." He looks to Manda, then back to me. "If you want him to. No pressure, love. That is your call, and I will…." He takes a shuddering breath, "I will support any decision that you make about Baby Boy."

"I wasn't sure if I was going to keep him, but when you found out about us, you didn't waste a second. You didn't fear me rejecting you, and to save your heart, reject me first. You laid it all out for me and told me you'd support any decision I made. I knew that you already loved me, but I could feel how much that love grew when you told me the truth. But when you took my hand and said I wouldn't be alone in raising this baby, that'd you be with me every step of the way, and we'd learn and grow together, I knew that I would be okay. I knew that being a mom would be something I could do because I had you. And I can't wait to tell him about how he wasn't made by love, but he was born into an abundance of it, and his grandpa is who loved him the most." Theo wraps himself up in her arms gently. "I also thought of a name for him. Since he is going to be part of a proper family that we never got growing up, I want to name him Theodore Storm Loveitt. I want him to be every bit as awesome as his Grandpa." Theo unabashedly sobbed, pulling Manda to him. I wrapped myself around both of them. We are all just sitting there holding one another, crying at that announcement.

"Sorry to disrupt you." A familiar voice called from the door.

Looking behind me stood Audrina, in her nice dress pants and flowing blouse. Her red curly hair rivaled mine in vibrance and bounce, but she still wore the same kind smile and soft eyes.

"Elvira, you seem to be everywhere these days. How is sweet Kelsey?" She took a few steps into the room.

"Audrina, it's so nice to see you. Kelsey is doing great. They think that she is going to be able to come home soon. She is almost completely off the drugs and is a lot more cognitive. It really should be any day now."

"That's wonderful," she gives me a small hug and turns towards Manda, "hello. My name is Audrina. I am going to be the Social Worker assigned to your case. How are you feeling?"

"Right now? I am nervous. Why are you here? Are you going to take my baby?" Manda says with a panic tone. I was about to reassure her that no, that wouldn't happen when Theo stepped in.

"No, babygirl. Hey, look at me. No one is taking Teddy from us, okay? You and that baby are mine, and you're coming home with me." Fatherhood looks good on him. He is already stepping into the role so well. "Right?" He turns to Audrina.

"Right. I am so sorry if I gave that impression. Your baby is yours. I am here to help get the ball rolling with your dad here to be able to legally claim you. I know a lot about your home life as I have spoken with Elvira in great detail. I can use the information that I have to help get this going so you can legally be a Loveitt."

"I am a Loveitt. I just need a stupid piece of paper to match. It's so dumb. He's my dad! We shouldn't have to fight this hard." Manda was getting upset, which I understood. Having just had a baby, those hormones are no joke and then finding out that her dad had to go through all these hoops just to have his name added to his birth certificate was already taking its toll on her.

"Sweetheart, I know you're upset, and you have every right to be, but please don't take it out on Audrina. I promise she is here to help you."

"You're right, momma. I'm sorry."

Her calling me momma was something that I needed to have a talk to her about. Or at least a talk with Theo. I was Momma El, more recently Momma, and Ken was Poppa Ken. Was this something that Theo would want her to stop?

"It's okay. It's not the worst thing that has ever been shouted at me, I promise." Audrina smiles and starts taking us through all the steps that we needed to take to get this going and make this all official. She had the birth certificate documents and helped Manda fill those out.

"Theodore Storm? I like that. That is an incredibly strong name for a strong little boy. Great choice." Manda beams up at Audrina. I could see how proud she was to name her son that. I glance over at Theo, and he has tears in his eyes again. As soon as little Teddy comes home, he is going to have his grandfather wrapped around his fingers.

"Okay, now that we've gotten this all taken care of, how about we get you up to see your grandson? It's my understanding that you haven't met him yet."

Theo takes a sharp inhale of breath, and I can feel the tears willing to spill. Manda is looking up at her father with pure joy.

"You can do that?" Theo asks her. I can tell he doesn't want to get his hopes up.

"I may or may not be able to pull some strings and get you in. But, you can't tell my secrets." She winks at him, and he just laughs. I can hear the cries that he is trying to hold back at the same time.

"Yes. Please. Let's do it. I want to see him more than anything."

"Alright. Come with me."

Theo

This was it. I was about to meet my grandson. My. Grandson. Finding out that I had a kid was already a shock to my system but finding out that my kid was having a kid, even more so.

She is so beautiful, though. Every time I look at her, I try to remember who her mother is. I try to think back to when and where I made her. The only answer I have is California. I am such a damn manwhore that I can't even remember her mother. What does that say about me? What am I going to say to her when she asks?

I had to shake the thoughts from my head, though. At this moment, I couldn't let it be overrun with the what-ifs and how comes. I needed to be here, in the now, here with my daughter and her son.

I still can't get over the fact that she named him after me. Theodore Storm Loveitt. She is embracing the fact that she is my child without hesitation. I couldn't have asked for anything better. I was terrified that she would reject me. That she would want nothing to do with me because I wasn't aware of her existence. I was prepared to fight for her and for him if I needed to. I have always cared about Manda. I care about all of the kids out at the ranch. I'm the fun uncle that they all love to hang out with. I think, deep down, that's why she was so open. We already had a relationship; now we get to let it blossom into something that it should have always been.

I am getting my second chance, though. I get to be here for my little guy. I get to help her raise him and teach him how to ride a bike, play ball, and build an engine. When he is old enough and most likely against his mother's wishes, I'll get him his first motorcycle, and I will teach him how to ride.

I couldn't wait for these moments. I also couldn't wait for the moments I was going to get to have with my daughter. She's only sixteen, so I still get to threaten her prom date, terrify her first serious boyfriend, begrudgingly give my permission for someone to marry her, walk her down the aisle and be there every step of the way when she has another kid, should she choose too.

I've missed a lot but starting now, I was going to be there for everything.

We get to the desk at the NICU, and Audrina does her thing. That's when I feel a hand grip mine. I look down, and I see that it's Manda. She looks up at me, and I can see the worry across her face.

"Hey, what's wrong?"

"I come up here, and I visit, but I can't get myself to stay very long. Momma El stays longer than me because it hurts too much to see him like this. I can't hold him yet, and there are so many wires and tubes sticking out of his little body. Did I fail him? Is that why he is here? It hurts to be down here."

"Hey, hey, hey. Don't go thinking like that. I know it's hard not to, but you did nothing wrong. It was just his time to come into the world. You are a strong, strong girl, and when you feel weak, you have so many people to fall back onto to help you stand back up. You are not alone in this. If it's too hard to see him like this, that's okay. Everyone handles situations like this differently. You need to process how you need to process. No one can tell you otherwise."

"I just, I feel so guilty. I cry so much, and I just want him to be okay."

"I know, and he will be. We have to trust the people here know what they're doing, and they will keep him safe."

She hugs me, and I can't help but hug her a little too tight, but she doesn't complain. I lean my body down to place my head on top of hers and just close my eyes. Basking in this feeling. I don't think I have ever felt this much love for another person before. This is on a new, higher level.

"Okay, follow me," Audrina says, pulling us out of my thoughts. We go through the process of washing our hands and arms, and she leads us back to his own little room. A nurse is in there checking his vitals, and when she sees us, she smiles.

"Hey there, Manda, El. He's doing great today. No issues or causes for concern. He is right on track. He's had about an ounce and a half to eat and needed a diaper change. Doing exactly what he should be doing," she turns her attention to me, "I'm sorry, I haven't met you yet. I'm Natalie. I'm baby boy's day nurse."

"I'm Theo. I'm grandpa."

"Well, it's nice to meet you. I'll leave you guys to your visit with baby boy."

"Actually," Manda pipes up, "I decided to name him Theodore Storm, Teddy for short."

"Oh, that's wonderful! I will make him a name tag right away." Natalie beams a beautiful smile. Once she is out of the room, we turn towards Teddy. I walk up to him, and even though he is covered in tubes and wires, he is the most beautiful baby I have ever seen.

I was wrong. This is the biggest amount of love I have ever felt. I don't know if my heart is going to be able to handle the amount of love I have for these two kids: my daughter and my grandson.

"Babygirl, he is perfect."

"But he's in here."

"That's okay," I tell her, "it's okay that he is in here. He just needs a little help, a little time, and a whole lot of love. He has that from you, from me, from El. You can tell that nurse of his cares a whole lot about him too. Trust me. He's perfect."

She gives me a hug, and I barely hear her when she says, "thanks, dad."

If I never have anything great happen to me ever again for the rest of my life, I will be okay knowing I have this.

TWENTY-EIGHT

JUDGE

-Present-

Despite Theo not being here, the club was running smoothly. Cowboy still had no idea that he had been nominated as Prez, and we were going to make the announcement later tomorrow night after Manda's welcome home party.

I was in the house watching El rush around the kitchen, checking cabinets, the pantry, and the freezer for all the food we're gonna need for the party. We are making it seem like it's Manda's welcome home/welcome to the family party. And in a way, it is to start with. But we are going to throw our first Biker party. Artem and his guys are going to be showing up, but only for a short while. He has some business to attend to in California.

"You don't need to stress about this, Firecracker. You are popping all over the place, and you need to calm yourself." I get up to stop her after her third trip to the boot room where the stand-up freezers are.

"This is a big deal Ken, you are retiring, my baby is taking over, and we have Theo moving back in with us. I know I suggested that, but him staying for a long dinner is taxing on my nerves…. He never leaves after dinner anymore, Ken. I will start drinking. I swear I will." I know she is kidding, but I still take her in my arms to try and settle her racing heart and frazzled nerves.

"You know this is different. He has a lot more going on and is rarely here long enough to eat or sleep. He and Manda will practically live at that hospital, and we will be here to help. Not take over, help." I tell her. I love my wife, but she has this take charge way about her and wants to do it all, so no one suffers.

"Ya Elvira! I am a big boy. I know what I am doing with my life!" Speak of the fucking devil.

"Shut up, Shit, Storm. I can't wait until you change that poo explosion diaper. I will record it all and send it to America's Funniest Home Videos! Bring in some good coin for me." El says, pulling away from me.

"Is that show still relevant?" I asked

"Shut up! What are you doing here anyway? Thought you were still at the hospital with Manda and Teddy."

"She sent me home to get her some clothes and a few things because they are sending her home today. I am going to go get her as soon as I take some time to steal our husband away from you for a quick chat." He comes over, putting his arm over me, leaving himself open for a nut shot, which I take.

"Don't touch me when I have my wife in my arms. Rules dude, boundaries!" I laugh at him while he is in the fetal position on the kitchen floor.

"Fucker," he groans, slowly getting up and adjusting his sack like he doesn't have mixed company in his presence. Yeah living with Theo again is going to take some getting used to. "I do want to talk to you, though, dude. Can you and I head to the office?"

I am about to answer when the buzzer for the front gate goes off. Elvira waves us off and heads to the camera and phone to let them in or turn them away. Walking into the office, I see Artem's car heading through the gate, wondering what he wants but still focus my attention on Theo sitting across from me at the big desk.

"What's shakin' bacon?" I asked, leaning back in my chair, feet propped up on the desk. He started pacing the office and had a worried look on his face. This put me on high alert instantly.

"Theo, what is it? Is it Manda, is it Teddy? Are they okay? Did something happen? Fuck. Lemme go get El." I fired off in rapid succession.

"What? No. Don't get it. Nothing happened to them. They're fine. We're all fine. She doesn't need to know what I am about to tell you."

"Okay. Dude, I'm not gonna fucking lie. You're scaring me. What the hell is going on?"

He keeps pacing and is now running his hands through his hair. He is stressed as hell, and it's obvious he doesn't want to tell me what he claims he wants to tell me. I make my way over to him and pull him into my embrace.

This is us. We have always been this way. He calms instantly, and I pull back, holding him by his upper arms. "Alright, man, you gotta tell me what's bothering you. You know that you can tell me anything. What's going on?"

He takes a deep breath before he sits down and gestures for me to sit as well.

"I have been thinking a lot. With Manda coming into my life and Teddy as well, I started to sit and really think about who I am as a person and how I was, how I hope to be. Do you know that I can't even tell you who her mother is? How fucked is that? She might have questions one day, and I won't be able to answer them."

"I get that, man. You have to be honest with her. Unfortunately, you don't know. But I am sure that there are ways that we can find out. It'll be alright." I tried to reassure him.

"That's not the only thing, though. Because trust me, I came to that conclusion also. Honesty. I decided that I needed to be honest with her no matter how hard the question was. I want her to get to know me and vice versa, and I can't do that if I keep things from her."

I was trying to figure out why he was telling me this. What significance did it have towards me? I completely agreed with him that he should be honest with her. That was the best case. But he's always been honest with me. Wait.

"Are you trying to tell me that you're keeping something from me?" I couldn't stop the hurt in my voice. I tell this man everything. To know that he hadn't done the same breaks a piece of me.

He shakes his head before he continues.

"After you aged out and I was by myself, a new kid came in. We did everything together. In a way, it was like what I had with you. What I missed so much. That connection, that friendship." I nod, and he continued. "After a while, Shay and I started having a relationship. Everything that we normally did became that much more intense. It was almost indescribable. I loved,"

He stops. I can tell that he is getting choked up about his feelings for this girl. I don't understand why he would keep her a secret all this time, but I don't say anything. I wait for him to continue.

"I loved Shay. With everything I had. We lost our virginity to each other, and we continued our relationship until the day I aged out. Once I turned eighteen, my foster family had my shit in a garbage bag ready to go when I woke up. I didn't get to say goodbye. Afterward, I didn't see Shay again. I searched for you and caught up with you, and by the time I pulled my head out of my ass, Shay was gone."

"What do you mean gone?"

"That piece of shit foster father found out about us. He took it all out on Shay. Ended up killing him."

"Wait, because you two were together, he killed her?"

Theo just stared at me for a moment, and I let it sink in as to what he said. *Him.* He said him.

"You're gay."

Theo just blew out a breath and rubbed his hands down his face. "No. I'm not gay. Shay is the only man I ever loved. The only man I ever felt anything for in any romantic capacity. Shay was my world. When I found out he died, I went on a bender and never got off. Sleeping with any woman that would offer herself up to me. I was addicted. At first, it was to numb the pain from losing Shay, and then it became a way to numb the pain from the pain. It took years before I got to the point of sleeping around simply because I wanted to. The point is, Manda's mom was one of those women I slept with to numb the pain of losing my boyfriend. The one I walked away from and allowed him to die."

He was crying now. Tears streaming down his face, and I did what I always did. I held him. Nothing changed between him and me. He needed to know that.

"Nothing that happened to Shay at the hands of that monster was your fault. You couldn't have known that it would happen. And I can see why this is a huge deal for you, but, I promise you, Manda is a lot tougher than anyone gives her credit for. She would be able to handle this truth. Trust in your daughter. She's half you, after all."

"Yeah, yeah, I can do that. But what about us?"

"What about us?"

"You…I just…I just told you I had a boyfriend. That doesn't bother you?"

"What bothers me is that you even have to ask me that. You're my other damn half, Theo. Nothing has changed."

"I don't know why I was so afraid to tell you."

"You're a dumbass, for starters." I can't even continue with all my points because Ellie comes tearing into the office, not even knocking.

"Daddy! You need to come out here quick!" Fuck, she hasn't called me daddy in years. Are those tears on her face?

"Ellie? Baby Girl, why are you crying?" My hackles are up; what the fuck is going on? What did Artem bring into my house now? It's not like I have enough shit on my plate.

"Follow me, I promise, I promise you will be happy. Uncle Artie brought a huge surprise for us!" She tears back out of the room, leaving Theo and me in her dust.

"I still can't believe she can call Artem Uncle Artie, and I can't even call him Mafia Man without the threat of a gun up my ass." Theo pouts.

"Well, I don't know why you are upset about that prospect. From the tone of our last convo, you like it up the bum." I shot back quickly, leaving the room before he can hit me.

I start speed walking making my way out the side kitchen door where a crowd has gathered. I was about to call out to them from the porch when I heard El start sobbing and calling for her baby. What the fuck is going on?

Theo and I take off for the crowd, and there in the middle is my woman wrapped around a muscular man, his hair cropped short. Then I saw the military-issued pants.

"Well fuck!" I say, wrapping my expansive arms around my wife and our boy. "Robert James! You came home."

'Well shit, the prodigal son returns. All this time, no phone call, no letters. What am I chopped liver?" Theo calls before joining the group hug.

"No, you're the asshole who told me only pussies join the Marines. Real men are bikers." R.J laughs, punching him in the shoulder when we all pull back. Well, when Theo and I pulled back, El was clinging to him like a lifeline, still crying.

"Marley, hide your crayons! Uncle R.J. is home!" J.J. calls out, rushing his brother in a bro hug. "Bout time you showed your face around here! We missed you. Not everyone can wing Theo like you can. But that last one was weak. You are losing your game, too much wax in your diet."

"How long are you staying? I can get a room ready for you. We can plan all kinds of things to do. I'm sure...."

"Mom. As much as I love all that, I have to leave tomorrow. Artem is taking me back to California. But I needed to see you guys. Needed a break. Shits been…shit."

I can tell that El wants to break down knowing that R.J will be leaving just as quickly as he got here. I can't have her being upset the whole time. I smack him on the shoulder again. "We got all our kids here. I say we make the most of it and get this party rollin'."

Everyone laughs and cheers, and I can see that El is excited, but I know that tomorrow, she will be a wreck again because eleven years gone is a fucking long time to be away and only get twenty-four hours to visit. If we're lucky to get the full twenty-four.

TWENTY-NINE

JUDGE

-Present-

It only took El, Ellie, Kathey-Rea, and Natasha just under two hours to get all the food started and set. Natasha stopped and picked steaks, hotdogs, and hamburgers up for us on her way over. I was at the grill. The guys came in early from the field to join us, the cattle were set for the night, and we were just going to enjoy tonight. I sent the lone prospect still here to check on the bar, Cowboys place, and oversee the shipment Artem's soldiers were dropping off in the storeroom out behind the homestead barn.

Life felt complete at home, settled. Looking out at my NOMC brothers mingling with the hired hands, the kids running around. It just felt right. It felt like this was what I needed. I needed to be home and enjoy this time while I had it. I knew the people you loved were not around forever. I had lost 75% of those that meant the most to me, some before I even met them.

Stepping back to be a soldier, a brother, a father, and a guiding force and let my boy come into his own and protect the people of Wyman and his family where I had failed was what was best. I know that I took on too much with everything, and I am man enough to admit I need help. Our goals are not being met, we started the MC to help those who cannot help themselves, and each brother here has stood by that.

But we were failing to get that threat under control to gain the information needed. There haven't been more OD's or issues due to the drugs, but that didn't mean the threat was gone. There was also the matter of Manda Foster Fuckers, the prospects have been on their tail, and so far, nothing has been shifty or shady, and they have not had any visitors or gone anywhere that didn't involve the kids.

Artem was talking with El and sticking close to R.J. while his Number Two was out talking to Cowboy and playing nice with Marley, who was attached to my boy like velcro. This was a good as night as any to share that I will be stepping back. I wonder if I should pull Artem aside and give him a warning that the change in leadership was coming. But that thought is fleeting; blindsiding him is always more fun. The grill is shut down, the plates are piled high, and the picnic tables are full of everyone and anyone we hold near and dear.

"May I have your attention," I call out, standing tall while everyone remained seated. "I am happy to say that this party was brought about by Manda and officially welcoming her to our family and back home to stay. We know your boy will be here in no time at all." The boys hoot and holler, and I level them all with a single look that quiets them down fast. "There has been a lot going on, and with everyone home and settled, it's time to make some changes.

Life has thrown us some crazy fucking curveballs lately. Some giving us trouble, some giving us life, some giving us more love than we ever thought possible. Manda, I know that you were terrified of what was going to happen with you and Teddy, but I promise you, you are at home baby girl, and you and your boy will be safe here, forever.

Elviria. You have given so much of yourself to everyone here. I am in awe of you. I thought that I was tough as shit before. I've realized that I don't hold a candle to you, but I sure as shit want to try. I want to be the man that you deserve.

There is so much more that I could say and drag this shit on forever, but I need to get to the most important part. Cowboy, can you come up here, please?"

J.J, my son, walks up to me with a look of confusion. He has zero idea as to what is about to happen. Almost everyone knows what's going on next, and I am excited to see how he reacts. Once he is standing next to me, I clap him on the shoulder and turn back towards the group.

"There is too much going on right now, and I can no longer give what this club deserves. Effective immediately, I am stepping down as the President of Nameless Order," I look to my son, "You have been everything that this club needs to move forward and take care of what needs to be handled. I am no longer that person, and I accept that. The club has voted and, if you choose to accept it, Cowboy, you are now the President of Nameless Order."

My son's face pales, and tears fill his eyes. If we went by the "natural procession," he would be third in line. But sometimes, that's not how things work. Everyone around us has erupted into cheers, shouts, and whistles. I look at my son and speak to where only he can hear me.

"What do you say, son? You wanna take over for your old man?"

"Dad. I. Are you sure? Shouldn't Theo be...I just, what if I mess up?"

"Son, you will. That's inevitable. What matters is how you handle it and how you get back up. You are more than capable of leading these men. You don't need to run the Ranch, MC, and Foster Home. You only need to focus on the MC. The drug problem and whatever else comes up. I am always here to help you. Whatever you need, I am here. You're not alone in this J.J. You can do this. I believe in you. The question is, do you believe in yourself?"

I could see the wheels turning in his head. I want him to accept this. I know that he can do it. The club knows what he can do. They believe in him as much as I do. He looks up at me, and he nods. Turning to the guys, I let out a loud whistle as they are still cheering and talking about the announcement.

"Hey! Listen up!" They all give their attention to Cowboy and me. "I want to be honest with you all. This decision to step down wasn't an easy one, but it's the right one. It's something that I have been thinking about for a while. I need to be the best man for my family, and this MC needs the best man. Cowboy is that man, and he has accepted our nomination to make him President."

The men go insane with cheers, and that's when Theo walks up to me with the next piece of this announcement.

"Chill the fuck out. We aren't done yet! Cowboy, this belongs to you." I hand him the patch that says Prez and bring him in for a hug. When we separate from each other, he has stopped his tears, but I can tell it's taking work on his part.

"Now, there is one more piece to cover." I look at Dizz, and he gives me a nod. I hoped that this announcement would be coming, and I am thankful that it is. I know that it is the right decision. "To take the place of Cowboy as Enforcer, the club has voted, and I just got the confirmation. Your new Enforcer is Dizz."

The crazy that had surrounded us before is back once again. I know that this is the best choice for this club. This club means the world to me, but it is time to step away. It's what's going to get this club to where they need to be and get this town clean of this mysterious drug that's slowly taking over.

The guys all get up and congratulate Cowboy and Dizz, and I make my way over to El and Theo. Theo claps me on the shoulder and gives me a tight hug.

"He's the right choice, man. We're going to be alright. Plus, you know I'll kick his ass if he does anything to put this club in jeopardy."

"I know, man. I know. I believe in him completely, but I know that he is going to have a hard time adjusting at first. You may have to lend a hand more than once, and he may take it wrong and…."

"Dude shut the fuck up. Do you forget that I've known him as long as you and helped raise that fucker? I've helped make his way up through the ranks just as much as you. I know how he is. He will be fine. Shit."

"Theo, don't be a dick. Right now, he is just a dad making sure he made the right choice for his son. You'll know exactly what he is going through soon enough with Manda and Teddy." El snaps at him. Fuck, I love this woman.

She comes up to me and wraps her arm around my waist. I put mine around her shoulders and bring my head down to kiss the top of hers. She's right. While I know making him Prez is the right choice from an MC standpoint, from a father standpoint, I am questioning everything. I want him to be the very best he can be. The last thing I want is to lead him down the wrong path.

"He will be fine, Ken," El says, almost as if she is reading my thoughts. "He was made for this. He's wanted nothing more than to be a part of this club after you started it. He is going to do everything he needs to to make sure that it runs the way it should. You chose well."

"I know, baby. It's just a lot to take in at the moment."

"How about you take me inside, and I make you forget about it?"

I dip down and throw her over my shoulder. She laughs, and I smack her square on her juicy ass. I will never tire of this woman, and I am still shocked every single day that she chose me to live this life with. I've never been given a greater gift.

"Hey! You can't leave in the middle of the party to fuck your woman, *boss.*" Butcher shouts out. "You don't see Abilene and me sneaking off." I stop and put her down. I kiss her on the nose, and I tell her to give me a moment. I turn around to retort before the woman in question beats me to it.

"I would if you could get it up." Abilene deadpans.

"I told you not to mention it in front of the guuuuuuys." He whines while dragging out his words. Everyone starts laughing, and Butcher sets his sights on all of them. "Wanna see that she's lying?" He starts to unbutton his pants, and before he can get them down, Abilene is behind him.

"If you ever wanna put that monster in me again, you'll remember that there are children here and stop right this second."

"But. But. Babe." She gives him a look that would kill him if that were possible. He stalks off with his head pointed down. That guy, I swear to fuck. I was about to walk back to grab El when I could hear R.J. giving his older brother shit. El and I can never let them know this, but we love their little fights. They dig into each other, but the shit they say is always pure gold. We walk over to them because all I can hope for is some of the stupid shit they used to say to each other.

"I don't know man, seems like a pretty piss poor choice if you ask me. I mean, the fuck you know about leading a group of guys?"

"Fuck you. You're just jealous."

"You're shitting me, right? I'm…."

"Who gives a fuck what you are! Don't fucking talk to my Prez like that. Who the fuck are you? You're jack shit here. Watch your fucking mouth before I shut your ass up." Turd says. Taking a step towards him. His hand is sitting on his gun. Fuck. I can tell that he is serious with what he is telling R.J.

"Ken, you need to stop him."

"Turd, man. Chill out." I tell him.

"Chill out? Chill out? This fuck face, which I have never fucking seen before, comes in here, into our home, and threatens our Prez. Do you expect me to just sit back and watch it fucking happen? I don't fucking think so."

"Listen, you twat. You're gonna wanna shut the fuck up before I make *you.*" R.J. says.

"Try me fucker." Before I can do anything, R.J. is going after Turd. Fists are flying, and they are each holding their own.

"Fifty on R.J.!" Butcher shouts.

"I'll take that. Fifty on Turd, he's a wirey mutha fucker ."Sever adds on.

"Both of you shut the fuck up!" I look over to Cowboy, "You gonna do anything about this? Or do I need to take my fucking title back?"

"You ain't taking shit, old man. Let him learn the hard way." Cowboy tells me.

I look around, and thankfully, the women had gotten the kids inside. At the moment, I see El coming back towards me. *When the fuck did she leave?* She has a broom and throws it up over her head, and starts smacking them. It does shit to stop them, though, and I pull her back before she gets hit.

"What the fuck, Ken. Stop them!"

"It's not my choice, darling. Talk to your son."

"Jonathan Jackson May! You make them stop right now."

"Ooo-wee boy. Momma brought out the full name. You may wanna stop this before your first act as Prez is getting out being grounded." Willie shouts out.

"Watch your damn mouth, Willie."

"Sure, Prez."

Already taking advantage of his title. While letting his brother and Turd fight is childish, I know that he's got this. The reaction the guys are having - Turd defending him, Willie conceding, I know that they are all going to give him the respect that he has earned.

"Enough." Cowboy shouts. When nothing happens, he starts up again. "I FUCKING SAID ENOUGH!" His voice booming. Turd and R.J. are in a twisted heap on the ground, and they both stop instantly. "Get the fuck up, both of you."

They push off each other and get up. "You both feel better now?" They look at each other, and Turd sneers at R.J. "Turd, meet my younger brother, R.J."

Turd's eye bug out of his head before looking back at R.J. and then to Cowboy, trying to see the similarities. "Sorry, Prez, but I wasn't about to sit back and let him disrespect you."

"This fucker is always talking shit. It's nothing new."

"Well, I didn't even know you had a brother."

"Did you have to kick his ass, though?"

"Fuck yeah, I win. Pay up fucker!" Sever yells out to Butcher. I look over, and Butcher reluctantly pulls money out of his wallet, placing it in Sever's hand.

"You," Cowboy turns to his brother, "you could have just told him who the fuck you were instead of trying to be the big man on campus. You haven't been around in how fucking long and then come in here and fight my guys? All because they were defending me? The fuck is wrong with you?"

R.J. tries to speak, but Cowboy just holds up his hand to stop him. "I don't wanna hear it, man. Get your shit together and hang out. You leave tomorrow, man, and fuck knows when I'll see you again. Stay the fuck away from each other, and let's party."

We're all about to go our own ways when I hear Turd tell R.J, "I still don't fucking like you."

"Yeah, well, I don't like you either, cocksucker."

R.J. walks away, and Turd stalks off towards the other end of the grounds. The fucking joys of MC life.

"Really, J.J., letting them fight?" El says, with her hands on her thick, delicious hips.

"Mom, I love you but, club business." El's mouth hangs open, and J.J. walks away. She turns towards me, and I just laugh. When she gets close enough to me, she swats at me. "It isn't funny, Ken."

"Oh baby, yeah, it is. Hey…come on now. Let him be. How bout we go finish what we tried to start earlier?"

She nods, and I capture her mouth with mine. When she lets out a moan, I know it's time to get the fuck out of here. After all, I ain't Prez anymore. There isn't one single reason why I need to be at an MC party any longer tonight.

THIRTY

JUDGE

-Present-

Waking up the next day after I stepped down as President was surreal. For the past fifteen-plus years, I was so consumed with the MC that not getting up and going straight into club business - I don't know what to do now.

I'm lost.

The MC was all I knew. Yeah, I helped run the ranch and help in the home, but with the ranch hands and El running the ranch and the home, my main focus was always the MC. I sigh loudly while rubbing my hands down my face. This is all new territory to me.

I'm lost.

"You are not lost. You have this," she gestures to the room.

"How the fuck did you know what I was thinking?"

She looks at me like I have just lost my mind, looking at me hard. "You said it out loud a second ago. Are you sure you're okay? Did you 'retire' from the MC for another reason? You going senile on me, old man?"

I pull her in close, resting my chin on the top of her head. Taking a deep calming breath, really trying to psych her out for some sick twisted reason.

"No, just trying to find that new balance. I worked long and hard on so many different things for so long that I am now just trying to find myself again with a few less balls in the air." I explain, feeling her body go from tense to relax as I explained myself. She then quickly pulled away from me, smacked me, and wandered into the bathroom, cursing me out and telling me not to follow her if I knew what was good for me. Which was code for she wanted angry shower sex.

I was more than happy to oblige. Before I could even make the three-foot walk to our bathroom, there was banging on our bedroom door. Fuck me, and I thought not being Prez meant I didn't get cock blocked, but *NOOOOOOO*, I had to have kids in my house.

I rip open our bedroom door with a loud and growly 'what?' looking to see a tearful Manda wrapped up in Kathy-Rea's arms. Kathy-Rea giving me a pleading look and passed the inconsolable new mom to me.

"What is going on? Where is your fu- uh, fudging father?" I hug her close as her partner in crime scurries away.

"He went to see Teddy early this morning. I woke up alone, with no one, and it made me realize that I am a single mom of a sick baby. What man is going to want me? I am going to be alone forever!" She throws herself deeper into my arms, still talking, but it's coming out garbled and incoherent with all the tears and the crying.

In our MC, we are all about embracing your feelings, and it's okay to cry. I mean, Theo is the king of emotions. But this was a level that I just could not get behind and did not know how she went from waking up in a room by herself to being alone forever. My brain cannot begin to understand those gymnastics to make that leap.

"Okay, Manda, baby girl, I am going to lead you to the bed, and then I am gonna go get El. I am sure she is better equipped to help you, through…. This." I start to gently guide her to the bed to get the one with these parts to help her.

"See! Even you don't want to be around me! I am going to be alone! FOREVER!" She wails, throwing herself in the middle of the bed.

I cannot handle this much hormonal female drama this early in the morning. I turn to get El, but she walks out in her ratty terry cloth housecoat to see Manda, a ball of tears, and most likely snot in our bed.

"Okay, Old man, I got this; you can go hide from the hormones and emotions now." She says, not even looking at me and laying beside the tearful girl. I hear her calming mom voice as I back away slowly, not to alert Manda that I am leaving her.

I make my way into the kitchen. I need coffee. Lots and lots of coffee. Once I have my mug full, I pull my phone out and call Theo. He finally picks up right before it was set to go to voicemail.

"What? I'm with Teddy."

"You need to get your ass back here now."

"Oh, hmmm. Let me think about it. No."

"No. What the fuck do you mean no. Get. Here."

"You ain't Prez anymore, *Ken.*"

"Mother fucker. Did you forget you have a kid here? She needs you, now. Get your ass here!"

"I'm on my way."

I know that he was just giving me shit because he could, but it definitely wasn't the time to be doing so.

It's not like he knew his daughter was freaking out. Yeah, but I don't care. He shouldn't have done it. Dude, give him a break. WHY THE FUCK AM I FIGHTING WITH MYSELF!

I shake out my head and gulp down my coffee. I'm not awake enough, I'm horny as fuck, and I have shit to do because I am nothing without the MC.

I am. Nothing. Without the MC.

Do I really believe that? I sit down at the table and bang my head against it. I can't think that. There's no way that it's true. I have so much. I am so much more than the Prez of an MC. What the hell is going on with me?

I'm starting to think that I can't do this. I was wrong to give it away so soon. I should have kept going. Fuuuuuuuuuuck.

"PawPaw! You're here for breakfast. Did'ed yous not gotta go to work today? We can play princess all day. But, yous gotta be the princess because I's the Queen!"

She hops into my lap and starts going into animated detail about how she is Queen Marley, and I start to relax. This right here. Moments like this. This is why I stepped down. I needed more time like this.

"Where is she?" Theo yells into the house.

"Okay, Queen Marley, I need to go help Funcle Theo with some stuff. I'll come to find you later."

"Pinky swear?" She holds out her tiny little pinky.

"Pinky swear." We lock pinkies, and then she runs off to do who knows what, and I head over to Theo. "She's in with El. She has it set in her mind that she is going to be alone forever because who the hell is going to want to be with a single teenage mom who has a sick kid?"

"Watch what you fucking say! That's my kid!"

"I didn't say it, asshole. *She* did. She is terrified that she is going to be alone. She woke up alone and went into a spiral. I didn't know what to do. I told her to sit so I could get El, and she freaked out, thinking that I didn't even want her around. Look, I know you want to be with your grandson, but I think, at least for a while, don't go unless you take her. She's just a kid, and even though she says she's okay, I don't think she is. She needs you here."

Theo lets out a shaky breath and just nods his head. He still isn't used to having a child, and all he wants is to be a part of both of their lives. He's afraid to miss any time with Teddy especially given his situation. But Manda, she needs him more than Teddy does.

"You're right, man. I just. I missed her life. The thought of missing a single moment of Teddy's, I don't want to. I don't want to miss any more of hers either, but he's…he's just so little, and I am so scared he won't make it. I can't be in two places at once. I thought if I went before she was up, it would be fine but, I guess not, which is okay. I should have asked. Fuck, being a parent is hard."

"I get it, man. I got my kids when they were around the same age. You know that you were fucking there all the damn time. It's a major adjustment. Yours is just harder because she just had a baby. Everything that she is feeling, thinking, it's all amplified to the max right now. She is pumping all day to feed her son and having to go to the hospital and not come home with him. I can imagine it's terrible for her every day that she walks in and then back out with no baby. Just be here for her and be with her. See Teddy together. You have the time away from the MC, and they know that Manda and Teddy are your top priority now. Do what you gotta do."

"You're right. Where is she at?"

"I'm right here, dad." Theo walks over to Manda and grips her tight into a hug. He kisses the top of her head and mumbles something in her hair. I make my way over to El.

"Okay?"

"She will be." She says and gives me a slight smile.

"Go get dressed, babe. I'll get breakfast started."

It's been about a week since I stepped down, and I am just as lost as ever, if not more so. I make my way to the clubhouse, which is the original homestead. That was one of the changes that Cowboy put into place. Everything, including Church, happens down there now. We had kept it close to the main house before, so I could easily go back and forth, but now that I don't have to, it's where it should have been all along.

I am still so lost. My mind is swirling, and I feel like I am slipping into a black hole. You never realize what you have until it's gone. I knew that the MC was a large part of who I was, but it didn't occur to me that it was the biggest part of me.

Which, at the same time, pissed me off that I was giving it so much of myself. I had El, and I had my home, my ranch, *my kids. Why* couldn't I let this go?

I walk into the clubhouse and make my way to the office that was mine that I hardly ever used, to begin with. The cut sluts are here. There is a bar in one corner. It's the shape of a giant L, and at the corner point, there is a circular stage and a stripper pole.

The club, while I would come down here on occasion, it was never my thing. I didn't need to be surrounded by naked women and the free for all sex. I have my wife. But I knew that being with the guys was important, so while it wasn't my thing, I'd drag my own ass down here.

As I try to make my way through the club to get to the office, a cut slut walks up to me and grips my arm. I jerk it away and just stare at her.

"Oh come on, Prez," which reminds me, I gotta take this patch off, "I can make you feel so good, baby."

"I'm married. The Prez is Cowboy. Find someone else."

"She doesn't have to know, sexy. I won't tell her." She tries once again to run her hands up my arm. I grip her wrists and give her a look that I save for the men we torture.

"Listen here, when someone says no, it fucking means no. I don't know who the fuck you are, but if you attempt to touch another person after being told to get the fuck away, I will shoot you."

Her face pales. "You...you wouldn't. You can't do that! You said you're not the Prez."

"Here's the thing. This is *MY* club. I am the founding member. Also, did you forget that you are in a goddamn MC clubhouse? I have the cops in my pocket, I work with the mafia, and I have multiple ways to dispose of your body. Disrespect the clubs and its rules again, and you're fucking dead. I'm not putting up with your shit."

Right at that moment, Rambo walks up and grips her arm, spinning her around. "What the hell do you think you're doing, Steffie?"

I'll give it to the girl. She changes tactics and puts on a show quickly. "Just offering to show him a good time, baby. You wanna have a good time?"

I look at Rambo and lift my brow to him. *Don't do it, man. This one is a loose cannon. Don't do it.*

"Hmm, yeah, baby, let's go."

He starts to pull her to one of the rooms we have here, and she looks back at me with a smug grin. I scoff. Why she thinks I give a shit is baffling. If she knew what my wife looked like, her confidence would plummet.

Normally, I wouldn't want a woman to feel that way, but something seriously bothers me about that woman. I just hope that I don't find out what it is too late.

I get to the office and knock on the door.

"Yeah."

I make my way in and see J.J. sitting at the desk, going over, whatever the fuck the issues are. Holy shit. The fact that I don't know. Fuck. Now I'm back in the headspace I don't want to be in.

"Hey, pops. What's going on?"

"I gotta talk to you, son. You got some time you can spare for your old man?"

"Dad, you know that I always do. What's going on? Are you okay?"

"Yeah, son, I'm fine. Well, no. That's a lie. I'm not fine. I am so lost now. I don't know what to do without this MC. I don't know what to do without the title."

"Are you trying to take my title from me?" He asks. His tone is full of obvious worry. Mixed with anger and pain

"What? No. Never. You earned that title. I just. Fuck I don't even know. I…I don't know. Who the hell am I if I'm not the Prez of this club?"

"You're my dad."

Those three words hit me right in my soul. I was so focused on everything I lost when I stepped down from the MC that I clouded my own vision to everything I had. It didn't matter what El told Theo or me. They would always tell me what I needed to hear and what I wanted to hear at times. While I think, deep down, I knew that everything they told me was true, I still didn't allow myself to believe it.

Growing this MC from the ground up was a huge accomplishment. One that I pride myself in but one of my biggest accomplishments was sitting right across from me, telling me everything I needed.

I knew this kid loved me, but when you're down and out and so unsure of what is needed of you, your kids always find a way to show you. I am needed because my son needs me. While I may no longer hold the title of Prez, I will always hold the title of Dad. No one can take that away from me.

“I’m your dad.”

EPILOGUE

COWBOY

I was sitting across from one of the strongest men I had ever known, seeing him go from broken and lost to complete again at one simple phrase.

"I'm Your Dad." He repeats back to me, a small smile creeping on his face.

"Ya, I mean, you were my dad before you were Prez. You showed me how to do this. Have faith that I am not going to walk away and leave you with a broken club you have to rebuild." I laugh at the idea. "I have plans to help this club, you and mom, even ways to expand Artem's reach. Do you have time to talk about it?"

I know that I am coming off like I know what I am doing, but I am flying by the seat of my pants. I don't have one fucking clue of what I am doing. But my formative teenage years were spent in the club, watching Ken, Judge, my dad, build it up to this. I am just trying to make him proud. I knew he didn't want the club's dirty business dealings to touch the Foster Home and kids for fear they would lose that designation. So moving the MC,

Church, and the threat of unwelcome visitors away from the main ranch was step one.

"For you, I will make time, but if your mother asks, I was in town at the diner with Artem. Not here at the bar with the Cut Sluts." He chuckles.

"Deal." I open the desk drawer and pull out a file folder; opening it, I lay out several pieces of paper. "I want to hire help for the Group home. I know mom runs a tight ship, but something is going to give at some point, and I don't want it to be her health or your sanity. Mom already thinks you are going senile for stepping down."

"Trust me, I know, I hear about it every night when I have been, and I quote, 'up her ass all damn day." He looks like he wants to make a joke about fucking my mom up the ass, but the horrified look on my face must remind him that I am her son and DO NOT need to hear about what they do behind closed doors. It was bad enough when Yaya was still alive, and we were roomed on the same fucking floor. I shudder at that memory.

"Okay, well.... Moving on, Natasha set me up online with a place that runs accredited background checks on all possible employees. Plus, we can get Knuckles to do his freaky dark web digging and run an even deeper background check on the top people, and from there, we can hire the least psychotic person. Cause lets face it, you need to be a little crazy to survive around here."

As if on cue, I hear Sever start yelling about something and Butcher laughing. I don't know what we will do with those two, but they make sure the day is never dull.

Dad takes the folder and starts flipping through and reading the resumes and checking my top picks, and I let my mind wander to the men outside. My men.

I am now in charge of this rag-tag bunch of fucking lunatics. They all come with their own quirks and fucked up qualities that make them fit. I mean, Butcher is fucking insane and knows how to torture, maim and kill and look like he was playing with a puppy. He also had started mentoring a former foster brother, Angel. He completed his prospecting two years ago and has learned the ways that are explained as Butcher. Then we had my VP, Storm, my uncle Theo. I don't even know what kind of shit he will give me once he comes back full-time, but I am ready and looking forward to it.

Sever looks like the scariest mother fucker you could ever come across, but I have seen him run from the bunkhouse shower buck naked because there was a centipede on his towel. But, he can handle business and likes to make sure those that cross him only do so once. They pay with limb or life. Wee Willie, I don't even know with that man, he is the best friend to everyone here. He joined when Dad and Theo founded, going from farm hand to MC Road Captain almost seemed too natural for him. He can hold his own when we move the product for Artem and knows how to trick the cops with his unassuming demeanor. He looked like a simple guy, talked like one too, but that fucker was smart and knew how to make us do whatever he needed.

Dad was taking his time looking when I heard more commotion outside the door, and I knew it was all in fun, so I made no move. When I heard the prospect squeal, I knew Butcher was showing him that stupid pressure point trick to drop a man so fast with just one finger. We don't even bother to know prospects' names. When you prospect, you are given a job to do and a number to be. Hell, when I started, I was prospect Number Two for nine months; I always said it's because I was the shit, but dad always knocked me back down.

We have three currently, and I am only sure about one of them. We will keep them working and see what happens. Omen oversees them, and I know he likes it cause he is a sneaky mother fucker and knows how to sneak up on you and watch you for hours before letting you know you are doing it wrong. Scared the crap out of Dizz and me more than once. Gears was another Foster Brother that took a liking to the bikes and knowing what made them click. Watching that man pull apart a bike and rebuild it was comparable to seeing a woman give birth. It was both beautiful and messy.

Bigfoot earned his name long before this MC, but I think it was because he looked like the mystical creature and hated people about the same. The second it was brought up for me to be the enforcer, he jumped at the chance to step down and oversee the prospects with Omen. Now that Omen is doing that, I see him stepping down soon as well, fucker is closing in on a hundred years old.

Knuckles is a computer nerd with a James Dean Attitude. He was always one to conduct business with his own two hands. His main focus was IT, but he had a mean streak in him that there was little self-control to stop when his fists began to fly. I have seen him crush a man's face in with just his own two hands. I am not even going to get started with Turd. What you see is what you get with that fucker.

Zombie was a drifter looking for a place, former military looking for that brotherhood again. Dad and Theo were quick to welcome him in, but I see him leaving when Bigfoot does. Dizz and Rambo are my best friends and brothers by choice. Rambo is younger than us but came from a similar background as Dizz, and when he started coming around more and more, I knew we were going to come through this whole thing together and alright.

"Her," Dad said, jolting me from my thoughts.

"Huh?" Sounding so smart.

"Her. She will be the best fit for your mama. Cause any of these other girls are too wishy-washy, and your mama will break them, mind, body, and soul. This one here, she's got something that will have her fitting in like the best of them." He finishes. Tossing the resume at me.

"Well, I will take your word on it. I mean, you are 'Judge' for a reason."

Before I could look at it any more, the office door bursts open, and there stands Artem, coming in a bit further and his number two, tossing a lifeless, broken, and bleeding fucker onto the floor. Then placing a baggy of something on my desk in front of Dad and me.

"Sorry to interrupt this father-son bonding moment, but it's time to put on your big boy panties and deal with this fucker. As well as those." Artem states as he gestures to the bag on the desk.

Looking at it closer, it seems to be coke, but it doesn't look as pure as the shit we hold and package for Artem. Well, shit, this job just got more interesting in only a week.

"Is he dead?" Butcher asks, peering over Artem's shoulder, causing him to jump.

"I don't know, maybe?" Rafe says, giving his foot a little kick to see if there is any reaction. "Doesn't look like it."

"Can my piggies have him?"

"Well, Prez, what are you gonna do now?" My dad asks, leaning back like there wasn't a possible dead body on the floor behind him.

ACKNOWLEDGMENTS

Clarebear, you are one of the sweetest ladies we have ever met! This pandemic and the Ruthless Underworld brought you to us, and we couldn't be more thankful for you. You are the kind hand we need every so often, but we all know the wild cat you are hiding! Thank you for being 100% who you are and always being honest with us. *#ArtemIsClares*

Libby, thank you for being that stern voice when we needed it. Telling us how it is and always being honest with us. We know everything you say comes from the heart, and we are so grateful for the amount of support that you constantly show us. *#JudgeIsLibbys*

Erica, my[Lee] child. Sorry not sorry you can't read the unedited version of these books. I know you know what it all is, but I refuse to hand it over to you. You do not need to know the depraved things your mother writes about for *at least* two more years. You support us so much, and you really are our biggest hype-man. I love you, to the moon and back, and honestly, still, more than you will ever know.

All the women that we have made friends with from the book world. You all keep us going, even if you don't know it. Your friendships are cherished. We all are miles, and some oceans, apart, but this whole entire book world makes us feel closer than ever. We love you all.

Christina, we are so thankful for your guiding hand and realistic views for what we trying to put out. You were one of the few who got a real inside look into what we are trying to accomplish with Nameless Order. You are one of our biggest supporters and hype women and we can never thank you enough for all that you do. You are amazing! *#TheoisChristinas*

Carolyn. Your support for this was beyond anything we can measure or say thank you for. You had no idea how much your words meant to us. Every time you'd say something or share something, it took a lot for us to not cry. Seriously. You're the best. Forever in our hearts. #NamelessSisterForever

To our kids, all seven of you, we love you.

Thank you, Mom[Michele]! For showing me that it's okay to like the dirtier things in life, even if it was by accident and I was only sixteen. Thank you and Dad for supporting me in this, even though I am sure you won't read what depravity we have come up with.

Bijoux, for being the furriest, most annoying writing buddy out there. Thanks for almost spilling my water many a time and causing computers to crash. You are the best asshole in my house.

To Ash and Brit….. You know why!

Those guys we're married to - you're cool - we guess.

Tanner - we've told you a million times how much you mean to us and we'll tell you a million times more. You're a light and we don't deserve you. The world deserves to experience your joy. Follow Willie on TikTok @wildhog_1800

Last but not at all least, Silla. You are a Godsend, and we aren't worthy of you. Everything you have told us and done for us is more than we could have ever asked for. You are one of the best people we have never met IRL, and we are so incredibly thankful that you found your way into our lives. Without you, we don't know where we would be. We love you so hard.

To all of you who made it this far, thank you! We are so excited for what is to come and can't wait for you to see it all unfold.

See you again in Cowboy.

PLAYLIST

Elvira - The Oak Ridge Boys
Face Down - The Red Jumpsuit Apparatus
Notice - Thomas Rhett
I Didn't Fall In Love with Your Hair - Brett Kissel & Carolyn Dawn Johnson
I Knew I Loved You - Savage Garden
Just A Kiss - Lady A
Begin Again - Taylor Swift
Things I Can't Say - Spencer Crandall & Julia Cole
Waiting For You - Russell Dickerson
Beautiful With You - Halestorm
This Is Us - Backstreet Boys
I'm Gonna Love You Through It - Martina McBride
Mirrors - Boyce Avenue, Fifth Harmony
Little Bit of Life - Craig Morgan

ABOUT THE AUTHOR

Michele Lee is made up of two moms that met through a reading group and found an instant connection via the books they love to read.

We started to talk daily and found that we both had been working on our own books. Sharing those books with each other, we realized that we have the same writing style and a few ideas stored away that we could combine and make into an amazing world.

So, that's what we did. We are currently working on multiple stories and have multiple plots written. Now, the struggle is finding the time to get it all out on paper.

With seven kids between us, two husbands, and day jobs, we are working on our stories as fast as possible. However, we are taking the time needed as well to produce the most amazing stories.

The most fun fact about us, though? We have NEVER met in person. Everything is done via text message, late-night video calls, multiple pages of notes, and hundreds of Google Docs.

It works, though, and our "date nights" are the best because they are productively *un*productive. Oops.

Connect with us

https://www.instagram.com/author_michele_lee/
https://www.facebook.com/authormichelelee
https://www.tiktok.com/authormichelelee
Newsletter
https://authormichelelee.wixsite.com/blog

ALSO BY MICHELE LEE

Cowboy – Coming Soon!

I was now the Prez. Keeping this club going was up to me. Finding out who was tarnishing this town now fell onto my shoulders and I was ready to take it on. However, that was just the first change that completely restructured my life.

An opportunity came, and I took it. It may not have been the best way to handle it, but I knew I needed to get what I wanted.

What I wanted was her.

Bri.

The woman that knocked me on my ass and made me see what it is to be loved—the woman who would give me everything in this life.

But life had other plans.

It broke me, and when you don't know how to handle that pain, what more can you do?

I've made my mistakes. I've paid for them. Starting now, I will be the man I was made to be—the man that Bri fell in love with and the man that will keep this club going.

After all, you can't find the monster that's hiding in the shadows if you stay broken.

Made in the USA
Coppell, TX
19 December 2021